The Short Stories

The Short Stories

Ian McEwan

JONATHAN CAPE
LONDON

This collection first published 1995

3 5 7 9 10 8 6 4

© Ian McEwan 1975, 1978

Ian McEwan has asserted his right
under the Copyright, Designs and Patents Act, 1988
to be identified as the author of this work

First published in this form in the United Kingdom in 1995
by Jonathan Cape
Random House, 20 Vauxhall Bridge Road, London SW1V 2SA

Random House Australia (Pty) Limited
20 Alfred Street, Milsons Point, Sydney,
New South Wales 2061, Australia

Random House New Zealand Limited
18 Poland Road, Glenfield,
Auckland 10, New Zealand

Random House South Africa (Pty) Limited
PO Box 337, Bergvlei, 2012 South Africa

Random House UK Limited Reg. No. 954009

A CIP catalogue record for this book
is available from the British Library

Papers used by Random House UK Limited are natural,
recyclable products made from wood grown in sustainable forests.
The manufacturing processes conform to the environmental
regulations of the country of origin.

ISBN 0–224–04258–0

Printed and bound in Great Britain by
Mackays of Chatham PLC, Chatham, Kent

Contents

First Love, Last Rites

To Elaine

Solid Geometry

In Melton Mowbray in 1875 at an auction of articles of
'curiosity and worth', my great-grandfather, in the company of M his friend, bid for the penis of Captain Nicholls
who died in Horsemonger jail in 1873. It was bottled in a
glass twelve inches long, and, noted my great-grandfather
in his diary that night, 'in a beautiful state of preservation'.
Also for auction was 'the unnamed portion of the late
Lady Barrymore. It went to Sam Israels for fifty guineas.'
My great-grandfather was keen on the idea of having the
two items as a pair, and M dissuaded him. This illustrates
perfectly their friendship. My great-grandfather the ex-
citable theorist, M the man of action who knew when to
bid at auctions. My great-grandfather lived for sixty-nine
years. For forty-five of them, at the end of every day, he
sat down before going to bed and wrote his thoughts in a
diary. These diaries are on my table now, forty-five
volumes bound in calf leather, and to the left sits Capt.
Nicholls in the glass jar. My great-grandfather lived on the
income derived from the patent of an invention of his
father, a handy fastener used by corset-makers right up till
the outbreak of the First World War. My great-grandfather liked gossip, numbers and theories. He also liked
tobacco, good port, jugged hare and, very occasionally,
opium. He liked to think of himself as a mathematician,

though he never had a job, and never published a
book. Nor did he ever travel or get his name in *The Times*,
even when he died. In 1869 he married Alice, only
daughter of the Rev. Toby Shadwell, co-author of a not
highly regarded book on English wild flowers. I believe my
great-grandfather to have been a very fine diarist, and
when I have finished editing the diaries and they are published I am certain he will receive the recognition due to
him. When my work is over I will take a long holiday,
travel somewhere cold and clean and treeless, Iceland or
the Russian Steppes. I used to think that at the end of it all
I would try, if it was possible, to divorce my wife Maisie,
but now there is no need at all.

Often Maisie would shout in her sleep and I would have
to wake her.

'Put your arm around me,' she would say. 'It was a
horrible dream. I had it once before. I was in a plane
flying over a desert. But it wasn't really a desert. I took the
plane lower and I could see there were thousands of
babies heaped up, stretching away into the horizon, all of
them naked and climbing over each other. I was running
out of fuel and I had to land the plane. I tried to find a
space, I flew on and on looking for a space...'

'Go to sleep now,' I said through a yawn. 'It was only a
dream.'

'No,' she cried. 'I mustn't go to sleep, not just yet.'

'Well, *I* have to sleep now,' I told her. 'I have to be up
early in the morning.'

She shook my shoulder. 'Please don't go to sleep yet,
don't leave me here.'

'I'm in the same bed,' I said. 'I won't leave you.'

'It makes no difference, don't leave me awake ...' But
my eyes were already closing.

Lately I have taken up my great-grandfather's habit.

Before going to bed I sit down for half an hour and think over the day. I have no mathematical whimsies or sexual theories to note down. Mostly I write out what Maisie has said to me and what I have said to Maisie. Sometimes, for complete privacy, I lock myself in the bathroom, sit on the toilet seat and balance the writing-pad on my knees. Apart from me there is occasionally a spider or two in the bathroom. They climb up the waste pipe and crouch perfectly still on the glaring white enamel. They must wonder where they have come to. After hours of crouching they turn back, puzzled, or perhaps disappointed they could not learn more. As far as I can tell, my great-grandfather made only one reference to spiders. On May 8th, 1906, he wrote, 'Bismarck is a spider.'

In the afternoons Maisie used to bring me tea and tell me her nightmares. Usually I was going through old newspapers, compiling indexes, cataloguing items, putting down this volume, picking up another. Maisie said she was in a bad way. Recently she had been sitting around the house all day glancing at books on psychology and the occult, and almost every night she had bad dreams. Since the time we exchanged physical blows, lying in wait to hit each other with the same shoe outside the bathroom, I had had little sympathy for her. Part of her problem was jealousy. She was very jealous ... of my great-grandfather's forty-five-volume diary, and of my purpose and energy in editing it. She was doing nothing. I was putting down one volume and picking up another when Maisie came in with the tea.

'Can I tell you my dream?' she asked. 'I was flying this plane over a kind of desert ...'

'Tell me later, Maisie,' I said. 'I'm in the middle of something here.' After she had gone I stared at the wall in front of my desk and thought about M, who came to talk and dine with my great-grandfather regularly over a period of fifteen years up until his sudden and unexplained departure one evening in 1898. M, whoever he might have been, was something of an academic, as well as a man of action. For example, on the evening of August 9th, 1870, the two of them are talking about positions for lovemaking and M tells my great-grandfather that copulation *a posteriori* is the most natural way owing to the position of the clitoris and because other anthropoids favour this method. My great-grandfather, who copulated about half-a-dozen times in his entire life, and that with Alice during the first year of their marriage, wondered out loud what the Church's view was and straight away M is able to tell him that the seventh-century theologian Theodore considered copulation *a posteriori* a sin ranking with masturbation and therefore worthy of forty penances. Later in the same evening my great-grandfather produced mathematical evidence that the maximum number of positions cannot exceed the prime number seventeen. M scoffed at this and told him he had seen a collection of drawings by Romano, a pupil of Raphael's, in which twenty-four positions were shown. And, he said, he had heard of a Mr F. K. Forberg who had accounted for ninety. By the time I remembered the tea Maisie had left by my elbow it was cold.

An important stage in the deterioration of our marriage was reached as follows. I was sitting in the bathroom one evening writing out a conversation Maisie and I had had about the Tarot pack when suddenly she was outside, rapping on the door and rattling the door-handle.

'Open the door,' she called out. 'I want to come in.'

I said to her, 'You'll have to wait a few minutes more. I've almost finished.'

'Let me in now,' she shouted. 'You're not using the toilet.'

'Wait,' I replied, and wrote another line or two. Now Maisie was kicking the door.

'My period has started and I need to get something.' I ignored her yells and finished my piece, which I considered to be particularly important. If I left it till later certain details would be lost. There was no sound from Maisie now and I assumed she was in the bedroom. But when I opened the door she was standing right in my way with a shoe in her hand. She brought the heel of it sharply down on my head, and I only had time to move slightly to one side. The heel caught the top of my ear and cut it badly.

'There,' said Maisie, stepping round me to get to the bathroom, 'now we are both bleeding,' and she banged the door shut. I picked up the shoe and stood quietly and patiently outside the bathroom holding a handkerchief to my bleeding ear. Maisie was in the bathroom about ten minutes and as she came out I caught her neatly and squarely on the top of her head. I did not give her time to move. She stood perfectly still for a moment looking straight into my eyes.

'You worm,' she breathed, and went down to the kitchen to nurse her head out of my sight.

During supper yesterday Maisie claimed that a man locked in a cell with only the Tarot cards would have access to all knowledge. She had been doing a reading that afternoon and the cards were still spread about the floor.

'Could he work out the street plan of Valparaiso from the cards?' I asked.

'You're being stupid,' she replied.

'Could it tell him the best way to start a laundry business, the best way to make an omelette or a kidney machine?'

'Your mind is so narrow,' she complained. 'You're so narrow, so predictable.'

'Could he', I insisted, 'tell me who M is, or why ...'

'Those things don't matter,' she cried. 'They're not necessary.'

'They are still knowledge. Could he find them out?'

She hesitated. 'Yes, he could.'

I smiled, and said nothing.

'What's so funny?' she said. I shrugged, and she began to get angry. She wanted to be disproved. 'Why did you ask all those pointless questions?'

I shrugged again. 'I just wanted to know if you really meant *everything*.'

Maisie banged the table and screamed, 'Damn you! Why are you always trying me out? Why don't you say something real?' And with that we both recognized we had reached the point where all our discussions led and we became bitterly silent.

Work on the diaries cannot proceed until I have cleared up the mystery surrounding M. After coming to dinner on and off for fifteen years and supplying my great-grand-father with a mass of material for his theories, M simply disappears from the pages of the diary. On Tuesday, December 6th, my great-grandfather invited M to dine on the following Saturday, and although M came, my great-grandfather in the entry for that day simply writes, 'M to dinner.' On any other day the conversation at these meals is recorded at great length. M had been to dinner on Monday, December 5th, and the conversation had been about geometry, and the entries for the rest of that week are entirely given over to the same subject. There is absolutely no hint of antagonism. Besides, my great-grandfather *needed* M. M provided his material, M knew what was going on, he was familiar with London and he had been on the Continent a number of times. He knew all about socialism and Darwin, he had an acquaintance in the free love movement, a friend of James Hinton. M was *in* the world in a way which my great-grandfather, who left Melton Mowbray only once in his lifetime, to visit Nottingham, was not. Even as a young man my great-grandfather preferred to theorize by the fireside; all he needed were the materials M supplied. For example, one evening in June 1884 M, who was just back from London, gave my great-grandfather an account of how the streets of the town were fouled and clogged by horse dung. Now in that same week my great-grandfather had been reading the essay by Malthus called 'On the Principle of Population'. That night he made an excited entry in the diary about a pamphlet he wanted to write and have published. It was to be called 'De Stercore Equorum'. The pamphlet was never published and probably never written, but there are detailed notes in the diary entries for the two weeks following that evening. In 'De Stercore Equorum' ('Concerning Horseshit') he assumes geometric growth in the horse population, and working from detailed street plans he predicted that the metropolis would be impassable by 1935. By impassable he took to mean an average thickness of one foot (compressed) in every major street. He described involved experiments outside his own stables to determine the compressibility of horse dung, which he managed to express mathematically. It was all pure theory, of course. His results rested on the assumption that no dung would be shovelled aside in the fifty years to come. Very likely it was M who talked my great-grandfather out of the project.

One morning, after a long dark night of Maisie's nightmares, we were lying side by side in bed and I said,

'What is it you really want? Why don't you go back to your job? These long walks, all this analysis, sitting around the house, lying in bed all morning, the Tarot pack, the nightmares ... what is it you want?'

And she said, 'I want to get my head straight,' which she had said many times before.

I said, 'Your head, your mind, it's not like a hotel kitchen, you know, you can't throw stuff out like old tin cans. It's more like a river than a place, moving and changing all the time. You can't make rivers flow straight.'

'Don't go through all that again,' she said. 'I'm not trying to make rivers flow straight, I'm trying to get my head straight.'

'You've got to *do* something,' I told her. 'You can't do nothing. Why not go back to your job? You didn't have nightmares when you were working. You were never so unhappy when you were working.'

'I've got to stand back from all that,' she said. 'I'm not sure what any of it means.'

'Fashion,' I said, 'it's all fashion. Fashionable metaphors, fashionable reading, fashionable malaise. What do you care about Jung, for example? You've read twelve pages in a month.'

'Don't go on,' she pleaded, 'you know it leads nowhere.'

But I went on.

'You've never been anywhere,' I told her, 'you've never done anything. You're a nice girl without even the blessing of an unhappy childhood. Your sentimental Buddhism, this junk-shop mysticism, joss-stick therapy, magazine astrology ... none of it is yours, you've worked none of it out for yourself. You fell into it, you fell into a swamp of respectable intuitions. You haven't the originality or passion to intuit anything yourself beyond your own unhappiness. Why are you filling your mind with other people's mystic banalities and giving yourself nightmares?' I got out of bed, opened the curtains and began to get dressed.

'You talk like this was a fiction seminar,' Maisie said. 'Why are you trying to make things worse for me?' Self-pity began to well up from inside her, but she fought it down. 'When you are talking,' she went on, 'I can feel myself, you know, being screwed up like a piece o paper.'

'Perhaps we *are* in a fiction seminar,' I said grimly. Maisie sat up in bed staring at her lap. Suddenly her tone changed. She patted the pillow beside her and said softly,

'Come over here. Come and sit here. I want to touch you, I want you to touch me ...' But I was sighing, and already on my way to the kitchen.

In the kitchen I made myself some coffee and took it through to my study. It had occurred to me in my night of broken sleep that a possible clue to the disappearance of M might be found in the pages of geometry. I had always skipped through them before because mathematics does not interest me. On the Monday, December 5th, 1898, M and my great-grandfather discussed the *vescia piscis*, which apparently is the subject of Euclid's first proposition and a profound influence on the ground plans of many ancient religious buildings. I read through the account of the conversation carefully, trying to understand as best I could the geometry of it. Then, turning the page, I found a lengthy anecdote which M told my great-grandfather that same evening when the coffee had been brought in and the cigars were lit. Just as I was beginning to read Maisie came in.

'And what about you,' she said, as if there had not been an hour break in our exchange, 'all you have is books. Crawling over the past like a fly on a turd.'

I was angry, of course, but I smiled and said cheerfully, 'Crawling? Well, at least I'm moving.'

'You don't speak to me any more,' she said, 'you play me like a pinball machine, for points.'

'Good morning, Hamlet,' I replied, and sat in my chair waiting patiently for what she had to say next. But she did not speak, she left, closing the study door softly behind her.

'In September 1870,' M began to tell my great-grand-father,

I came into the possession of certain documents which not only invalidate everything fundamental to our science of solid geometry but also undermine the whole canon of our physical laws and force one to redefine one's place in Nature's scheme. These papers outweigh in importance the combined work of Marx and Darwin. They were entrusted to me by a young American mathematician, and they are the work of David Hunter, a mathematician too and a Scotsman. The American's name was Goodman. I had corresponded with his father over a number of years in connection with his work on the cyclical theory of menstruation which, incredibly enough, is still widely discredited in this country. I met the young Goodman in Vienna where, along with Hunter and mathematicians from a dozen countries, he had been attending an international conference on mathematics. Goodman was pale and greatly disturbed when I met him, and planned to return to America the following day even though the conference was not yet half complete. He gave the papers into my care with instructions that I was to deliver them to David Hunter if I was ever to learn of his whereabouts. And then, only after much persuasion and insistence on my part, he told me what he had witnessed on the third day of the conference. The conference met every morning at nine thirty when a paper was read and a general discussion ensued. At eleven o'clock refreshments were brought in and many of the mathematicians would get up from the long, highly polished table round which they were all gathered and stroll about the large, elegant room and engage in informal discussions with their colleagues. Now, the conference lasted two weeks, and by a long-standing arrangement the most eminent of the mathematicians read their papers first, followed by the slightly less eminent, and and so on, in a descending hierarchy throughout the two weeks, which caused, as it is wont to do among highly intelligent men, occasional but intense jealousies. Hunter, though a brilliant mathematician, was young and virtually unknown outside his university, which was Edinburgh. He had applied to deliver what he described as a very important paper on solid geometry, and since he was of little account in this pantheon he was assigned to read to the conference on the last day but one, by which time many of the most important figures would have returned to their respective countries. And so on the third morning, as the servants were bringing in the refreshments, Hunter stood up suddenly and addressed his colleagues just as they were rising from their seats. He was a large, shaggy man and, though young, he had about him a certain presence which reduced the hum of conversation to a complete silence.

'Gentlemen,' said Hunter, 'I must ask you to forgive this improper form of address, but I have something to tell you of the utmost importance. I have discovered the plane without a surface.' Amid derisive smiles and gentle bemused laughter, Hunter picked up from the table a large white sheet of paper. With a pocket-knife he made an incision along its surface about three inches long and slightly to one side of its centre. Then he made some rapid, complicated folds and, holding the paper aloft so all could see, he appeared to draw one corner of it through the incision, and as he did so it disappeared.

'Behold, gentlemen,' said Hunter, holding out his empty hands towards the company, 'the plane without a surface.'

Maisie came into my room, washed now and smelling faintly of perfumed soap. She came and stood behind my chair and placed her hands on my shoulders.

'What are you reading?' she said.

'Just bits of the diary which I haven't looked at before.' She began to massage me gently at the base of my neck. I would have found it soothing if it had still been the first year of our marriage. But it was the sixth year and it generated a kind of tension which communicated itself the length of my spine. Maisie wanted something. To restrain her I placed my right hand on her left, and, mistaking this for affection, she leaned forward and kissed under my ear. Her breath smelled of toothpaste and toast. She tugged at my shoulder.

'Let's go in the bedroom,' she whispered. 'We haven't made love for nearly two weeks now.'

'I know,' I replied. 'You know how it is ... with my work.' I felt no desire for Maisie or any other woman. All I wanted to do was turn the next page of my great-grandfather's diary. Maisie took her hands off my shoulders and stood by my side. There was such a sudden ferocity in her silence that I found myself tensing like a sprinter on the starting line. She stretched forward and picked up the sealed jar containing Capt. Nicholls. As she lifted it his penis drifted dreamily from one end of the glass to the other.

'You're so COMPLACENT,' Maisie shrieked, just before she hurled the glass bottle at the wall in front of my table. Instinctively I covered my face with my hands to shield off the shattering glass. As I opened my eyes I heard myself saying,

'Why did you do that? That belonged to my great-grandfather.' Amid the broken glass and the rising stench of formaldehyde lay Capt. Nicholls, slouched across the leather covers of a volume of the diary, grey, limp and menacing, transformed from a treasured curiosity into a horrible obscenity.

'That was a terrible thing to do. Why did you do that?' I said again.

'I'm going for a walk,' Maisie replied, and slammed the door this time as she left the room.

I did not move from my chair for a long time. Maisie had destroyed an object of great value to me. It had stood in his study while he lived, and then it had stood in mine, linking my life with his. I picked a few splinters of glass from my lap and stared at the 160-year-old piece of another human on my table. I looked at it and thought of all the homunculi which had swarmed down its length. I thought of all the places it had been, Cape Town, Boston, Jerusalem, travelling in the dark, fetid inside of Capt. Nicholls's leather breeches, emerging occasionally into the dazzling sunlight to discharge urine in some jostling public place. I thought also of all the things it had touched, all the molecules, of Captain Nicholls's exploring hands on lonely unrequited nights at sea, the sweating walls of cunts of young girls and old whores, their molecules must still exist today, a fine dust blowing from Cheapside to Leicestershire. Who knows how long it might have lasted in its glass jar. I began to clear up the mess. I brought the rubbish bucket in from the kitchen. I swept and picked up all the glass I could find and swabbed up the formaldehyde. Then, holding him by just one end, I tried to ease Capt. Nicholls on to a sheet of newspaper. My stomach heaved as the foreskin began to come away in my fingers. Finally, with my eyes closed, I succeeded, and wrapping him carefully in the newspaper, I carried him into the garden and buried him under the geraniums. All this time I tried to prevent my resentment towards Maisie filling my mind. I wanted to continue with M's story. Back in my chair I dabbed at a few spots of formaldehyde which had blotted the ink, and read on.

For as long as a minute the room was frozen, and with each successive second it appeared to freeze harder. The first to speak was Dr Stanley Rose of Cambridge University, who had much to lose by Hunter's plane without a surface. His reputation, which was very considerable indeed, rested upon his 'Principles of Solid Geometry'.

'How dare you, sir. How dare you insult the dignity of this assembly with a worthless conjuror's trick.' And bolstered by the rising murmur of concurrence behind him, he added, 'You should be ashamed, young man, thoroughly ashamed.' With that, the room erupted like a volcano. With the exception of young Goodman, and of the servants who still stood by with the refreshments, the whole room turned on Hunter and directed at him a senseless babble of denunciation, invective and threat. Some thumped on the table in their fury, others waved their clenched fists. One very frail German gentlemen fell to the floor in an apoplexy and had to be helped to a chair. And there stood Hunter, firm and outwardly unmoved, his head inclined slightly to one side, his fingers resting lightly on the surface of the long polished table. That such an uproar should follow a worthless conjuror's trick clearly demonstrated the extent of the underlying unease, and Hunter surely appreciated this. Raising his hand, and the company falling suddenly silent once more, he said,

'Gentlemen, your concern is understandable and I will effect another proof, the ultimate proof.' This said, he sat down and removed his shoes, stood up and removed his jacket, and then called for a volunteer to assist him, at which Goodman came forward. Hunter strode through the crowd to a couch which stood along one of the walls, and while he settled himself upon it he told the mystified Goodman that when he returned to England he should take with him Hunter's papers and keep them there until he came to collect them. When the mathematicians had gathered round the couch Hunter rolled on to his stomach and clasped his hands behind his back in a strange posture to fashion a hoop with his arms. He asked Goodman to hold his arms in that position for him, and rolled on his side where he began a number of strenuous jerking movements which enabled him to pass one of his feet through the hoop. He asked his assistant to turn him on his other side, where he performed the same movements again and succeeded in passing his other foot between his arms, and at the same time bent his trunk in such a way that his head was able to pass through the hoop in the opposite direction to his feet. With the help of his assistant he began to pass his legs and head past each other through the hoop made by his arms. It was then that the distinguished assembly vented, as one man, a single yelp of utter incredulity. Hunter was beginning to disappear, and now, as his legs and head passed through his arms with greater facility, seemed even to be drawn through by some invisible power, he was almost gone. And now ... he was gone, quite gone, and nothing remained.

M's story put my great-grandfather in a frenzy of excitement. In his diary that night he recorded how he tried 'to prevail upon my guest to send for the papers upon the instant' even though it was by now two o'clock in the morning. M, however, was more sceptical about the whole thing. 'Americans', he told my great-grandfather, 'often indulge in fantastic tales.' But he agreed to bring along the papers the following day. As it turned out M did not dine with my great-grandfather that night because of another engagement, but he called round in the late afternoon with the papers. Before he left he told my great-grandfather he had been through them a number of times and 'there was no sense to be had out of them'. He did not realize then how much he was underestimating my great-grandfather as an amateur mathematician. Over a glass of sherry in front of the drawing-room fire the two men arranged to dine together again at the end of the week, on Saturday. For the next three days my great-grandfather hardly paused from his reading of Hunter's theorems to eat or sleep. The diary is full of nothing else. The pages are covered with scribbles, diagrams and symbols. It seems that Hunter had to devise a new set of symbols, virtually a whole new language, to express his ideas. By the end of the second day my great-grandfather had made his first breakthrough. At the bottom of a page of mathematical scribble he wrote, 'Dimensionality is a function of consciousness'. Turning to the entry for the next day I read the words, 'It disappeared in my hands'. He had reestablished the plane without a surface. And there, spread out in front of me, were step by step instructions on how to fold the piece of paper. Turning the next page I suddenly understood the mystery of M's disappearance. Undoubtedly encouraged by my great-grandfather, he had taken part that evening in a scientific experiment, probably in a spirit of great scepticism. For here my great-grandfather had drawn a series of small sketches illustrating what at first glance looked like yoga positions. Clearly they were the secret of Hunter's disappearing act.

My hands were trembling as I cleared a space on my desk. I selected a clean sheet of typing paper and laid it in front of me. I fetched a razor blade from the bathroom. I rummaged in a drawer and found an old pair of compasses, sharpened a pencil and fitted it in. I searched through the house till I found an accurate steel ruler I had once used for fitting window panes, and then I was ready. First I had to cut the paper to size. The piece that Hunter had so casually picked up from the table had obviously been carefully prepared beforehand. The length of the sides had to express a specific ratio. Using the compasses I found the centre of the paper and through this point I drew a line parallel to one of the sides and continued it right to the edge. Then I had to construct a rectangle whose measurements bore a particular relation to those of the sides of the paper. The centre of this rectangle occurred on the line in such a way as to dissect it by the Golden Mean. From the top of this rectangle I drew intersecting arcs, again of specified proportionate radii. This operation was repeated at the lower end of the rectangle, and when the two points of intersection were joined I had the line of incision. Then I started work on the folding lines. Each line seemed to express, in its length, angle of incline and point of intersection with other lines, some mysterious inner harmony of numbers. As I intersected arcs, drew lines and made folds, I felt I was blindly operating a system of the highest, most terrifying form of knowledge, the mathematics of the Absolute. By the time I had made the final fold the piece of paper was the shape of a geometric flower with three concentric rings arranged round the incision at the centre. There was something so tranquil and perfect about this design, something so remote and compelling, that as I stared into it I felt myself going into a light trance and my mind becoming clear and inactive. I shook my head and glanced away. It was time now to turn the flower in on itself and pull it through the incision. This was a delicate operation and now my hands were trembling again. Only by staring into the centre of the design could I calm myself. With my thumbs I began to push the sides of the paper flower towards the centre, and as I did so I felt a numbness settle over the back of my skull. I pushed a little further, the paper glowed whiter for an instant and then it *seemed* to disappear. I say 'seemed' because at first I could not be sure whether I could feel it still in my hands and not see it, or see it but not feel it, or whether I could sense it had disappeared while its external properties remained. The numbness had spread right across my head and shoulders. My senses seemed inadequate to grasp what was happening. 'Dimensionality is a function of consciousness,' I thought. I brought my hands together and there was nothing between them, but even when I opened them again and saw nothing I could not be sure the paper flower had completely gone. An impression remained, an after-image not on the retina but

on the mind itself. Just then the door opened behind me,
and Maisie said,

'What are you doing?'

I returned as if from a dream to the room and to the
faint smell of formaldehyde. It was a long, long time ago
now, the destruction of Capt. Nicholls, but the smell re-
vived my resentment, which spread through me like the
numbness. Maisie slouched in the doorway, muffled in a
thick coat and woollen scarf. She seemed a long way off,
and as I looked at her my resentment merged into a
familiar weariness of our marriage. I thought, why did she
break the glass? Because she wanted to make love?
Because she wanted a penis? Because she was jealous of my
work, and wanted to smash the connection it had with my
great-grandfather's life?

'Why did you do it?' I said out loud, involuntarily.
Maisie snorted. She had opened the door and found me
hunched over my table staring at my hands.

'Have you been sitting there all afternoon,' she asked,
'thinking about *that*?' She giggled. 'What happened to it,
anyway? Did you suck it off?'

'I buried it,' I said, 'under the geraniums.'

She came into the room a little way and said in a serious
tone, 'I'm sorry about that, I really am. I just did it before
I knew what was happening. Do you forgive me?' I
hesitated, and then, because my weariness had blossomed
into a sudden resolution, I said,

'Yes, of course I forgive you. It was only a prick in
pickle,' and we both laughed. Maisie came over to me and
kissed me, and I returned the kiss, prising open her lips
with my tongue.

'Are you hungry?' she said, when we were done with
kissing. 'Shall I make some supper?'

'Yes,' I said. 'I would love that.' Maisie kissed me on the

top of my head and left the room, while I turned back to my studies, resolving to be as kind as I possibly could to Maisie that evening.

Later we sat in the kitchen eating the meal Maisie had cooked and getting mildly drunk on a bottle of wine. We smoked a joint, the first one we had had together in a very long time. Maisie told me how she was going to get a job with the Forestry Commission planting trees in Scotland next summer. And I told Maisie about the conversation M and my great-grandfather had had about *a posteriori*, and about my great-grandfather's theory that there could not be more than the prime number seventeen positions for making love. We both laughed, and Maisie squeezed my hand, and lovemaking hung in the air between us, in the warm fug of the kitchen. Then we put our coats on and went for a walk. It was almost a full moon. We walked along the main road which runs outside our house and then turned down a narrow street of tightly packed houses with immaculate and minute front gardens. We did not talk much, but our arms were linked and Maisie told me how very stoned and happy she was. We came to a small park which was locked and we stood outside the gates looking up at the moon through the almost leafless branches. When we came home Maisie took a leisurely hot bath while I browsed in my study, checking on a few details. Our bedroom is a warm, comfortable room, luxurious in its way. The bed is seven foot by eight, and I made it myself in the first year of our marriage. Maisie made the sheets, dyed them a deep, rich blue and embroidered the pillow cases. The only light in the room shone through a rough old goatskin lampshade Maisie bought from a man who came to the door. It was a long time since I had taken an interest in the bedroom. We lay side by side in the tangle of sheets and rugs, Maisie

voluptuous and drowsy after her bath and stretched full
out, and I propped up on my elbow. Maisie said sleepily,
'I was walking along the river this afternoon. The trees
are beautiful now, the oaks, the elms ... there are two
copper beeches about a mile past the footbridge, you
should see them now ... ahh, that feels good.' I had eased
her on to her belly and was caressing her back as she
spoke. 'There are blackberries, the biggest ones I've ever
seen, growing all along the path, and elderberries, too. I'm
going to make some wine this autumn ...' I leaned over her
and kissed the nape of her neck and brought her arms
behind her back. She liked to be manipulated in this way
and she submitted warmly. 'And the river is really still,'
she was saying. 'You know, reflecting the trees, and the
leaves are dropping into the river. Before the winter comes
we should go there together, by the river, in the leaves. I
found this little place. No one goes there ...' Holding
Maisie's arms in position with one hand, I worked her legs
towards the 'hoop' with the other. '... I sat in this place for
half an hour without moving, like a tree. I saw a water-rat
running along the opposite bank, and different kinds of
ducks landing on the river and taking off. I heard these
plopping noises in the river but I didn't know what they
were and I saw two orange butterflies, they almost came
on my hand.' When I had her legs in place Maisie said,
'Position number eighteen,' and we both laughed softly.
'Let's go there tomorrow, to the river,' said Maisie as I
carefully eased her head towards her arms. 'Careful, careful, that hurts,' she suddenly shouted, and tried to struggle.
But it was too late now, her head and legs were in place in
the hoop of her arms, and I was beginning to push them
through, past each other. 'What's happening?' cried
Maisie. Now the positioning of her limbs expressed the
breathtaking beauty, the nobility of the human form, and,

as in the paper flower, there was a fascinating power in its symmetry. I felt the trance coming on again and the numbness settling over the back of my head. As I drew her arms and legs through, Maisie appeared to turn in on herself like a sock. 'Oh God,' she sighed, 'what's happening?' and her voice sounded very far away. Then she was gone ... and not gone. Her voice was quite tiny, 'What's happening?' and all that remained was the echo of her question above the deep-blue sheets.

Homemade

I can see now our cramped, overlit bathroom and Connie
with a towel draped round her shoulders, sitting on the
edge of the bath weeping, while I filled the sink with warm
water and whistled – such was my elation – 'Teddy Bear'
by Elvis Presley, I can remember, I have always been able
to remember, fluff from the candlewick bedspread swirling
on the surface of the water, but only lately have I fully
realized that if this was the *end* of a particular episode, in so
far as real-life episodes may be said to have an end, it was
Raymond who occupied, so to speak, the beginning and
middle, and if in human affairs there are no such things as
episodes then I should really insist that this story is about
Raymond and not about virginity, coitus, incest and self-
abuse. So let me begin by telling you that it was ironic, for
reasons which will become apparent only very much later
– and you must be patient – it was ironic that Raymond of
all people should want to make me aware of my virginity.
On Finsbury Park one day Raymond approached me, and
steering me across to some laurel bushes bent and unbent
his finger mysteriously before my face and watched me
intently as he did so. I looked on blankly. Then I bent and
unbent my finger too and saw that it was the right thing to
do because Raymond beamed.

'You get it?' he said. 'You get it!' Driven by his

exhilaration I said yes, hoping then that Raymond would leave me alone now to bend and unbend my finger, to come at some understanding of his bewildering digital allegory in solitude. Raymond grasped my lapels with unusual intensity.

'What about it, then?' he gasped. Playing for time, I crooked my forefinger again and slowly straightened it, cool and sure, in fact so cool and sure that Raymond held his breath and stiffened with its motion. I looked at my erect finger and said,

'That depends,' wondering if I was to discover today what it was we were talking of.

Raymond was fifteen then, a year older than I was, and though I counted myself his intellectual superior – which was why I had to pretend to understand the significance of his finger – it was Raymond who *knew* things, it was Raymond who conducted my education. It was Raymond who initiated me into the secrets of adult life which he understood himself intuitively but never totally. The world he showed me, all its fascinating detail, lore and sin, the world for which he was a kind of standing master of ceremonies, never really suited Raymond. He knew that world well enough, but it – so to speak – did not want to know him. So when Raymond produced cigarettes, it was I who learned to inhale the smoke deeply, to blow smoke-rings and to cup my hands round the match like a film star, while Raymond choked and fumbled; and later on when Raymond first got hold of some marihuana, of which I had never heard, it was I who finally got stoned into euphoria while Raymond admitted – something I would never have done myself – that he felt nothing at all. And again, while it was Raymond with his deep voice and wisp of beard who got us into horror films, he would sit through the show with his fingers in his ears and his eyes

shut. And that was remarkable in view of the fact that in
one month alone we saw twenty-two horror films. When
Raymond stole a bottle of whisky from a supermarket in
order to introduce me to alcohol, I giggled drunkenly for
two hours at Raymond's convulsive fits of vomiting. My
first pair of long trousers were a pair belonging to Raymond which he had given to me as a present on my
thirteenth birthday. On Raymond they had, like all his
clothes, stopped four inches short of his ankles, bulged at
the thigh, bagged at the groin and now, as if a parable for
our friendship, they fitted me like tailor-mades, in fact so
well did they fit me, so comfortable did they feel, that I
wore no other trousers for a year. And then there were the
thrills of shoplifting. The idea as explained to me by
Raymond was quite simple. You walked into Foyle's bookshop, crammed your pockets with books and took them to
a dealer on the Mile End Road who was pleased to give
you half their cost price. For the very first occasion I
borrowed my father's overcoat which trailed the pavement
magnificently as I swept along. I met Raymond outside the
shop. He was in shirtsleeves because he had left his coat on
the Underground but he was certain he could manage
without one anyway, so we went into the shop. While I
stuffed into my many pockets a selection of slim volumes of
prestigious verse, Raymond was concealing on his person
the seven volumes of the Variorum Edition of the Works of
Edmund Spenser. For anyone else the boldness of the act
might have offered some chance of success, but Raymond's
boldness had a precarious quality, closer in fact to a complete detachment from the realities of the situation. The
under-manager stood behind Raymond as he plucked the
books from the shelf. The two of them were standing by
the door as I brushed by with my own load, and I gave
Raymond, who still clasped the tomes about him, a

conspiratorial smile, and thanked the under-manager who automatically held the door open for me. Fortunately, so hopeless was Raymond's attempt at shoplifting, so idiotic and transparent his excuses, that the manager finally let him go, liberally assuming him to be, I suppose, mentally deranged.

And finally, and perhaps most significantly, Raymond acquainted me with the dubious pleasures of masturbation. At the time I was twelve, the dawn of my sexual day. We were exploring a cellar on a bomb site, poking around to see what the dossers had left behind, when Raymond, having lowered his trousers as if to have a piss, began to rub his prick with a coruscating vigour, inviting me to do the same. I did and soon became suffused with a warm, indistinct pleasure which intensified to a floating, melting sensation as if my guts might at any time drift away to nothing. And all this time our hands pumped furiously. I was beginning to congratulate Raymond on his discovery of such a simple, inexpensive yet pleasurable way of passing the time, and at the same time wondering if I could not dedicate my whole life to this glorious sensation – and I suppose looking back now in many respects I have – I was about to express all manner of things when I was lifted by the scruff of the neck, my arms, my legs, my insides, haled, twisted, racked, and producing for all this two dollops of sperm which flipped over Raymond's Sunday jacket – it was Sunday – and dribbled into his breast pocket.

'Hey,' he said, breaking with his action, 'what did you do that for?' Still recovering from this devastating experience I said nothing, I could not say anything.

'I show you how to do this,' harangued Raymond, dabbing delicately at the glistening jissom on his dark jacket, 'and all you can do is spit.'

And so by the age of fourteen I had acquired, with

Raymond's guidance, a variety of pleasures which I rightly associated with the adult world. I smoked about ten cigarettes a day, I drank whisky when it was available, I had a connoisseur's taste for violence and obscenity, I had smoked the heady resin of *cannabis sativa* and I was aware of my own sexual precocity, though oddly it never occurred to me to find any use for it, my imagination as yet unnourished by longings or private fantasies. And all these pastimes were financed by the dealer in the Mile End Road. For these acquired tastes Raymond was my Mephistopheles, he was a clumsy Virgil to my Dante, showing me the way to a Paradiso where he himself could not tread. He could not smoke because it made him cough, the whisky made him ill, the films frightened or bored him, the cannabis did not affect him, and while I made stalactites on the ceiling of the bomb-site cellar, he made nothing at all.

'Perhaps,' he said mournfully as we were leaving the site one afternoon, 'perhaps I'm a little too old for that sort of thing.'

So when Raymond stood before me now intently crooking and straightening his finger I sensed that here was yet another fur-lined chamber of that vast, gloomy and delectable mansion, adulthood, and that if I only held back a little, concealing, for pride's sake, my ignorance, then shortly Raymond would reveal and then shortly I would excel.

'Well, that depends.' We walked across Finsbury Park where once Raymond, in his earlier, delinquent days had fed glass splinters to the pigeons, where together, in innocent bliss worthy of the 'Prelude', we had roasted alive Sheila Harcourt's budgerigar while she swooned on the grass nearby, where as young boys we had crept behind bushes to hurl rocks at the couples fucking in the arbour;

across Finsbury Park then, and Raymond saying,

'Who do you know?' Who did I know? I was still blundering, and this could be a change of subject, for Raymond had an imprecise mind. So I said, 'Who do *you* know?' to which Raymond replied, 'Lulu Smith,' and made everything clear – or at least the subject matter, for my innocence was remarkable. Lulu Smith! Dinky Lulu! the very name curls a chilly hand round my balls. Lulu Lamour, of whom it was said she would do anything, and that she had done everything. There were Jewish jokes, elephant jokes and there were Lulu jokes, and these were mainly responsible for the extravagant legend. Lulu Slim – but how my mind reels – whose physical enormity was matched only by the enormity of her reputed sexual appetite and prowess, her grossness only by the grossness she inspired, the legend only by the reality. Zulu Lulu! who – so fame had it – had laid a trail across north London of frothing idiots, a desolation row of broken minds and pricks spanning Shepherds Bush to Holloway, Ongar to Islington. Lulu! Her wobbling girth and laughing piggy's eyes, blooming thighs and dimpled finger-joints, this heaving, steaming leg-load of schoolgirl flesh who had, so reputation insisted, had it with a giraffe, a humming-bird, a man in an iron lung (who had subsequently died), a yak, Cassius Clay, a marmoset, a Mars Bar and the gear stick of her grandfather's Morris Minor (and subsequently a traffic warden).

Finsbury Park was filled with the spirit of Lulu Smith and I felt for the first time ill-defined longings as well as mere curiosity. I knew approximately what was to be done, for had I not seen heaped couples in all corners of the park during the long summer evenings, and had I not thrown stones and water bombs? – something I now superstitiously regretted. And suddenly there in Finsbury

Park, as we threaded our way through the pert piles of dog shit, I was made aware of and resented my virginity; I knew it to be the last room in the mansion, I knew it to be for certain the most luxurious, its furnishings more elaborate than any other room, its attractions more deadly, and the fact that I had never had it, made it, done it, was a total anathema, my malodorous albatross, and I looked to Raymond, who still held his forefinger stiff before him, to reveal what I must do. Raymond was bound to know ...

After school Raymond and I went to a cafe near Finsbury Park Odeon. While others of our age picked their noses over their stamp collections or homework, Raymond and I spent many hours here, discussing mostly easy ways of making money, and drinking large mugs of tea. Sometimes we got talking to the workmen who came there. Millais should have been there to paint us as we listened transfixed to their unintelligible fantasies and exploits, of deals with lorry drivers, lead from church roofs, fuel missing from the City Engineer's department, and then of cunts, bits, skirt, of strokings, beatings, fuckings, suckings, of arses and tits, behind, above, below, in front, with, without, of scratching and tearing, licking and shitting, of juiced cunts streaming, warm and infinite, of others cold and arid but worth a try, of pricks old and limp, or young and ebullient, of coming, too soon, too late or not at all, of how many times a day, of attendant diseases, of pus and swellings, cankers and regrets, of poisoned ovaries and destitute testicles; we listened to who and how the dustmen fucked, how the Co-op milkmen fitted it in, what the coalmen could hump, what the carpet-fitter could lay, what the builders could erect, what the meter man could inspect, what the bread man could deliver, the gas man sniff out, the plumber plumb, the electrician connect, the doctor inject, the lawyer solicit, the furniture man install –

and so on, in an unreal complex of timeworn puns and innuendo, formulas, slogans, folklore and bravado. I listened without understanding, remembering and filing away anecdotes which I would one day use myself, putting by histories of perversions and sexual manners – in fact a whole sexual morality, so that when finally I began to understand, from my own experience, what it was all about, I had on tap a complete education which, augmented by a quick reading of the more interesting parts of Havelock Ellis and Henry Miller, earned me the reputation of being the juvenile connoisseur of coitus to whom dozens of males – and fortunately females, too – came to seek advice. And all this, a reputation which followed me into art college and enlivened my career there, all this after only one fuck – the subject of this story.

So it was there in the cafe where I had listened, remembered and understood nothing that Raymond now relaxed his forefinger at last to curl it round the handle of his cup, and said,

'Lulu Smith will let you see it for a shilling.' I was glad of that. I was glad we were not rushing into things, glad that I would not be left alone with Zulu Lulu and be expected to perform the terrifyingly obscure, glad that the first encounter of this necessary adventure would be reconnaissance. And besides, I had only ever seen two naked females in my life. The obscene films we patronized in those days were nowhere near obscene enough, showing only the legs, backs and ecstatic faces of happy couples, leaving the rest to our tumescent imaginations, and clarifying nothing. As for the two naked women, my mother was vast and grotesque, the skin hanging from her like flayed toad-hides, and my ten-year-old sister was an ugly bat whom as a child I could hardly bring myself to look at, let along share the bath-tub with. And after all, a shilling was no expense at all, considering that Raymond and I were richer than most of the workmen in the cafe. In fact I was richer than any of my many uncles or my poor overworked father or anyone else I knew in my family. I used to laugh when I thought of the twelve-hour shift my father worked in the flour mill, of his exhausted, blanched, ill-tempered face when he got home in the evening, and I laughed a little louder when I thought of the thousands who each morning poured out of the terraced houses like our own to labour through the week, rest up on Sunday and then back again on Monday to toil in the mills, factories, timber yards and quaysides of London, returning each night older, more tired and no richer; over our cups of tea I laughed with Raymond at this quiescent betrayal of a lifetime, heaving, digging, shoving, packing, checking, sweating and groaning for the profits of others, at how, to reassure themselves, they made a virtue of this lifetime's grovel, at how they prized themselves for never missing a day in the inferno; and most of all I laughed when uncles Bob or Ted or my father made me a present of one of their hard-earned shillings – and on special occasions a ten-shilling note – I laughed because I knew that a good afternoon's work in the bookshop earned more than they scraped together in a week. I had to laugh discreetly, of course, for it would not do to mess up a gift like that, especially when it was quite obvious that they derived a great deal of pleasure from giving it to me. I can see them now, one of my uncles or my father striding the tiny length of the front parlour, the coin or banknote in his hand, reminiscing, anecdoting and advising me on Life, poised before the luxury of giving, and feeling good, feeling so good that it was a joy to watch. They felt, and for that short period they were, grand, wise, reflective, kind-hearted and expansive, and perhaps, who knows, a little divine; patricians dispensing to their son or nephew in the wisest, most generous way, the fruits of their sagacity and wealth – they were gods in their own temple and who was I to refuse their gift? Kicked in the arse round the factory fifty hours a week they needed these parlour miracle-plays, these mythic confrontations between Father and Son, so I, being appreciative and sensible of all the nuances of the situation, accepted their money, at the risk of boredom played along a little and suppressed my amusement till afterwards when I was made weak with tearful, hooting laughter. Long before I knew it I was a student, a promising student, of irony.

A shilling then was not too much to pay for a glimpse at the incommunicable, the heart of mystery's mystery, the Fleshly Grail, Dinky Lulu's pussy, and I urged Raymond to arrange a viewing as soon as possible. Raymond was already sliding into his role of stage manager, furrowing his brow in an important way, humming about dates, times, places, payments, and drawing ciphers on the back of an envelope. Raymond was one of those rare people who not only derive great pleasure from organizing events, but also are forlornly bad at doing it. It was quite possible that we would arrive on the wrong day at the wrong time, that there would be confusion about payment or the length of viewing time, but there was one thing which was ultimately more certain than anything else, more certain than the sun rising tomorrow, and that was that we would finally be shown the exquisite quim. For life was undeniably on Raymond's side; while in those days I could not have put my feelings into so many words, I sensed that in the cosmic array of individual fates Raymond's was cast diametrically opposite mine. Fortuna played practical jokes on Raymond, perhaps she even kicked sand in his eyes, but she never spat in his face or trod deliberately on his existential corns – Raymond's mistakings, losses, betrayals and injuries were all, in the final estimate, comic rather than tragic. I remember one occasion when Raymond paid seventeen pounds for a two-ounce cake of hashish which turned out not to be hashish at all. To cover his losses Raymond took the lump to a well-known spot in Soho and tried to sell it to a plainclothes man who fortunately did not press a charge. After all, there was, at that time at least, no law against dealing in powdered horse-dung, even if it was wrapped in tinfoil. Then there was the cross-country. Raymond was a mediocre runner and was among ten others chosen to represent the school in the sub-counties meeting. I always went along to the meetings. In fact there was no other sport I watched with such good heart, such entertainment and elation as a good cross-country. I loved the racked, contorted faces of the runners as they came up the tunnel of flags and crossed the finishing line; I found especially interesting those who came after the first fifty or so, running harder than any of the other contestants and competing demoniacally among themselves for the hundred and thirteenth place in the field. I watched them stumble up the tunnel of flags, clawing at their throats, retching, flailing their arms and falling to the grass, convinced that I had before me here a vision of human futility. Only the first thirty runners counted for anything in the contest and once the last of these had arrived the group of spectators began to disperse, leaving the rest to fight their private battles – and it was at this point that my interest pricked up. Long after the judges, marshals and time-keepers had gone home I remained at the finishing line in the descending gloom of a late winter's afternoon to watch the last of the runners crawl across the end marker. Those who fell I helped to their feet, I gave handkerchiefs to bloody noses, I thumped vomiters on the

back, I massaged cramped calves and toes – a real
Florence Nightingale, in fact, with the difference that I felt
an elation, a gay fascination with the triumphant spirit of
human losers who had run themselves into the ground for
nothing at all. How my mind soared, how my eyes swam,
when, after having waited ten, fifteen, even twenty minutes
in that vast, dismal field, surrounded on all sides by
factories, pylons, dull houses and garages, a cold wind
rising, bringing the beginnings of a bitter drizzle, waiting
there in that heavy gloom – and then suddenly to discern
on the far side of the field a limp white blob slowly making
its way to the tunnel, slowly measuring out with numb feet
on the wet grass its micro-destiny of utter futility. And
there beneath the brooding metropolitan sky, as if to unify
the complex totality of organic evolution and human purpose and place it within my grasp, the tiny amoebic blob
across the field took on human shape and yet still it held to
the same purpose, staggering determinedly in its pointless
effort to reach the flags – just life, just faceless, self-
renewing life to which, as the figure jack knifed to the
ground by the finishing line, my heart warmed, my spirit
rose in the fulsome abandonment of morbid and fatal
identification with the cosmic life process – the Logos.

'Bad luck, Raymond,' I would say cheerily as I handed
him his sweater, 'better luck next time.' And smiling wanly
with the sure, sad knowledge of Arlecchino, of Feste, the
knowledge that of the two it is the Comedian, not the
Tragedian, who holds the Trump, the twenty-second
Arcanum, whose letter is Than, whose symbol is Sol,
smiling as we left the now almost dark field, Raymond
would say,

'Well, it was only a cross-country, only a game, you
know.'

Raymond promised to confront the divine Lulu Smith

with our proposition the following day after school, and since I was pledged to look after my sister that evening while my parents were at the Walthamstow dog track, I said goodbye to Raymond there at the cafe. All the way home I thought about cunt. I saw it in the smile of the conductress, I heard it in the roar of the traffic, I smelt it in the fumes from the shoe-polish factory, conjectured it beneath the skirts of passing housewives, felt it at my finger tips, sensed it in the air, drew it in my mind and at supper, which was toad-in-the-hole, I devoured, as in an unspeakable rite, genitalia of batter and sausage. And for all this I still did not know just exactly what a cunt was. I eyed my sister across the table. I exaggerated a little just now when I said she was an ugly bat – I was beginning to think that perhaps she was not so bad-looking after all. Her teeth protruded, that could not be denied, and if her cheeks were a little too sunken it was not so you would notice in the dark, and when her hair had been washed, as it was now, you could almost pass her off as plain. So it was not surprising that I came to be thinking over my toad-in-the-hole that with some cajoling and perhaps a little honest deceit Connie could be persuaded to think of her-self, if only for a few minutes, as something more than a sister, as, let us say, a beautiful young lady, a film star and maybe, Connie, we could slip into bed here and try out this rather moving scene, now you get out of these clumsy pyjamas while I see to the light ... And armed with this comfortably gained knowledge I could face the awesome Lulu with zeal and abandon, the whole terrifying ordeal would pale into insignificance, and who knows, perhaps I could lay her out there and then, halfway through the peepshow.

I never enjoyed looking after Connie. She was petulant, demanding, spoiled and wanted to play games all the while instead of watching the television. I usually managed to get her to bed an hour early by winding the clock forward. Tonight I wound it back. As soon as my mother and father had left for the dog track I asked Connie which games she would like to play, she could choose anything she liked.

'I don't want to play games with you.'

'Why not?'

'Because you were staring at me all the time through supper.'

'Well, of course I was, Connie. I was trying to think of the games you liked to play best and I was just looking at you, that was all.' Finally she agreed to play hide and seek, which I had suggested with special insistence because our house was of such a size that there were only two rooms you could hide in, and they were both bedrooms. Connie was to hide first. I covered my eyes and counted to thirty, listening all the while to her footsteps in my parents' bedroom directly above, hearing with satisfaction the creak of the bed – she was hiding under the eiderdown, her second favourite place. I shouted 'Coming' and began to mount the stairs. At the bottom of the stairs I do not think I had decided clearly what I was about to do; perhaps just look around, see where things were, draw a mental plan for future reference – after all it would not do to go scaring my little sister who would not think twice about telling my father everything, and that would mean a scene of some sort, laborious lies to invent, shouting and crying and that sort of thing, just at a time when I needed all my energy for the obsession in hand. By the time I reached the top of the stairs, however, the blood having drained from brain to groin, literally, one might say, from sense to sensibility, by the time I was catching my breath on the top stair and closing my moist hand round the bedroom door-handle, I had decided to rape my sister. Gently I pushed the door open and called in a sing-song voice,

'Connieee, where aaare you?' That usually made her giggle, but this time there was no sound. Holding my breath I tip-toed over to the bedside and sang,

'I knooow where youuu are,' and bending down by the tell-tale lump under the eiderdown, I whispered,

'I'm coming to get you,' and began to peel the bulky cover away, softly, almost tenderly, peeking into the dark warmth underneath. Dizzy with expectation I drew it right back, and there, helplessly and innocently stretched out before me were my parents' pyjamas, and even as I was leaping back in surprise I received a blow in the small of my back of such unthinking vigour as can only be inflicted by a sister on her brother. And there was Connie dancing with mirth, the wardrobe door swinging open behind her.

'I saw you, I saw you and you didn't see me!' To relieve my feelings I kicked her shins and sat on the bed to consider what next, while Connie, predictably histrionic, sat on the floor and boo-hooed. I found the noise depressing after a while so I went downstairs and read the paper, certain that soon Connie would follow me down. She did, and she was sulking.

'What game do you want to play now?' I asked her. She sat on the edge of the sofa pouting and sniffing and hating me. I was even considering forgetting the whole plan and giving myself up to an evening's television when I had an idea, an idea of such simplicity, elegance, clarity and formal beauty, an idea which wore the assurance of its own success like a tailor-made suit. There is a game which all home-loving, unimaginative little girls like Connie find irresistible, a game which, ever since she had learned to speak the necessary words, Connie had plagued me to play with her, so that my boyhood years were haunted by her pleadings and exorcised by my inevitable refusals; it was a game, in short, which I would rather be burned at the stake for than have my friends see me play it. And now at last we were going to play Mummies and Daddies.

'*I* know a game you'd like to play, Connie,' I said. Of course she would not reply, but I let my words hang there in the air like bait. 'I know a game *you*'d like to play.' She lifted her head.

'What is it?'

'It's a game you're always wanting to play.'

She brightened. 'Mummies and Daddies?' She was transformed, she was ecstatic. She fetched prams, dolls, stoves, fridges, cots, teacups, a washing machine and a kennel from her room and set them up around me in a flutter of organizational zeal.

'Now you go here, no there, and this can be the kitchen and this is the door where you come in and don't tread on there because there's a wall and I come in and see you and I say to you and then you say to me and you go out and I make lunch.' I was plunged into the microcosm of the dreary, everyday, ponderous banalities, the horrifying, niggling details of the life of our parents and their friends, the life that Connie so dearly wanted to ape. I went to work and came back, I went to the pub and came back, I posted a letter and came back, I went to the shops and came back, I read a paper, I pinched the Bakelite cheeks of my progeny, I read another paper, pinched some more cheeks, went to work and came back. And Connie? She just cooked on the stove, washed up in the sink unit, washed, fed, put to sleep and roused her sixteen dolls and then poured some more tea – and she was happy. She was the inter-galactic-earth-goddess-housewife, she owned and controlled all around her, she saw all, she knew all, she told me when to go out, when to come in, which room I was in, what to say, how and when to say it. She was happy. She was complete, I have never seen another human so complete, she smiled, wide open, joyous and innocent smiles which I have never seen since – she tasted paradise on earth. And one point she was so blocked with the wonder, the ecstasy of it all, that mid-sentence her words choked up and she sat back on her heels, her eyes glistening, and breathed one long musical sigh of rare and wonderful happiness. It was almost a shame I had it in mind to rape her. Returning from work the twentieth time that half hour I said,

'Connie, we're leaving out one of the most important things that Mummies and Daddies do together.' She could hardly believe we had left anything out and she was curious to know.

'They fuck together, Connie, surely you know about that.'

'Fuck?' On her lips the word sounded strangely meaningless, which in a way I suppose it was, as far as I was concerned. The whole idea was to give it some meaning.

'Fuck? What does that mean?'

'Well, it's what they do at night, when they go to bed at night, just before they go to sleep.'

'Show me.' I explained that we would have to go upstairs and get into bed.

'No, we don't. We can pretend and this can be the bed,' she said, pointing at a square made by the design of the carpet.

'I cannot pretend and show it to you at the same time.' So once again I was climbing the stairs, once again my blood pounding and my manhood proudly stirring. Connie was quite excited too, still delirious with the happiness of the game and pleased at the novel turn it was taking.

'The first thing they do', I said, as I led her to the bed, 'is to take off all their clothes.' I pushed her on to the bed and, with fingers almost useless with agitation, unbuttoned her pyjamas till she sat naked before me, still sweet-smelling from her bath and giggling with the fun of it all. Then I got undressed too, leaving my pants on so as not to alarm her, and sat by her side. As children we had seen enough of each other's bodies to take our nakedness for granted, though that was some time ago now and I sensed her unease.

'Are you sure this is what they do?'

My own uncertainty was obscured now by lust. 'Yes,' I said, 'it's quite simple. You have a hole there and I put my weenie in it.' She clasped her hand over her mouth, giggling incredulously.

'That's silly. Why do they want to do that?' I had to admit it to myself, there was something unreal about it.

'They do it because it's their way of saying they like each other.' Connie was beginning to think that I was making the whole thing up, which, again, in a way I suppose I was. She stared at me, wide-eyed.

'But that's daft, why don't they just tell each other?' I was on the defensive, a mad scientist explaining his new crack-pot invention – coitus – before an audience of sceptical rationalists.

'Look,' I said to my sister, 'it's not only that. It's also a very nice feeling. They do it to get that feeling.'

'To get the feeling?' She still did not quite believe me. 'Get the feeling? What do you mean, get the feeling?'

I said, 'I'll show you.' And at the same time I pushed Connie on to the bed and lay on top of her in the manner I had inferred from the films Raymond and I had seen together. I was still wearing my underpants. Connie stared blankly up at me, not even afraid – in fact, she might have been closer to boredom. I writhed from side to side, trying to push my pants off without getting up.

'I still don't get it,' she complained from underneath me. 'I'm not getting any feeling. Are you getting any feeling?'

'Wait,' I grunted, as I hooked the underpants round the end of my toes with the very tips of my fingers, 'if you just wait a minute I'll show you.' I was beginning to lose my temper with Connie, with myself, with the universe, but mostly with my underpants which snaked determinedly round my ankles. At last I was free. My prick was hard and sticky on Connie's belly and now I began to manœuvre it between her legs with one hand while I supported the weight of my body with the other. I searched her tiny crevice without the least notion of what I was looking for, but half expecting all the same to be transformed at any moment into a human whirlwind of sensation. I think perhaps I had in mind a warm fleshy chamber, but as I prodded and foraged, jabbed and wheedled, I found nothing other than tight, resisting skin. Meanwhile Connie just lay on her back, occasionally making little comments.

'Ooh, that's where I go wee-wee. I'm sure *our* mummy and daddy don't do this.' My supporting arm was being seared by pins and needles, I was feeling raw and yet still I poked and pushed, in a mood of growing despair. Each time Connie said, 'I still don't get any feeling,' I felt another ounce of my manhood slip away. Finally I had to rest. I sat on the edge of the bed to consider my hopeless failure, while behind me Connie propped herself up on her elbows. After a moment or two I felt the bed begin to shake with silent spasms and, turning, I saw Connie with tears spilling down her screwed-up face, inarticulate and writhing with choked laughter.

'What is it?' I asked, but she could only point vaguely in my direction and groan, and then she lay back on the bed, heaving and helpless with mirth. I sat by her side, not knowing what to think but deciding, as Connie quaked behind me, that another attempt was now out of the question. At last she was able to get out some words. She sat up and pointed at my still erect prick and gasped, 'It looks so ... it looks so ...' sank back in another fit, and then managed in one squeal, *So silly, it looks so silly,* after which she collapsed again into a high-pitched, squeezed-out titter. I sat there in lonely detumescent blankness, numbed by this final humiliation into the realization that this was no real girl beside me, this was no true representative of that sex; this was no boy, certainly, nor was it finally a girl – it was my sister, after all. I stared down at my limp prick, wondering at its hang-dog look, and just as I was thinking of getting my clothes together, Connie, silent now, touched me on the elbow.

'I know where it goes,' she said, and lay back on the bed, her legs wide apart, something it had not occurred to me to ask her to do. She settled herself among the pillows. 'I know where the hole is.'

I forgot my sister and my prick rose inquisitively, hopefully, to the invitation which Connie was whispering. It was all right with her now, she was at Mummies and Daddies and controlling the game again. With her hand she guided me into her tight, dry little-girl's cunt and we lay perfectly still for a while. I wished Raymond could have seen me, and I was glad he had brought my virginity to my notice, I wished Dinky Lulu could have seen me, in fact if my wishes had been granted I would have had all my friends, all the people I knew, file through the bedroom to catch me in my splendorous pose. For more than sensation, more than any explosion behind my eyes, spears through my stomach, searings in my groin or rackings of my soul – more than any of these things, none of which I felt anyway, more then than even the thought of these things, I felt proud, proud to be fucking, even if it were only Connie, my ten-year-old sister, even if it had been a crippled mountain goat I would have been proud to be lying there in that manly position, proud in advance of being able to say 'I have fucked', of belonging intimately and irrevocably to that superior half of humanity who had known coitus, and fertilized the world with it. Connie lay quite still too, her eyes half-closed, breathing deeply – she was asleep. It was way past her bedtime and our strange game had exhausted her. For the first time I moved gently backwards and forwards, just a few times, and came in a miserable, played-out, barely pleasurable way. It woke Connie into indignation.

'You've wet inside me,' and she began to cry. Hardly noticing, I got up and started to get dressed. This may have been one of the most desolate couplings known to copulating mankind, involving lies, deceit, humiliation, incest, my partner falling asleep, my gnat's orgasm and the sobbing which now filled the bedroom, but I was pleased with it, myself, Connie, pleased to let things rest a while, to let the matter drop. I led Connie to the bathroom and began to fill the sink – my parents would be back soon and Connie should be asleep in her bed. I had made it into the adult world finally, I was pleased about that, but right then I did not want to see a naked girl, or a naked anything for a while yet. Tomorrow I would tell Raymond to forget the appointment with Lulu, unless he wanted to go it alone. And I knew for a fact that he would not want that at all.

Last Day of Summer

❖❖❖

I am twelve and lying near-naked on my belly out on the back lawn in the sun when for the first time I hear her laugh. I don't know, I don't move, I just close my eyes. It's a girl's laugh, a young woman's, short and nervous like laughing at nothing funny. I got half my face in the grass I cut an hour before and I can smell the cold soil beneath it. There's a faint breeze coming off the river, the late afternoon sun stinging my back and that laugh jabbing at me like it's all one thing, one taste in my head. The laughing stops and all I can hear is the breeze flapping the pages of my comic, Alice crying somewhere upstairs and a kind of summer heaviness all over the garden. Then I hear them walking across the lawn towards me and I sit up so quickly it makes me dizzy, and the colours have gone out of everything. And there's this fat woman, or girl, walking towards me with my brother. She's so fat her arms can't hang right from her shoulders. She's got rubber tyres round her neck. They're both looking at me and talking about me, and when they get really close I stand up and she shakes my hand and still looking right at me she makes a kind of yelping noise like a polite horse. It's the noise I heard just now, her laugh. Her hand is hot and wet and pink like a sponge, with dimples at the base of each finger. My brother introduces her as Jenny. She's going to take the attic bedroom. She's got a very large face, round like a red moon, and thick glasses which make her eyes as big as golf balls. When she lets go of my hand I can't think of one thing to say. But my brother Peter talks on and on, he tells her what vegetables we are growing and what flowers, he makes her stand where she can get a view of the river between the trees and then he leads her back to the house. My brother is exactly twice my age and he's good at that sort of thing, just talking.

Jenny takes the attic. I've been up there a few times looking for things in the old boxes, or watching the river out of the small window. There's nothing much in the boxes really, just cloth scraps and dressmaking patterns. Perhaps some of them actually belonged to my mother. In one corner there's a pile of picture frames without pictures. Once I was up there because it was raining outside, and downstairs there was a row going on between Peter and some of the others. I helped José clear out the place ready for a bedroom. José used to be Kate's boyfriend and then last spring he moved his things out of Kate's bedroom and moved into the spare room next to mine. We carried the boxes and frames to the garage, we stained the wooden floor black and put down rugs. We took apart the extra bed in my room and carried it up. With that, a table and a chair, a small cupboard and the sloping ceiling, there is just room for two people standing up. All Jenny has for luggage is a small suitcase and a carrier bag. I take them up to her room for her and she follows, breathing harder and harder and stopping half way up the third set of stairs to get a rest. My brother Peter comes up behind and we squeeze in as if we are all going to be living there and we're seeing it for the first time. I point out the window for her so she can see the river. Jenny sits with her big elbows on the table. Sometimes she dabs at her damp red face with a large white handkerchief while she's listening to some story of Peter's. I'm sitting on the bed behind her looking at how immense her back is, and under her chair I can see her thick pink legs, how they taper away and squeeze into tiny shoes at the bottom. Everywhere she's pink. The smell of her sweat fills the room. It smells like the new cut grass outside, and I get this idea that I mustn't breathe it in too deeply or I'll get fat too. We stand up to go so she can get on with her unpacking and she's saying thank you for everything, and as I go through the door she makes her little yelp, her nervous laugh. Without meaning to I glance back at her through the doorway and she's looking right at me with her magnified golf-balls eyes.

'You don't say much, do you?' she says. Which sort of makes it even harder to think of something to say. So I just smile at her and carry on down the stairs.

Downstairs it's my turn to help Kate cook the supper. Kate is tall and slim and sad. Really the opposite of Jenny. When I have girl friends I'm going to have them like Kate. She's very pale, though, even at this time in the summer. She has strange-coloured hair. Once I heard Sam say it was the colour of a brown envelope. Sam is one of Peter's friends who also lives here and who wanted to move his things into Kate's bedroom when José moved his out. But Kate is sort of haughty and she doesn't like Sam because he's too noisy. If Sam moved into Kate's room he'd always be waking up Alice, Kate's little girl. When Kate and José are in the same room I always watch them to see if they ever look at each other, and they never do. Last April I went into Kate's room one afternoon to borrow something and she and José were in bed asleep. José's parents come from Spain and his skin is very dark. Kate was lying on her back with one arm stretched out, and José was lying on her arm, snuggling up to her side. They didn't have pyjamas on, and the sheet came up to their waists. They were so black and so white. I stood at the foot of the bed a long time, watching them. It was like some secret I'd found out. Then Kate opened her eyes and saw me there and told me very softly to get out. It seems pretty strange to me that they were lying there like that and now they don't even look at each other. That wouldn't happen with me if I was lying on some girl's arm. Kate doesn't like cooking. She has to spend a lot of time making sure Alice doesn't put knives in her mouth or pull boiling pots off the stove. Kate prefers dressing-up and going out, or talking for hours on the telephone, which is what I would rather do if I was a girl. Once she stayed out late and my brother Peter had to put Alice to bed. Kate always looks sad when she speaks to Alice, when she's telling her what to do she speaks very softly as if she doesn't really want to be speaking to Alice at all. And it's the same when she talks to me, as if it's not really talking at all. When she sees my back in the kitchen she takes me through to the downstairs bathroom and dabs calamine lotion over me with a piece of cotton wool. I can see her in the mirror, she doesn't seem to have any particular expression on her face. She makes a sound between her teeth, half a whistle and half a sigh, and when she wants a different part of my back towards the light she pushes or pulls me about by my arm. She asks me quickly and quietly what the girl upstairs is like, and when I tell her, 'She's very fat and she's got a funny laugh,' she doesn't make any reply. I cut up vegetables for Kate and lay the table. Then I walk down to the river to look at my boat. I bought it with some money I got when my parents died. By the time I get to the jetty it's past sunset and the river is black with scraps of red like the cloth scraps that used to be in the attic. Tonight the river is slow and the air is warm and smooth. I don't untie the boat, my back is too sore from the sun to row. Instead I climb in and sit with the quiet rise and fall of the river, watching the red cloth sink in the black water and wondering if I breathed in too much of Jenny's smell.

When I get back they are about to start eating. Jenny is sitting next to Peter and when I come in she doesn't look up from her plate, even when I sit down on the other side of her. She's so big beside me, and yet so bowed down over her plate, looking as if she doesn't really want to exist, that I feel sorry for her in a way and I want to speak to her. But I can't think of anything to say. In fact no one has anything to say this meal, they're all just pushing their knives and forks backwards and forwards over their plates, and now and then someone murmurs for something to be passed. It doesn't usually happen like this when we're eating, there's usually something going on. But Jenny's here, more silent than any of us, and bigger, too, and not looking up from her plate. Sam clears his throat and looks down our end of the table at Jenny, and everyone else looks up too, except for her, waiting for something. Sam clears his throat again and says,

'Where were you living before, Jenny?' Because no one's been speaking it comes out flat, as if Sam's in an office filling in a form for her. And Jenny, still looking down at her plate, says,

'Manchester.' Then she looks at Sam. 'In a flat.' And she gives a little yelp of a laugh, probably because we're all listening and looking at her, and then she sinks back into her plate while Sam's saying something like, 'Ah, I see,' and thinking of the next thing to say. Upstairs, Alice starts crying so Kate goes and brings her down and lets her sit on her lap. When she stops crying she points at each one of us in turn and shouts, 'UH, UH, UH,' and so on right round the table while we all sit there eating and not speaking. It's like she's telling us off for not thinking of things to say. Kate tells her to be quiet in the sad way she always has when she's with Alice. Sometimes I think she's like that because Alice doesn't have a father. She doesn't look at all like Kate, she has very fair hair and ears that are too large for her head. A year or two ago when Alice was very little I used to think that José was her father. But his hair is black, and he never pays much attention to Alice. When everybody's finished the first course and I'm helping Kate collect the dishes, Jenny offers to have Alice on her lap. Alice is still shouting and pointing at different things in the room, but once she's on Jenny's lap she goes very quiet. Probably because it's the biggest lap she's ever seen. Kate and I bring in fruit and tea, and when we are peeling oranges and bananas, eating the apples from our tree in the garden, pouring tea and passing cups with milk and sugar round, everyone starts talking and laughing like they usually do, like there never was anything holding them back. And Jenny is giving Alice a really good time on her lap, making her knees gallop like a horse, making her hand swoop down like a bird on to Alice's belly, showing her tricks with her fingers, so that all the time Alice is shouting for more. It's the first time I've heard her laugh like that. And then Jenny glances down the table at Kate who's been watching them play with the same kind of look she might have on her face if she was watching the telly. Jenny carries Alice to her mother like she's suddenly feeling guilty about having Alice on her lap for such a long time and having so much fun. Alice is shouting, 'More, more, more,' when she's back at the other end of the table, and she's still shouting it five minutes later when her mother carries her up to bed.

Because my brother asks me to, I take coffee up to Jenny's room early next morning. When I go in she's already up, sitting at her table putting stamps on letters. She looks smaller than she did last night. She has her window wide open and her room is full of morning air, it feels like she's been up for a long time. Out of her window I can see the river stretching between the trees, light and quiet in the sun. I want to get outside, I want to see my boat before breakfast. But Jenny wants to talk. She makes me sit on her bed and tell her about myself. She doesn't ask me any questions and since I'm not sure how to start off telling someone about myself I sit there and watch while she writes addresses on her letters and sips her coffee. But I don't mind, it's all right in Jenny's room. She's put two pictures on the wall. One is a framed photograph taken in a zoo of a monkey walking upside down along a branch with its baby hanging on to its stomach. You can tell it is a zoo because in the bottom corner there's a zoo-keeper's cap and part of his face. The other is a colour picture taken out of a magazine of two children running along the sea shore holding hands. The sun is setting and everything in the picture is deep red, even the children. It's a very good picture. She finishes with her letters and asks me where I go to school. I tell her about the new school I'm going to when the holidays are over, the big comprehensive in Reading. But I haven't been there yet, so there isn't much I can tell her about it. She sees me looking out the window again.

'Are you going down to the river?'

'Yes, I have to see my boat.'

'Can I come with you? Will you show me the river?' I wait for her by the door, watching her squeeze her round, pink feet into small, flat shoes and brush her very short hair with a brush which has a mirror on the back. We walk across the lawn to the kissing gate at the bottom of the garden and along the path through the high ferns.

Half way down I stop to listen to a yellow-hammer, and she tells me that she doesn't know the song of one bird. Most grown-up people will never tell you that they don't know things. So farther on down the path just before it opens out on to the jetty we stop under an old oak tree so she can hear a blackbird. I know there's one up there, it's always up there singing this time in the morning. Just as we get there it stops and we have to wait quietly for it to begin again. Standing by that half-dead old trunk I can hear other birds in other trees and the river just round the corner washing under the jetty. But our bird is taking a rest. Something about waiting in silence makes Jenny nervous and she pinches her nose tight to stop her yelp of a laugh getting out. I want her to hear the blackbird so much I put my hand on her arm, and when I do that she takes her hand away from her nose and smiles. Just a few seconds after that the blackbird sets out on its long complicated song. It was waiting all the time for us to get settled. We walk out on to the jetty and I show her my boat tied up at the end. It's a rowing boat, green on the outside and red on the inside like a fruit. I've been down here every day all this summer to row it, paint it, wipe it down, and sometimes just to look at it. Once I rowed it seven miles upstream and spent the rest of the day drifting back down. We sit on the edge of the jetty looking at my boat, the river and the trees on the other side. Then Jenny looks downstream and says,

'London's down there.' London is a terrible secret I try to keep from the river. It doesn't know about it yet while it's flowing past our house. So I just nod and say nothing. Jenny asks me if she can sit in the boat. It worries me at first that she's going to be too heavy. But of course I cannot tell her that. I lean over the jetty and hold the painter rope for her to climb in. She does it with a lot of grunting and rocking around. And since the boat doesn't look any lower now than it usually does, I get in too and we watch the river from this new level where you can see how strong and old it really is. We sit talking for a long time. First I tell her about how my parents died two years ago in a car crash and how my brother had ideas for turning the house into a kind of commune. At first he was going to have over twenty people living here. But now I think he wants to keep it down to about eight. Then Jenny tells me about the time she was a teacher in a big school in Manchester where all the children were always laughing at her because she was fat. She doesn't seem to mind talking about it, though. She has some funny stories of her time there. When she's telling me of the time when the children locked her in a book cupboard we both laugh so much the boat rocks from side to side and pushes small waves out into the river. This time Jenny's laugh is easy and kind of rhythmic, not hard and yelping like before. On the way back she recognizes two blackbirds by their songs, and when we're crossing the lawn she points out another. I just nod. It's a song-thrush really, but I'm too hungry to tell her the difference.

Three days later I hear Jenny singing. I'm in the back yard trying to put together a bicycle out of bits and pieces and I hear her through the open kitchen window. She's in there cooking lunch and looking after Alice while Kate visits friends. It's a song she doesn't know the words for, half way between happy and sad, and she's singing like an old croaky Negress to Alice. New morning man la-la, la-la-la-, l'la, new morning man la-la-la, la-la, l'la, new morning man take me 'way from here. That afternoon I row her out on the river and she has another song with the same kind of tune, but this time with no words at all. Ya-la-la, ya-laaa, ya-eeeee. She spreads her hands out and rolls her big magnified eyes around like it's a serenade especially for me. A week later Jenny's songs are all over the house, sometimes with a line or two if she can remember it, most often with no words at all. She spends a lot of her time in the kitchen and that's where she does most of her singing. Somehow she makes more space in there. She scrapes paint off the north window to let in more light. No one can think why it was painted over in the first place. She carries out an old table, and when it's out everyone realizes that it was always in the way. One afternoon she paints the whole of one wall white to make the kitchen look bigger, and she arranges the pots and plates so that you always know where they are and even I can reach them. She makes it into the kind of kitchen you can sit around in when you've got nothing else to do. Jenny makes her own bread and bakes cakes, things we usually go to the shop for. On the third day she's here I find clean sheets on my bed. She takes the sheets I've been using all summer and most of my clothes away for washing. She spends all of one afternoon making a curry, and that night I eat the best meal in two years. When the others tell her how good they think it is Jenny gets nervous and does her yelping laugh. I can see the others are still bothered when she does it, they sort of look away as if it is something disgusting that would be rude to look at. But it doesn't worry me at all when she does that laugh, I don't even hear it except when the others are there at the table looking away. Most afternoons we go out on the river together and I try to teach her to row, and listen to her stories of when she was teaching, and when she was working in a supermarket, how she used to watch old people come in each day to shoplift bacon and butter. I teach her some more birdsongs, but the only one she can really remember is the first one, the blackbird. In her room she shows me pictures of her parents and her brother and she says,

'I'm the only fat one.' I show her some pictures of my parents, too. One of them was taken a month before they died, and in it they are walking down some steps holding hands and laughing at something outside the picture. They were laughing at my brother who was fooling around to make them laugh for the picture I was taking. I had just got the camera for my tenth birthday and that was one of the first pictures I took with it. Jenny looks at it for a long time and says something about her looking like a very nice woman, and suddenly I see my mother as just a woman in a picture, it could be any woman, and for the first time she's far off, not in my head looking out, but outside my head being looked at by me, Jenny or anyone who picks up the photo. Jenny takes it out of my hand and puts it away with the others in the shoe box. As we go downstairs she starts off on a long story about a friend of hers who was producing a play which ended strangely and quietly. The friend wanted Jenny to start off the clapping at the end but Jenny got it all wrong somehow and started everyone clapping fifteen minutes before the end during a quiet bit so that the last part of the play was lost and the clapping was all the louder because no one knew what the play was about. All this, I suppose, is to make me stop thinking about my mother, which it does.

Kate spends more time with her friends in Reading. One morning I'm in the kitchen when she comes in very smartly dressed in a kind of leather suit and high leather boots. She sits down opposite me to wait for Jenny to come down so she can tell her what food to give Alice that day, and what time she'll be back. It reminds me of another morning almost two years ago when Kate came into the kitchen in the same kind of suit. She sat down at the table, undid her blouse and started to knead with her fingers blueish-white milk into a bottle from one tit and then the other. She didn't seem to notice me sitting there.

'What are you doing that for?' I asked her.

She said, 'It's for Janet to give to Alice later on today. I've got to go out.' Janet was a black girl who used to be living here. It was strange watching Kate milk herself into a bottle. It made me think how we're just animals with clothes on doing very peculiar things, like monkeys at a tea party. But we get so used to each other most of the time. I wonder if Kate is thinking of that time now, sitting with me in the kitchen first thing in the morning. She's got orange lipstick on and her hair tied back and that makes her look even thinner than usual. Her lipstick is sort of fluorescent, like a road sign. Every minute she looks at her watch and her leather creaks. She looks like some beautiful woman from outer space. Then Jenny comes down, wearing a huge old dressing-gown made out of patches and yawning because she's just got out of bed, and Kate speaks to her very quickly and quietly about Alice's food for the day. It's as if it makes her sad, talking about that sort of thing. She picks up her bag and runs out the kitchen and calls, ''Bye,' over her shoulder. Jenny sits down at the table and drinks tea and it's like she really is the big mama left behind at home to look after the rich lady's daughter. Yo' daddy's rich and yo' mama's goodlookin', lah la-la-la la-la don' yo' cry. And there's something in the way the others treat Jenny. Like she's outside things, and not really a person like they are. They've got used to her cooking big meals and making cakes. No one says anything about it now. Sometimes in the evenings Peter, Kate, José and Sam sit around and smoke hashish in Peter's homemade water-pipe and listen to the stereo turned up loud. When they do that Jenny usually goes up to her room, she doesn't like to be with them when they're doing that, and I can see they sort of resent it. And though she's a girl she's not beautiful like Kate or Sharon, my brother's girl friend. She doesn't wear jeans and Indian shirts like they do, either, probably because she can't find any to fit her. She wears dresses with flowers on and ordinary things like my mother or the lady in the post office wear. And when she gets nervous about something and does her laugh I can tell they think of her like some sort of mental patient, I know that by the way they turn their eyes away. And they still think about how fat she is. Sometimes when she's not there Sam calls her Slim Jim, and it always makes the others laugh. It's not that they're unfriendly to her or anything like that, it's just that in some way that's hard to describe they keep her apart from themselves. One time we're out on the river she asks me about hashish.

'What do you think about it all?' she says, and I tell her my brother won't let me try it till I'm fifteen. I know she's dead against it, but she doesn't mention it again. It's that same afternoon I take a photograph of her leaning by the kitchen door holding Alice and squinting a little into the sun. She takes mine too, riding no-hands round the back yard on the bicycle I put together out of bits and pieces.

It's hard to say exactly when Jenny becomes Alice's mother. At first she's just looking after her while Kate visits friends. Then the visits get more often till they are almost every day. So the three of us, Jenny, Alice and me, spend a lot of time together by the river. By the jetty there's a grass bank which slopes down on to a tiny sand beach about six feet across. Jenny sits on the bank playing with Alice while I do things to my boat. When we first put Alice in the boat she squeals like a baby pig. She doesn't trust the water. It's a long time before she'll stand on the small beach, and when she does at last she never takes her eyes off the water's edge to make sure it doesn't creep up on her. But when she sees Jenny waving to her from the boat, and quite safe, she changes her mind and we make a trip to the other side of the river. Alice doesn't mind about Kate being away because she likes Jenny, who sings her the bits of songs she knows and talks to her all the time when they are sitting on the grass bank by the river. Alice does not understand a word of it but she likes the sound of Jenny's voice going on and on. Sometimes Alice points up to Jenny's mouth and says, 'More, more.' Kate is always so quiet and sad with her she doesn't hear many voices speaking right at her. One night Kate stays away and doesn't come back till the next morning. Alice is sitting on Jenny's knee spreading her breakfast across the kitchen table when Kate comes running in, scoops her up, hugs her and asks over and over again without giving anyone time to reply,

'Has she been all right? Has she been all right? Has she been all right?' The same afternoon Alice is back with Jenny because Kate has to go off somewhere again. I'm in the hall outside the kitchen when I hear her tell Jenny she'll be back in the early evening, and a few minutes later I see her walking down the drive carrying a small suitcase. When she gets back two days later she just puts her head round the door to see if Alice is still there, and then she goes up to her room. It's not always such a good thing having Alice with us all the time. We can't go very far in the boat. After twenty minutes Alice gets suspicious of the water again and wants to be back on the shore. And if we want to walk somewhere Alice has to be carried most of the way. It means I can't show Jenny some of my special places along the river. By the end of the day Alice gets pretty miserable, moaning and crying about nothing be-cause she's tired. I get fed up spending so much time with

Alice. Kate stays up in her room most of the day. One afternoon I take her up some tea and she's sitting in a chair asleep. With Alice there so much of the time Jenny and I don't talk together as much as we did when she first came. Not because Alice is listening, but because all Jenny's time is taken up with her. She doesn't think of anything else, really, it seems like she doesn't want to talk with anyone but Alice. One evening we are all sitting around in the front room after supper. Kate is in the hall having a long argument with someone on the telephone. She finishes, comes in, sits down in a noisy kind of way and carries on reading. But I can see she's angry and not really reading at all. No one speaks for a while, then Alice starts crying upstairs and shouting for Jenny. Jenny and Kate both look up at once and stare at each other for a moment. Then Kate gets up and leaves the room. We all pretend to go on reading but really we are listening to Kate's footsteps on the stairs. We hear her walk into Alice's room, which is right over this one, and we hear Alice shout louder and louder for Jenny to come up. Kate comes back down the stairs, this time quickly. When she comes in the room Jenny looks up and they stare at each other again. And all the time Alice goes on shouting for Jenny. Jenny gets up and squeezes past Kate at the door. They don't speak. The rest of us, Peter, Sam, José and me, we carry on with our pretend reading and listen to Jenny's footsteps upstairs. The crying stops and she stays up there a long time. When she comes down Kate is back in her chair with her magazine. Jenny sits down and no one looks up, no one speaks.

Suddenly the summer is over. Jenny comes into my room early one morning to drag the sheets off my bed and all the clothes she can find in the room. Everything has to be washed before I go to school. Then she gets me to clean out my room, all the old comics and plates and cups which have been collecting under my bed all summer, all the dust and the pots of paint I've been using on my boat. She finds a small table in the garage and I help her carry it to my room. It's going to be my desk for doing homework on. She takes me into the village for a treat, and she won't tell me what it is. When we get there it turns out to be a haircut. I'm about to walk away when she puts her hand on my shoulder.

'Don't be silly,' she says. 'You can't go to school looking like that, you won't last a day.' So I sit still for the barber and let him cut away my whole summer while Jenny sits behind me, laughing at me scowling at her in the mirror. She gets some money from my brother Peter and takes me on the bus into town to buy a school uniform. It's strange having her tell me what to do all of a sudden after our times out on the river. But I don't mind, really, I can't think of any good reasons for not doing the things she says. She steers me through the main shopping streets, into shoe shops and outfitters, she buys me a red blazer and a cap, two pairs of black leather shoes, six pairs of grey socks, two pairs of grey trousers and five grey shirts, and all the time she's saying, 'Do you like these ones? Do you like this?' and since I don't have any special feeling for one particular shade of grey, I agree with whatever she thinks is the best. It's all over in an hour. That evening she empties my drawers of my rock collection to make room for the new clothes, and she gets me to put on the whole uniform. They all laugh downstairs, especially when I put the red cap on. Sam says I look like an inter-galactic postman. For three nights in a row she has me scrubbing my knees with a nail-brush to get the dirt out from under the skin.

Then on Sunday, the day before I start back at school, I go down to the boat with Jenny and Alice for the last time. In the evening I'm going to help Peter and Sam drag my boat up the path and across the lawn into the garage for the winter. Then we're going to build another jetty, a stronger one. It's the last boat trip of the summer. Jenny lifts Alice in and climbs in herself while I hold the boat steady from the jetty. As I'm pushing us off with an oar, Jenny starts one of her songs. Jeeesus won't you come on down, Jeeesus won't you come on down, Jeeesus won't you come on down, lah, la-la-la-lah, la-la. Alice stands between Jenny's knees watching me row. She thinks it's funny, the way I strain backwards and forwards. She thinks it's a game I'm playing with her, moving close up to her face and away again. It's strange, our last day on the river. When Jenny's finished her song no one speaks for a long time. Just Alice laughing at me. It's so still on the river, her laugh carries across the water to nowhere. The sun is a kind of pale yellow like it's burnt out at the end of summer, there's no wind in the trees on the banks, and no birdsong. Even the oars make no sound in the water. I row upstream with the sun on my back, but it's too pale to feel it, it's too pale to make shadows, even. Up ahead there's an old man standing under an oak tree, fishing. When we are level with him he looks up and stares at us in our boat and we stare back at him on the bank. His face does not change when he's looking at us. Our faces do not change, either, no one says hello. He has a long piece of grass in his mouth and when we've passed he takes it out and spits quietly into the river. Jenny trails her hand in the thick water and watches the bank as if it's something she's only seeing in her mind. It makes me think she doesn't really want to be out there on the river with me. She only came because of all the other times we've been rowing together, and because this is the last time this summer. It sort of makes me sad, thinking that, it makes it harder to row. Then after we've been going for about half an hour she looks at me and smiles and I can tell it's all in my head about her not wanting to be on the river because she starts talking about the summer, about all the things we've been doing. She makes it sound really great, much better than it was really. About the long walks we went on, and paddling at the edge of the river with Alice, how I tried to teach her to row and remember different birdsongs, and the times we used to get up while the others were still asleep and row on the river before breakfast. She gets me going too, remembering all the things we did, like the time we thought we saw a waxwing, and another time we waited one evening behind a bush for a badger to come out of its hole. Pretty soon we get really excited about what a summer it's been and the things we're going to do next year, shouting and laughing into the dead air. And then Jenny says,

'And tomorrow you put on your red cap and go to school.' There's something in the way she says it, pretending to be serious and telling me off, with one finger wagging in the air, that makes it the funniest thing I ever heard. And the idea of it too, of doing all those things in the summer and then at the end of it putting on a red cap and going to school. We start laughing and it seems like we're never going to stop. I have to put down the oars. Our hooting and cackling gets louder and louder because the still air doesn't carry it across the water and the noise of it stays with us in the boat. Each time we catch the other's eye we laugh harder and louder till it begins to hurt down my sides, and more than anything I want to stop. Alice starts to cry because she doesn't know what's happening, and that makes us laugh more. Jenny leans over the side of the boat so she can't see me. But her laugh is getting tighter and drier, little hard yelps like pieces of stone from her throat. Her big pink face and her big pink arms are shaking and straining to catch a mouthful of air, but it's all

going out of her in little pieces of stone. She leans back into
the boat. Her mouth is laughing but her eyes look kind of
scared and dry. She drops to her knees, holding her
stomach with the pain of laughing, and knocks Alice down
with her. And the boat tips over. It tips over because Jenny
falls against the side, because Jenny is big and my boat is
small. It goes over quickly, like the click of my camera
shutter, and suddenly I'm at the deep green bottom of the
river touching the cold soft mud with the back of my hand
and feeling the reeds on my face. I can hear laughter like
sinking pieces of stone by my ear. But when I push upwards to the surface I feel no one near me. When I come
up it's dark on the river. I've been down a long time.
Something touches my head and I realize I'm inside the
upturned boat. I go down again and up the other side. It
takes me a long time to get my breath. I work my way
round the boat shouting over and over for Jenny and Alice.
I put my mouth in the water and shout their names. But
no one answers, nothing breaks the surface. I'm the only
one on the river. So I hang on to the side of the boat and
wait for them to come up. I wait a long time, drifting along
with the boat, with the laughter still in my head, watching
the river and the yellow patches on it from the sun getting
low. Sometimes great shivers run through my legs and
back, but mostly I'm calm, hanging on to the green shell
with nothing in my mind, nothing at all, just watching the
river, waiting for the surface to break and the yellow
patches to scatter. I drift past the place where the old man
was fishing and it seems like a very long time ago. He's
gone now, there's just a paper bag in the place where he
was standing. I get so tired I close my eyes and it feels like
I'm at home in bed and it's winter and my mother's
coming into my room to say goodnight. She turns out the
light and I slip off the boat into the river. Then I remember

and I shout for Jenny and Alice and watch the river again and my eyes start to close and my mother comes into my room and says goodnight and turns out the light and I sink back into the water again. After a long time I forget to shout for Jenny and Alice, I just hang there and drift down. I'm looking at a place on the bank I used to know very well a long time ago. There's a patch of sand and a grass bank by a jetty. The yellow patches are sinking into the river when I push away from the boat. I let it drift on down to London and I swim slowly through the black water to the jetty.

Cocker at the Theatre

There was dust on the boards, the backdrops were half painted and they were all naked on the stage, with the bright lights to keep them warm and show up the dust in the air. There was nowhere to sit so they shuffled about miserably. They had no pockets to put their hands in, and there were no cigarettes.

'Is this your first time?' It was everybody's first time, only the director knew that. Only friends spoke, softly and not continuously. The rest were silent. How do naked strangers begin a conversation? No one knew. The professional men – for professional reasons – glanced at each other's parts, while the others, friends of friends of the director and needing some cash, regarded the women without appearing to. Jasmin called from the back of the auditorium where he had been talking with the costume designer, he called out in Welsh Camp Cockney,

'Have you all masturbated, boys? Well done.' (No one had spoken.) 'The first hard-on I see and out you go. This is a respectable show.' Some of the women giggled, the unprofessional men wandered out of the lights, two A.S.M.s carried a rolled carpet on stage. They said, 'Mind your backs,' and they all felt more naked than before. A man with a bush hat and a white shirt set up a tape recorder in the pit. He was scornful as he threaded the tape. It was the copulation scene.

'I want G.T.C., Jack,' Jasmin said to him. 'Let them hear it first.' There were four large loudspeakers, there was no escaping.

'Well, you've heard about the privacy of the sex-uu-aal act,
 Let me tell you people, just for a fact,
 Riiiight acroooss the nay-ay-ation
 It's the in-out one-two-three Grand Time Copulation.'

There were soaring violins and a military band, and after the chorus a march in exultant two-time with trombones, snare drums and a glockenspiel. Jasmin came down the aisle towards the stage.

'That's your fucking-music, boys and girls.' He undid the top button of his shirt. He wrote this one himself.

'Where's Dale? I want Dale.' Out of the dark came the choreographer. She had a stylish trenchcoat on, tied in the middle with a wide belt. She had a small waist, sunglasses and a sticky-bun hairdo. She walked like a pair of scissors. Without turning round Jasmin called out to the man who was leaving by a door at the back of the auditorium.

'I *want* those wigs, Harry dear. I *want* those wigs. No wigs, no Harry.' Jasmin sat down in the front row. He made a steeple under his nose with his hands and crossed his legs. Dale climbed on the stage. She stood in the middle of the large carpet spread across the boards, one hand on her hip. She said, 'I want the girls squatting in a V shape, five on each side.' She stood where the apex was to be, moving her arms. They sat at her feet and she clipped up and down the middle leaving a trail of musk. She made the V deeper, then shallow again, she made it a horseshoe and a crescent and then a shallow V once more.

'Very nice, Dale,' said Jasmin. The V pointed back-stage. Dale moved a girl from the middle and replaced her with a girl from the edge. She did not speak to them, she took them by the elbow, leading them from this place to that place. They could not see her eyes through her glasses and they did not always know what she wanted. She guided a man across to each woman and pressed on his shoulders to make him sit down opposite. She fitted the legs together of each couple, she straightened their backs, she put their heads in position and made the partners clasp forearms. Jasmin lit a cigarette. There were ten couples in the V shape on the carpet, which really belonged in the foyer.

At last Dale said, 'I am clapping my hands, you are rocking backwards and forwards in time.'

They began to rock like children playing at ships. The director walked to the back of the auditorium.

'I think closer together, darling, it looks like nothing at all from here.' Dale pressed the couples closer together. When they began to move again their pubic hair rasped. It was hard to keep time. It was very much a matter of practice. One couple fell sideways and the girl banged her head on the floor. She rubbed her head and Dale came over and rubbed it too and reassembled them. Jasmin skipped down the aisle.

'We'll try it with the music. Jack, please. And remember, boys and girls, after the singing you go into two-time.'

'Well, you've heard about the privacy of the sex-uu-aal act ...'

The boys and girls began to rock while Dale clapped her hands. One, two, three, four. Jasmin stood half way up the aisle, his arms crossed. He uncrossed them, and screamed,

'Stop. Enough.' It was suddenly very quiet. The couples stared into the blackness beyond the lights and waited. Jasmin came down the steps slowly, and when he reached the stage he spoke softly.

'I know it's hard, but you have to look as if you are enjoying this thing.' (His voice rose.) 'Some people do, you know. It's a fuck, you understand, not a funeral.' (His voice sank.) 'Let's have it again, with some enthusiasm this time. Jack, please.' Dale realigned those units rocked out of position and the director climbed the stairs again. It was better, there was no doubt that this time it was better. Dale stood by Jasmin and watched. He put his hand on her shoulder and smiled at her glasses.

'Darling, it's good, it's going to be good.'

Dale said, 'The two on the end are moving well. If they were all like that I would be out of a job.'

'It's the in-out one-two-three Grand Time Copulation.'

Dale clapped to help them with the new rhythm. Jasmin sat down in the front row and lit a cigarette. He called back to Dale,

'Them on the end ...' She put her finger to her ear to show him she could not hear, and walked down the steps towards him.

'Them on the end, they're going too fast, what do you think?' They watched together. It was true, the two who had been moving well, they were a little out of time. Jasmin made another steeple under his nose and Dale scissored on to the stage. She stood over them and clapped.

'One two, one two,' she shouted. They did not seem to hear Dale, or the trombones, snare drums and glockenspiel.

'One fucking two,' screamed Dale. She appealed to Jasmin. 'I expect them to have some sense of rhythm.'

But Jasmin did not hear because he was screaming too.

'Cut! Stop! Turn that thing off, Jack.' All the couples creaked to a standstill except the couple on the end. Everyone watched the couple on the end, who were rocking faster now. They had their own sinuous rhythm.

'My God,' said Jasmin, 'they're fucking.' He shouted at the A.S.M.s. 'Get them apart, will you, and get those grins off your faces or you won't work in London again.' He shouted at the other couples. 'Clear off, back in half an hour. No, no, stay here.' He turned to Dale, his voice was hoarse. 'I'm sorry about this, darling. I know just how you feel. It's disgusting and obscene, and it's all my fault. I should have checked them all first. It won't happen again.' And while he was talking Dale snipped up the aisle and disappeared. Meanwhile the couple rocked on without music. There was only the creaking of boards beneath the carpet and the woman's low moans. The A.S.M.s stood about, not sure what to do.

'Pull them apart,' Jasmin shouted again. One of the A.S.M.s tugged at the man's shoulders, but they were sweaty and there was nowhere to hold on. Jasmin turned away, tears in his eyes. It was hard to believe. The others were glad of the break, they stood around and watched. The A.S.M. who had tugged at the shoulders brought on a bucket of water. Jasmin blew his nose.

'Don't be pathetic,' he croaked, 'they might as well finish it now.' They juddered to an end as he was speaking. They pushed apart and the girl ran off to the dressing-room, leaving the man standing alone. Jasmin climbed on stage, trembling with sarcasm.

'Well, well, Portnoy, did you get your little poke?

Feeling better now?' The man stood with his hands behind his back. His prick was angry and gluey, it let itself down in little throbs.

'Yes, thank you, Mr Cleaver,' the man said.

'What's your name, dear?'

'Cocker.' Jack snorted in his pit, the closest he ever came to laughing. The rest sucked their lips. Jasmin took a deep breath.

'Well, Cocker, you and the little man stuck on the end of you can crawl off this stage, and take shagging Nellie with you. I hope you find a gutter big enough for two.'

'I'm sure we will, Mr Cleaver, thank you.' Jasmin climbed down into the auditorium.

'Positions, the rest of you,' he said. He sat down. There were days when he could weep, really weep. But he did not, he lit a cigarette.

Butterflies

I saw my first corpse on Thursday. Today it was Sunday and there was nothing to do. And it was hot. I have never known it so hot in England. Towards midday I decided on a walk. I stood outside the house, hesitating. I was not sure whether to go left or right. Charlie was on the other side of the street, underneath a car. He must have seen my legs for he called out,

'How's tricks?' I never have ready answers to questions like that. I fumbled in my mind for several seconds, and said,

'How are you, Charlie?' He crawled out. The sun was on my side of the street, straight into his eyes. He shielded them with his hand, and said,

'Where you off to now?' Again I did not know. It was Sunday, there was nothing to do, it was too hot ...

'Out,' I said. 'A walk ...' I crossed over and looked at the car's engine, although it meant nothing to me. Charlie is an old man who knows about machines. He repairs cars for the people in the street and their friends. He came round the side of the car carrying a heavy tool kit in two hands.

'She died, then?' He stood there wiping a spanner with cotton waste for something to do. He knew it already, of course, but he wanted to hear my story.

'Yes,' I told him. 'She's dead.' He waited for me to go

on. I leaned against the side of the car. Its roof was too hot to touch. Charlie prompted me.

'You saw her last ...'

'I was on the bridge. I saw her running by the canal.'

'You saw her ...'

'I didn't see her fall in.' Charlie put the spanner back in the box. He was getting ready to crawl back under the car, his way of telling me the conversation was over. I was still deciding which way to walk. Before Charlie disappeared he said,

'Shame, great shame.'

I walked off to the left because that was the way I was facing. I walked down several streets, between privet hedges and hot, parked cars. Down each street there was the same smell of lunch cooking. I heard the same radio programme through open windows. I saw cats and dogs but very few people, and only from a distance. I took off my jacket and carried it over my arm. I wanted to be near trees and water. There are no parks in this part of London, only car parks. And there is the canal, the brown canal which goes between factories and past a scrap heap, the canal little Jane drowned in. I walked to the public library. I knew in advance it would be closed but I prefer to sit on the steps outside. I sat there now, in a shrinking patch of shade. A hot wind was blowing down the street. It stirred the litter round my feet. I watched a sheet of newspaper blown along the centre of the road, a piece out of the *Daily Mirror*. It stopped and I could read a part of a headline ... 'MAN WHO' ... There was nobody about. Round the corner I heard the tinkle of an ice-cream van and I realized I was thirsty. It was playing something out of a Mozart piano sonata. It stopped abruptly, in the middle of a note, as if someone had kicked the machine. I walked quickly up the street but when I got to the corner it had gone. A moment later I heard it again, and it sounded a long way off.

I saw no one on the way back. Charlie had gone inside and the car he had been working on was no longer there. I drank water from the kitchen tap. I read somewhere that a glass of water from a London tap has been drunk five times before. It tasted metallic. It reminded me of the stainless steel table they put the little girl on, her corpse. They probably use tap water to clean the mortuary table tops. I was due to meet the girl's parents at 7 p.m. It was not my idea, it was the idea of one of the police sergeants, the one who took my statement. I should have been firm, but he got round me, he frightened me. When he spoke he held me by the elbow. It could be a trick they learn at police school to give them the power they need. He caught me as I was leaving the building and steered me into a corner. I could not shake him off without wrestling with him. He spoke kindly, urgently, in a cracked whisper.

'You were the last one to see the little girl before she died …' He lingered over this last word. '… And the parents, you know, of course they'd like to meet you.' He frightened me with his implications, whatever they were, and while he touched me he had the power. He tightened his hold a little. 'So I said you'd be along. You're almost next door to them, aren't you?' I think I looked away and nodded. He smiled, and it was fixed. Still, it was something, a meeting, an event to make sense of the day. In the late afternoon I decided to take a bath and dress up. I had time to kill. I found a bottle of cologne I had never opened before, and a clean shirt. While the bath ran I took off my clothes and stared at my body in the mirror. I am a suspicious-looking person, I know, because I have no chin. Although they could not say why, they suspected me at the police station before I even made a statement. I told them I was standing on the bridge and that I saw her from the bridge, running along the canal. The police sergeant said,

'That was quite a coincidence, then, wasn't it? I mean, her living in the same street as you.' My chin and my neck are the same thing, and it breeds distrust. My mother's was like that, too. Only after I had left home did I find her grotesque. She died last year. Women do not like my chin, they won't come near me. It was the same for my mother, she never had friends. She went everywhere alone, even on holidays. Each year she went to Littlehampton and sat in a deck-chair by herself, facing out to sea. Towards the end of her life she became vicious and thin, like a whippet.

Until last Thursday when I saw Jane's corpse I never had special thoughts about death. I saw a dog run over once. I saw the wheel go over its neck and its eyeballs burst. It meant nothing to me at the time. And when my mother died I stayed away, from indifference, mainly, and a distaste for my relatives. I had no curiosity either about seeing her dead, thin and grey among the flowers. I imagine my own death to be something like hers. But at that time I had not seen a corpse. A corpse makes you compare living with dead. They led me down a stone staircase and along a corridor. I thought the mortuary would stand by itself, but it was in an office building, seven storeys high. We were in the basement. I heard typewriters from the foot of the stairs. The sergeant was there, and a couple of others in suits. He held the swing doors open for me. I did not really think she was going to be there. I forget now what I was expecting, a photograph, perhaps, and some documents to sign. I had not thought the matter out. But she was there. There were five high stainless-steel tables in a row. And there were fluorescent lights in green tin hoods hanging on long chains from the ceiling.

She was on the table nearest the door. She was on her back, palms turned upwards, legs together, mouth wide open, eyes wide open, very pale, very quiet. Her hair was still a little damp. Her red dress looked newly washed. She smelled faintly of the canal. I suppose it was nothing exceptional if you had seen enough corpses, like the police sergeant. There was a small bruise over her right eye. I wanted to touch her but I had the feeling they were watching me closely. Like a secondhand-car salesman, the man in the white coat said briskly,

'Only nine years old.' No one responded, we all looked at her face. The sergeant came round my side of the table with some papers in his hand.

'O.K.?' he said. We went back down the long corridor. Upstairs I signed the papers which said that I had been walking across the footbridge by the railway lines and that I had seen a girl, identified as the one downstairs, running along the canal towpath. I looked away and a little later I saw something red in the water which sank out of sight. Since I cannot swim I fetched a policeman, who peered into the water and said he could see nothing. I gave my name and address and went home. An hour and a half later they pulled her up from the bottom with a dragline. I signed three copies of the statement. After that I did not leave the building for a long time. In one of the corridors I found a moulded plastic chair and sat in it. Opposite me, through an open doorway, I could see two girls typing in their office. They saw me watching them and spoke to each other and laughed. One of them came out smiling and asked me if I was being seen to. I told her I was just sitting and thinking. The girl went back into her office, leaned across her desk and told her friend. They glanced at me uneasily. They suspected me of something, they always do. I was not really thinking about the dead girl downstairs. I had confused images of her, alive and dead, but I tried not to reconcile them. I sat there all afternoon because I did not feel like going anywhere else. The girls closed their office door. I finally left because everyone had gone home and they wanted to lock up. I was the last to leave the building.

I took a long time getting dressed. I ironed my black suit, I thought black was appropriate. I chose a blue tie because I did not want to go too far with the black. Then, as I was about to leave the house, I changed my mind. I went back upstairs and took off the suit, shirt and tie. I was suddenly annoyed at myself for my preparations. Why was I so anxious to have their approval? I put on the old trousers and sweater I was wearing before. I regretted taking a bath and I tried to wash the cologne off the back of my neck. But there was another smell, that of the scented soap I had used in the bath. I used the same soap on Thursday, and that was the first thing the little girl said to me,

'You smell like flowers.' I was walking past her small front garden, setting off on a walk. I ignored her. I avoid talking to children, I find it hard to get the right tone with them. And their directness bothers me, it cramps me. I had seen this one many times before playing in the street, usually by herself, or watching Charlie. She came out of her garden and followed me.

'Where are you going?' she said. Again I ignored her, hoping she would lose interest in me. Furthermore, I had no clear idea where I was walking to. She asked me again, 'Where are you going?'

After a pause I said, 'Never you mind.' She walked right behind me where I could not see her. I had the feeling she was imitating my walk but I did not turn round to look.

'Are you going to Mr Watson's shop?'

'Yes I'm going to Mr Watson's shop.'

She came up level with me. 'Because it's closed today,' she said, 'it's Wednesday.' I had no reply to this. When we came to the corner at the end of the street she said,

'Where are you going really?' I looked at her closely for the first time. She had a long delicate face and large mournful eyes. Her fine brown hair was tied in bunches in red ribbon to match her red cotton dress. She was beautiful in a strange almost sinister way, like a girl in a Modigliani painting. I said,

'I don't know, I'm just going for a walk.'

'I want to come.' I said nothing, and we walked together towards the shopping centre. She was silent too, and walked a little behind me as if she was waiting for me to tell her to turn back. She brought out a game which all the children have round here. They have two hard balls on the ends of pieces of string which they knock together rapidly by some motion of their hand. It makes a clacking sound like a football rattle. I think she was doing it to please me. It made it harder to send her away. And I had spoken to no one in several days.

When I came downstairs after changing my clothes again it was a quarter past six. Jane's parents lived twelve houses away on my side of the street. Since I had finished my preparations forty-five minutes early, I decided on a walk to kill time. The street was in shadow now. I hesitated by the front door, thinking of the best route. Charlie was across the road repairing another car. He saw me, and without particularly wanting to I walked over to him. He looked up without smiling.

'Where you off to this time?' He spoke to me as if I were a child.

'Taking some air,' I said, 'taking some evening air.'

Charlie likes to know what is happening in the street. He knows everyone along here, including all the children. I had often seen the little girl out there with him. The last time she was holding a spanner for him. For some reason Charlie held her death against me. He had had all Sunday to think about it. He wanted to hear my story, but he could not bring himself to ask direct questions.

'Seeing her parents, then? Seven o'clock?'

'Yes, seven o'clock.' He waited for me to go on. I circled round the car. It was large, old and rusty, a Ford Zodiac, the kind of car you get in this street. It belonged to the Pakistani family who ran the small shop at the end of the street. For their own reasons they called the shop 'Watson's'. Their two sons were beaten up by local skinheads. They were saving money now to return to Peshawar. The old man used to tell me about it when I went to his shop, how he was taking his family home because of violence and bad weather in London. Charlie said to me from the other side of Mr Watson's car,

'She was their only.' He was accusing me.

'Yes,' I said, 'I know. Great shame.' We circled round the car. Then Charlie said,

'It was in the paper. Did you see it? It said you saw her go down.'

'That's right.'

'Couldn't reach her, then?'

'No, I couldn't. She sank.' I made my circle round the car wider and edged off. I knew Charlie's eyes were on me all the way down the street, but I did not turn round to acknowledge his suspicion.

At the end of the street I pretended to look up at an aeroplane and glanced back over my shoulder. Charlie was standing by the car, hands on hips, still watching me. There was a large black-and-white cat sitting at his feet.

I saw all this in a glimpse and turned the corner. It was half past six. I decided to walk to the library to use up the remaining time. It was the same walk I took earlier on. There were more people about now. I passed a group of West Indian boys playing football in the street. Their ball rolled towards me and I stepped over it. They stood about waiting while one of the younger boys collected the ball. As I edged past them they were silent, and watching me closely. As soon as I was past, one of them threw a small stone along the road at my feet. Without turning and almost without looking I trapped it neatly with my foot. It was an accident I did it so well. They all laughed at this and clapped and cheered me, so that for one elated moment I thought I could go back and join in their game. The ball was returned and they started to play again. The moment passed and I walked on. My heart was beating fast from the excitement of it. Even when I came to the library and sat down on the steps I could feel the thumping of my pulse in my temples. Such opportunities are rare for me. I do not meet many people, in fact the only ones I talk to are Charlie and Mr Watson. I speak to Charlie because he is there when I leave my front door; he is always the one to speak first, and there is no avoiding him if I want to leave the house. I do not talk to Mr Watson so much as listen, and I listen because I have to go into his shop to buy groceries. To have someone walking along with me on Wednesday was something of an opportunity, too, even if it was only a little girl with nothing to do. Although I would not have admitted it at the time, I felt pleased that she was genuinely curious about me, and I was attracted to her. I wanted her to be my friend.

But I was uneasy at first. She was walking a little behind me, playing with her toy and, for all I knew, making gestures behind my back the way children do. Then, when we came to the main shopping street, she came up to my side.

'Why don't you go to work?' she said. 'My dad goes to work every day except Sunday.'

'I don't need to go to work.'

'Have you got lots of money already?' I nodded. 'Really lots?'

'Yes.'

'Could you buy me something if you wanted to?'

'If I wanted to.' She was pointing at a toyshop window.

'One of those, please, go on, one of those, go on.' She was hanging on my arm, she was making a greedy little dance on the pavement and trying to push me towards the shop. No one had touched me intentionally like that for a long time, not since I was a child. I felt a cold thrill in my stomach and I was unsteady on my legs. I had some money in my pocket and I could see no reason why I should not buy her something. I made her wait outside while I went in the shop and bought her what she wanted, a small, pink, naked doll, moulded from one piece of plastic. Once she had it she seemed to lose interest in it. Farther down the same street she asked me to buy her an ice cream. She stood in the doorway of the shop waiting for me to follow. She did not touch me this time. Of course, I hesitated, I was not sure what was happening. But I was curious about her now, and the effect she was having on me. I gave her enough money to buy ices for both of us and let her go in and get them. She was obviously used to gifts. When we were a little farther down the street I asked her in the friendliest way,

'Don't you say thank you when someone gives you things?' She looked at me scornfully, her thin, pale lips circled with ice cream:

'No.'

I asked her her name. I wanted our conversation to be amiable.

'Jane.'

'What happened to the doll I bought you, Jane?' She glanced down at her hand.

'I left it in the sweet shop.'

'Didn't you want it?'

'I forgot it.' I was about to tell her to run back and get it when I realized how much I wanted her to stay with me, and how close we were to the canal.

The canal is the only stretch of water near here. There is something special about walking by water, even brown stinking water running along the backs of factories. Most of the factories overlooking the canal are windowless and deserted. You can walk a mile and a half along the tow-path and usually you meet no one. The path goes by an old scrap yard. Up until two years ago a quiet old man watched over the pile of junk from a small tin hut outside which, chained to a post, he kept a large Alsatian dog. It was too old to bark. Then the hut, the old man and the dog disappeared and the gate was padlocked. Gradually the surrounding fence was trampled down by the local kids, so that now only the gate stands. The scrap yard is the only thing of interest in that mile and a half because for the rest of the walk the path runs close to the factory walls. But I like the canal and I find it less of a confinement there by the water than anywhere else in this part of town. After walking with me in silence for a while Jane asked me again,

'Where are you going? Where are you going to walk?'

'Along the canal.'

She thought about this for a minute. 'I'm not allowed by the canal.'

'Why not?'

'Because.' She was walking slightly in front of me now. The white ring around her mouth had dried. My legs were weak and I felt suffocated by the sun's heat rising off the pavement. It had become a necessity to persuade her to walk along the canal with me. I sickened at the idea. I threw the rest of my ice cream away, and said,

'I walk along the canal nearly every day.'

'Why?'

'It's very peaceful there ... and there are all kinds of things to look at.'

'What things?'

'Butterflies.' The word was out before I could retrieve it. She turned round to me, suddenly interested. Butterflies could never survive near the canal, the stench would dissolve them. It would not take her long to find that out.

'What colour butterflies?'

'Red ones ... yellow ones.'

'What else is there?'

I hesitated. 'There's a scrap yard.' She wrinkled her nose. I continued quickly, 'And boats, too, boats on the canal.'

'Real boats?'

'Yes, of course, real boats.' Again this was not what I had intended. She stopped walking and I stopped too. She said,

'You won't tell on me if I come, will you?'

'No, I won't tell anyone, but you have to keep close to me when we're walking along the canal, understand?' She nodded. 'And wipe the ice cream off your mouth.' She trailed the back of her hand vaguely across her face. 'Come here, let me do it.' I pulled her towards me and cupped my left hand round the back of her neck. I wetted the forefinger of the other hand, the way I had seen parents do it, and ran it round her lips. I had never touched another person's lips before, nor had I experienced this kind of pleasure. It rose painfully from my groin to my chest and lodged itself there, like a fist pushing against my ribs. I wetted the same finger again and tasted the sticky sweetness on the end of it. I rubbed it round her lips once more and this time she pulled away.

'You hurt me,' she said. 'You pressed too hard.' We walked on, and now she kept close by me.

To get down to the towpath we had to cross the canal first by a narrow black bridge with high walls. Half way across, Jane stood on tiptoe and tried to look over the wall.

'Lift me up,' she said, 'I want to look at the boats.'

'You can't see them from here.' But I placed my hands round her waist and lifted her up. Her short red dress rode up over her backside and I felt the fist in my chest again. She called over her shoulder to me,

'The river's very dirty.'

'It's always been dirty,' I said, 'it's a canal.' As we walked down the stone steps to the towpath Jane moved closer to me. I had the feeling she was holding her breath. Usually the canal flows north, but today it was completely still. On the surface there were patches of yellow scum, and they did not move either because there was no wind to push them along. Occasionally a car passed on the bridge above us and beyond that there was the distant sound of London traffic. Apart from that it was very quiet by the canal. Because of the heat the canal smell was stronger today, an animal rather than a chemical smell given off by the scum. Jane whispered,

'Where are the butterflies?'

'They're not far. We have to go under two bridges first.'

'I want to go back. I want to go back.' We were now

over a hundred yards from the stone steps. She wanted to stop but I was urging her along. She was too frightened to leave my side and run back to the steps by herself.

'Not far now and we'll see the butterflies. Red ones, yellow ones, sometimes green ones.' I abandoned myself to the lie, I did not care what I told her now. She put her hand in mine.

'And what about the boats?'

'You'll see them. Farther up.' We walked on and I thought of nothing but of how to keep her with me. At certain points along the canal there are tunnels under factories, roads and railway lines. The first of these we came to was formed by a three-storey building which connects the factories on either side of the canal. It was empty now, like all the factories, and all the nearer windows were broken. At the entrance to this tunnel Jane tried to pull back.

'What's that noise? Let's not go in there.' She could hear water dripping from the roof of the tunnel into the canal, it echoed in a strange, hollow way.

'It's only water,' I said. 'Look, you can see through to the other side.' The path was very narrow in the tunnel so I made her walk in front of me and kept my hand on her shoulder. She was shivering. At the far end she stopped suddenly and pointed. Where the sunlight entered the tunnel a little way there was a flower growing from between the bricks. It looked like some kind of dandelion, growing out of a small tuft of grass.

'It's coltsfoot,' she said, and picked it and put it in her hair, behind her ear. I said,

'I've never seen flowers along here before.'

'There have to be flowers,' she explained, 'for the butterflies.'

For the next quarter of an hour we walked in silence.

Jane spoke once to ask me again about the butterflies. She seemed less afraid of the canal now and let go of my hand. I wanted to touch her but I could think of no way of doing that without frightening her. I tried to think of a conversation we might have but my mind was blank. The path was beginning to widen out to our right. Round the next bend of the canal in an immense space between a factory and a warehouse was the scrap yard. There was black smoke in the sky ahead of us, and as we came round the bend I saw that it was coming from the scrap yard. A group of boys stood round the fire they had built. They were some kind of gang, they all wore the same blue jackets and cropped hair. As far as I could tell they were preparing to roast a live cat. The smoke hung above them in the still air, behind them the scrapheap towered like a mountain. They had the cat tied up by its neck to a post, the same post the Alsatian dog used to be tied to. The cat's front and back legs were tied together. They were con- structing a cage over the fire made up of pieces of wire fencing and as we came past one of them was dragging the cat by the string around its neck towards the fire. I took Jane's hand and walked faster. They were working intently and in silence, and they hardly paused to glance up at us. Jane kept her eyes on the ground. Through her hand I could feel her whole body shaking.

'What were they doing to that cat?'

'I don't know.' I looked back over my shoulder. It was difficult to see what they were doing now because of the black smoke. We were leaving them far behind and our path was once more along the factory walls. Jane was almost crying, and her hand was only in mine because I I was holding it hard. It was not necessary really for there was nowhere she would dare run by herself. Back along the path past the scrap yard, or forwards into the tunnel we were approaching. I had no idea what was going to happen when we came to the end of the path. She would want to run home, and I just knew I could not let her go. I put it out of my mind. At the entrance to the second tunnel, Jane stopped.

'There aren't any butterflies, are there?' Her voice rose at the end because she was about to cry. I started to tell her that perhaps it was too hot for them. But she was not listening to me, she was wailing,

'You said a lie, there aren't any butterflies, you said a lie.' She started to cry in a half-hearted, miserable way and tried to pull her hand free from mine. I reasoned with her but she would not listen. I tightened my grip on her hand and pulled her into the tunnel. She was screaming now, a piercing continuous sound echoing back from the walls and roof of the tunnel and filling my head. I carried and dragged her right into the tunnel, about half way. And there, suddenly, her screams were drowned out by the thunder of a train going over our heads, and the air and the ground shook together. It took a long time for the train to pass. I held her arms at her sides, but she did not struggle, the din was overpowering her. When the last echoes had died away she said dully,

'I want my mummy.' I unzipped my fly. I did not know if she could see in the dark what was stretching out towards her.

'Touch it,' I said, and shook her gently by the shoulder. She did not move, so I shook her again.

'Touch me, go on. You know what I mean, don't you?' It was quite a simple thing I wanted really. This time I took her in both hands and shook her hard and shouted.

'Touch it, touch it.' She reached out her hand and her fingers briefly brushed my tip. It was enough, though. I doubled up and came, I came into my cupped hands. Like the train, it took a long time, pumping it all out into my hand. All the time I spent by myself came pumping out, all the hours walking alone and all the thoughts I had had, it all came out into my hand. When it was over I remained in that position for several minutes, bent up with my cupped hands in front of me. My mind was clear, my body was relaxed and I was thinking of nothing. I lay on my stomach, reached down and washed my hands in the canal. It was difficult to get the stuff off in cold water. It stuck to my fingers like scum. I picked it off in bits. Then I remembered the girl, she was no longer with me. I could not let her run home now, not after this. I would have to go after her. I stood and saw her silhouetted against the end of the tunnel. She was walking slowly along the edge of the canal in a daze. I could not run quickly because I could not see the ground in front of me. The nearer I got to the sunlight at the end of the tunnel, the harder it was to see. Jane was almost out of the tunnel. When she heard my footsteps behind her she turned round and gave a kind of yelp. She started to run too, and immediately lost her footing. From where I was it was difficult to see what happened to her, her silhouette against the sky suddenly disappeared into the black. She was lying face down when I reached her, with her left leg trailing off the path almost into the water. She had banged her head going down and there was a swelling over her right eye. Her right arm was stretched out in front of her and almost reached into the sunlight. I bent down to her face and listened to her breathing. It was deep and regular. Her eyes were closed tight and the lashes were still wet from crying. I no longer wanted to touch her, that was all pumped out of me now, into the canal. I brushed away some dirt from her face and some more from the back of her red dress.

'Silly girl,' I said, 'no butterflies.' Then I lifted her up gently, as gently as I could so as not to wake her, and eased her quietly into the canal.

I usually sit by the library steps, I prefer it to going inside and reading books. There is more to learn outside. I sat there now, Sunday evening, listening to my pulse slow down to its daily rhythm. Over and over again I ran through what had happened, and what I should have done. I saw the stone skimming along the road, and I saw myself trap it neatly with my foot, almost without turning. I should have turned round then, slowly, acknowledging their applause with a faint grin. Then I should have kicked the stone back, or better, stepped over it and walked casually towards them, and then, when the ball came back, I would be with them, one of them, in a team. I would play with them out there in the street most evenings, learn all their names and they would know mine. I would see them in town during the day and they would call out to me from the other side of the street, cross over and chat. At the end of the game one of them comes over to me and grips my arm.

'See you tomorrow, then ...'

'Yes, tomorrow.' We would go out drinking together when they were older, and I would learn to like beer. I stood up and began to walk slowly back the way I had come. I knew I would not be joining any football games. The opportunities are rare, like butterflies. You stretch your hand out and they are gone. I went along the street where they had been playing. It was deserted now and the stone I had stopped with my foot was still in the middle of the road. I picked it up and put it in my pocket, and then walked on to keep my appointment.

Conversation With a Cupboard Man

You ask me what I did when I saw this girl. Well, I'll tell you. You see that cupboard there, it takes up most of the room. I ran all the way back here, climbed inside and tossed myself off. Don't think I thought about the girl while I did it. No, I couldn't bear that. I went back in my mind till I was three feet high. That made it come quicker. I can see you think I'm dirty and bent. Well, I washed my hands afterwards, which is more than some people. And I felt better too. Do you see what I mean, I unwound. The way things have been up here in this room what else is there? It's all right for you. I bet you live in a clean house and your wife washes the sheets and the government pays you to find out about people. All right, I know you're a … what is it? … a social worker and you're trying to help, but you can do me no good except by listening. I won't change now, I've been me too long. But it's good to talk so I'll just tell you about myself.

I never saw my father because he died before I was born. I think problems started right there – it was my mother who brought me up and no one else. We lived in a huge house near Staines. She was twisted up, you know, that's where I got it from. All she wanted was to have children but she wouldn't think of getting married again so that left only me; I had to be all the children she had ever wanted. She tried to stop me growing up and for a long time she succeeded. Do you know, I didn't learn to speak properly till I was eighteen. I got no schooling, she kept me home because she said it was a rough area. She had her arms round me day and night. She didn't like it when I got too big for my cot so she went out and bought a crib bed from a hospital auction. That was the sort of thing she would do. Right up until I left I was still sleeping in that thing. I couldn't go to sleep in an ordinary bed, I thought I was going to fall out and I could never get to sleep. When I was two inches taller than her she was still trying to tie a bib round my neck. She was insane. She got a hammer and nails and some pieces of wood and tried to make a kind of high chair for me to sit in, and that was when I was fourteen. Well, you can imagine, the thing just fell to bits as soon as I sat in it. But Christ! The mush she used to feed me on. That's why I get these stomach troubles. She wouldn't let me do anything for myself, even tried to stop me from being clean. I could hardly move without her, and she loved it, the bitch.

Why didn't I run off then when I was older? You might think there was nothing to stop me. But listen, it never occurred to me. I didn't know any other life, I didn't think I was different. Anyway, how could I run away when I would be shitting myself with terror before I got fifty yards down the street? And where'd I go? I could hardly tie my own shoelaces, let alone get a job. Do I sound bitter about it now? I'll tell you a funny thing. I wasn't unhappy, you know. She was all right really. She used to read me stories and that, and we used to make things out of cardboard. We had a kind of theatre we made ourselves out of a fruit box, and we made the people out of paper and card. No, I wasn't unhappy till I found out what other people thought about me. I suppose I could have spent the whole of my life living my first two years over and over again and still not think I was unhappy. She was a good woman really, my mother. Just twisted, that's all.

How did I become an adult? I'll tell you, I never did learn. I have to pretend. All the things you take for granted I have to do it all consciously. I'm always thinking about it, like I was on the stage. I'm sitting in this chair with my arms folded, that's all right, but I'd rather be lying on the floor gurgling to myself than be talking to you. I can see you think I'm joking. It still takes me a long time to get dressed in the morning, and lately I haven't bothered anyway. And you've seen how clumsy I am with a knife and fork. I'd rather someone came and patted me on the back and fed me with a spoon. Do you believe me? Do you think it's disgusting? Well, I do. It's the most disgusting thing I know. That's why I spit on the memory of my mother because she made me this way.

I'll tell you how I came to learn to pretend to be an adult. When I was seventeen my mother was just thirty-eight. She was still an attractive woman and looked much younger. If it wasn't for her obsession with me she could have got married as easy as that. But she was too busy trying to push me back up her womb to think of things like that. That was until she met this bloke, and then it all changed, just like that. Overnight she just swapped obsessions and all the sex she'd missed out on caught up with her. She went mad for this fellow, as if she wasn't mad enough already. She wanted to bring him home but she didn't dare in case he saw me, a seventeen-year-old baby. That's why in two months I had a lifetime's growing up to do. She started hitting me when I spilt food or pronounced words wrongly or even when I was just standing there watching her doing something. And then she started going out in the evenings, leaving me alone in the house. This intensive training really threw me. To have someone all over you for seventeen years and then find yourself at war. I started getting these headaches. And then the fits, especially when she was getting ready to go out in the evenings. My arms and legs would go right out of control, my tongue did things by itself as if it belonged to someone else. It was a nightmare. Then everything went as black as hell. When I came round my mother would have gone out anyway and I'd be lying there in my own shit in that dark house. It was a bad time.

I think the fits became less frequent because one day she brought her man home. I was fairly presentable by that time. My mother passed me off as mentally subnormal, which I suppose I was. I can't remember much about the bloke except that he was very large with long hair greased back. He always wore blue suits. He owned a garage in Clapham and because he was big and successful he hated me at first sight. You can imagine how I looked then, I had hardly been out of the house in my life. I was thin and bloodless, even thinner and weaker than I am now. I hated him too because he had taken my mother. First time he just nodded when my mother introduced me to him and after that he never said a word to me. He didn't even notice me. He was so big and strong and full of himself I suppose he couldn't bear to think that people like me existed.

He came to our house pretty regularly, usually to take my mother out somewhere for the evening. I watched the telly. I got pretty lonely then. When the programmes had finished for the night I used to sit in the kitchen and wait up for my mother, and though I was seventeen I used to cry a lot. One morning I came down and found my mother's boyfriend having his breakfast in his dressing-gown. He didn't even look up at me when I came in the kitchen. When I looked at my mother she just pretended to be busy at the sink. After that his stays became more and more frequent till he was sleeping in our house every night. One afternoon they got dressed up smart and went out. When they came back they were laughing and falling about all over the place. They must have been drinking a lot. That night my mother told me they had got married and that I had to call him Father. That was the end. I had a fit, the worst one ever. I can't explain how bad it really was, it seemed to last for days, though it was only an hour or so. When it finished I opened my eyes and saw the look on my mother's face, complete disgust it was. You've no idea how much a person can change in such a short time. When I saw that look I realized she was as much a stranger to me as my father.

I stayed with them three months before they found a home to put me into. They were too busy with each other to notice me. They hardly spoke to me at all and they never spoke to each other when I was in the room. You know, I was pretty glad to get out of that place, even though it was my home, and I did cry a little when I left. But mostly I was glad to get away from them. And I suppose they were glad to see the last of me. It wasn't bad at the home they took me to. I didn't care where I was really. But they taught me to look after myself better and I even started to learn to read and write, though I've forgotten most of that now. I couldn't read that form you sent me, could I? That was pretty stupid. Anyway, it wasn't a bad life at this place. There were all kinds of weird people there and that made me feel more sure of myself. Three times a week they took me and a few others in a bus to a workshop place where we learned how to repair watches and clocks. The idea was that when I left I would be able to stand by myself and earn a living. I've never earned a penny from it yet. You go for a job and they ask you where you got your training. When you tell them they don't want to know about it. One of the best things about the place was that I met Mr Smith. I know it doesn't sound much of a name, and he looked pretty ordinary so you wouldn't expect him to be anything special. But he was. He was in charge of the home and it was him who tried to teach me to read. I did all right. By the time I left I had just finished reading *The Hobbit* and I enjoyed that. But once I was outside I didn't have much time for that sort of thing. Still, old Smith had a good try at teaching me. And he taught me a lot of other things. I was still slurring my words when I arrived there and he corrected me every time I spoke. Then I had to repeat it the way he said it. And then he used to say I needed more grace. Yes, grace! In his room he had this enormous record player and he would put on records and make me dance. I felt bloody stupid about that at first. He told me to forget where I was and relax my body and drift about to the feel of the music. So I pranced round the room waving my arms and kicking my legs and hoping that no one could see me through the window. And then I started to enjoy it. It was almost like having a fit, you know, except that it was pleasant. I mean I could really lose myself, if you can imagine that. Then the record stopped and I'd be standing there sweating and catching my breath, feeling a bit of a nutter. Old Smith didn't mind, though. I danced for him twice a week, Mondays and Fridays. There were days when he played the piano instead of the records. I didn't enjoy that so much but I never said a word because I could see from his face that he was enjoying it.

And he started me on painting. Not ordinary painting, mind. Say, if you wanted to paint a tree you'd probably make a brown bit down and a green blob on the top. He said this was all wrong. There was a big garden at this place and one morning he took me out by some old trees. We stopped under one of them, a massive one it was. He said he wanted me to ... what was it ... I had to sense the tree and then re-create it. It was a long time before I saw what he was getting at. I went on painting in my own way. Then he showed me what he meant. He said suppose I wanted to paint that oak tree. What did I think of? Bigness, solidity, darkness. He painted thick black lines on the paper. I got the idea then and started painting things the way I felt about them. He told me to paint a picture of myself, and I painted these strange shapes in yellow and white. And after that my mother, and I made large red mouths all over the paper – that was her lipstick – and in the mouths I painted it black. That was because I hated her. Though I didn't really. I've never done any painting since I left, there isn't room for that sort of thing outside a place like that.

If I'm boring you just say so, I know you have to see a lot of people. No reason why you should sit with me. All right then. It was one of the rules of the home that you had to leave when you were twenty-one. I remember they made me a cake by way of compensation, except that I don't like cake so I gave it to the other kids. They gave me letters of introduction and the names and addresses of people to go and see. I didn't want to know about that. I wanted to be on my own. It means a lot when you've had people looking after you all your life, even if they are good to you. So I came to London. I managed it at first, I felt strong in my mind, you know, I felt as though I could take on London. It was all new then and exciting for someone who had never been there in his life before. I found a room in Muswell Hill and started looking for a job. The only kind of jobs I came near to getting were lifting and carrying or digging. They'd take one look at me and tell me to forget it. Finally I found a job in a hotel, washing-up. It was a swanky place – the bit where the guests were, I mean. Deep red carpets and cut-glass chandeliers and a small orchestra playing in one corner of the hallway. I walked in the front bit by mistake on my first day. The kitchen wasn't so fine. Christ, no, it was a filthy shit-hole. They must have been understaffed because I was the only one washing-up. Or perhaps they saw me coming. Whatever it was, I had to do it all by myself, twelve hours a day with forty-five minutes for lunch.

I wouldn't have minded the hours of the work, I was pleased to be earning my own living for the first time in my life. No, it was the chief cook who really got me. He paid the wages and he was always cutting me short. The money of course went straight into his own pocket. He was an ugly bastard too. You never saw such spots. Over his face and forehead, under his chin, round by his ears, even on his ear lobes. Great puffy spots and scabs, red and yellow ones, I don't know why they let him near the food. Still, they didn't care too much about that sort of thing in that kitchen. They would have cooked the cockroaches if they had known how to catch them. The chief cook really got me. He used to call me scarecrow, and that was a great joke. 'Hey Scarecrow! Scared any more birds away?' He was one to talk. There could be no woman who would go near all that pus. His head was full of pus because he was a dirty-minded bastard. Always slobbering over his magazines. He used to chase after the women who were meant to keep the kitchen clean. They were all hags, none of them were under sixty, most of them black and ugly. I can see him now, giggling and spitting and running his hands up their skirts. The women didn't dare say anything because he could throw them out. You might say that at least he was normal. But I'd rather be me any day.

Because I didn't laugh at his jokes like the others, Pusface started getting really nasty. He went out of his way to find me more work to do, all the dirty jobs were mine. I was getting sick of all the scarecrow jokes, too, so one day when he'd made me scour all the pots three times over I said, 'Fuck off, Pus-face.' That really stung him. No one ever called him that to his face before. He left me alone for the rest of that day. But first thing next morning he came over to me and said, 'Get and clean the main oven.' There was this enormous cast-iron oven, see, and it got cleaned once a year, I think. Its walls were covered with a thick black scum. To get it off you had to get inside with a bowl of water and a scraper. It smelled like rotten cats inside that oven. I got a bowl of water and some scourers and crawled inside. You couldn't breath through your nose or you'd throw up. I had been in there ten minutes when the oven door shut. Pus-face had locked me in. I could just hear him laughing through the iron walls. He kept me in there five hours, till after my lunch break. Five hours in that stinking black oven, and after that he made me do the washing-up. You can imagine how furious I was. I wanted to keep my job so there was nothing I could say.

The very next morning Pus-face came up to me as I was beginning to wash up the breakfast plates. 'I thought I told you to clean that oven, Scarecrow.' So once again I got my things and crawled inside. And as soon as I was in the door slammed. I went mad. I screamed every name I could think of at Pus-face, and I hammered on the walls till my hands were raw. But I couldn't hear anything so

after a while I calmed down and tried to get comfortable.
I had to keep moving my legs so as not to get cramp. After
I had been in there what seemed six hours I heard Pus-face
laughing outside. Then it started to get hot. I couldn't
believe it at first, I thought I was imagining things. Pus-
face had turned on the oven at its lowest marking. It soon
got too hot to sit down and I had to crouch. I could feel
it burning through my shoes, it was burning my face and
up my nostrils. The sweat was running off me and every
mouthful of air scorched my throat. I couldn't bang on the
walls because they were too hot to touch. I wanted to
scream but I couldn't afford the air. I thought I was going
to die because I knew Pus-face was capable of roasting me
alive. In the late afternoon he let me out. I was almost
unconscious but I heard him say, 'Ah, Scarecrow, where've
you been all day? I wanted you to clean out the oven.'
Then he laughed and the others joined in, only because
they were scared of him. I got a taxi home and went to
bed. I was in a real mess. The next morning I was worse.
There were blisters on my feet and down my spine where I
must have leaned against the oven wall. And I was throw-
ing up. There was one thing I was sure of in my mind,
and that was that I had to get to work to even up with
Pus-face, if it meant dying in the attempt. It was torture
to walk so I took another taxi. Somehow I managed to get
through the first part of the morning until break. Pus-face
left me alone. During the break he was sitting by himself
reading one of his dirty magazines. Just before it was time
I lit the gas under one of the chip pans. It held about four
pints and when the oil was boiling I carried it over to
where Pus-face was sitting. The pain in the soles of my
feet made me want to cry out. My heart was thumping
because I knew I was going to get Pus-face. I came up
level with his chair. He glanced up and by the look on my

face he knew exactly what was going to happen to him. But he didn't have time to move. I let the oil fall right into his lap, and for the benefit of anyone watching I pretended to slip. Pus-face howled like a wild animal, I never heard a man make a noise like that. His clothes seemed to dissolve and I could see his balls red and swelling and then turning white. It was all down his legs. He was screaming for twenty-five minutes before the doctor came and gave him morphine. I found out later that Pus-face spent nine months in hospital while they picked out the bits of clothing from his flesh. That was how I sorted Pus-face out.

I was too ill to stay in my job after that. I had paid my rent in advance and saved a little money. The next two weeks I spent hobbling from my room to the doctor's surgery each day. When the blisters had gone I started looking for another job. But by this time I didn't feel so strong. London was becoming too much for me. I found it hard to get out of bed in the mornings. It was better under the bedclothes, I was safer there. I was depressed by the thought of facing thousands of people, thundering traffic, queues and things like that. I began to think back to the old days when I was with my mother. I wished I was back there. The old cotton-wool life when everything was done for me, warm and safe. It sounds pretty stupid, I know, but I started thinking that perhaps my mother had got tired of that man she had married and that if I went back we could carry on the old life. Well, this was on my mind for days until I became obsessed by it. I thought of nothing else. I convinced myself that she was waiting for me, perhaps she had the police out looking for me. I had to go home and then she would take me in her arms, she would feed me with a spoon, we would make another cardboard theatre together. One evening I was thinking of this when I decided to go to her. What was I waiting for? I ran out of doors and all the way down the street. I was almost singing with joy. I caught the train to Staines and I ran from the station to our house. It was going to be all right again. I slowed down when I turned down our road. The downstairs lights were on in the house. I rang the bell. My legs were trembling so much that I had to lean against the wall. The person who came to the door was not my mother. It was a girl, a very pretty girl of about eighteen. I couldn't think what to say. There was a stupid silence while I thought of something. Then she asked me who I was. I told her I used to live in the house and that I was looking for my mother. She said she had been living there with her parents for two years. She went inside to find out if any address had been left. While she was gone I was staring into the hallway. Everything was different. There were large book cases and another wall-paper, and a telephone which we never used to have. I felt really sad that it was changed, I felt cheated. The girl came back to tell me that no addresses had been left behind. I said goodnight and walked back down the pathway. I was left out. That house was really my own, and I wanted the girl to ask me inside, in the warm. If only she had put her arms round my neck and said, 'Come and live with us.' It sounds pretty stupid, but that was what I was thinking as I walked back to the station.

So I went back to looking for a job. I think it was the oven that did it. I mean it was the oven that made me think I could go back to Staines as if nothing had happened. I thought about that oven a lot. I made up daydreams about being made to stay inside an oven. That sounds incredible, especially after what I did to Pus-face. It was what I felt, though, and I couldn't help that. The more I thought about it, the more I realized that when I went to clean the oven the second time I was secretly wanting to be shut in. I was sort of hoping it without knowing it, do you see what I mean? I wanted to be frustrated. I wanted to be where I couldn't get out. That was at the bottom of my mind. When I was actually in the oven I was too worried about getting out and too furious with Pus-face to enjoy anything. It was in my mind afterwards, that was all.

I had no luck with finding a job and as my money was running out I started stealing from shops. You might think that was an idiotic thing to do but it was dead easy. And what else could I do? I had to eat. I only took a little from each shop, usually from supermarkets. I wore a long overcoat with large pockets. I stole things like frozen meat and tins of things. I also had to pay the rent so I started taking more valuable things and selling them in secondhand shops. This was working quite nicely for about a month. I had all I wanted, and if I wanted something different all I had to do was put it in my pocket. But then I must have got careless because a store detective caught me stealing a watch from a counter. He didn't stop me there as I was doing it. No, he let me take it and then followed me out into the street. I was at the bus stop when he caught me by the arm and told me to come back to the shop. They got the police in and I had to appear in court. It turned out that they had been watching me for quite a while, so I was up for a number of things. Since I had never done anything before they made me report to a probation officer twice a week. That was lucky. I could have got six months straight away. That's what the police sergeant said.

Being on probation didn't get me food or pay the rent. The officer was all right, I suppose, he did his best. There were so many people on his books that he couldn't remember my name from Monday to Thursday. In all the jobs he tried to get me they wanted someone who could read and write, and any other sort of job needed strength for lifting. Anyway, I didn't really want another job. I didn't want to meet any more people and get called Scarecrow again. So what could I do? I started stealing again. More carefully this time and never twice in the same place. But you know, I got caught almost immediately after about a week. I took an ornamental knife from a department store and because my coat pockets had carried so much they must have worn away. Just as I was going through the door the knife went straight out the bottom of my coat on to the floor. There were three of them on to me before I could even turn. I was back in front of the same magistrate again, and this time I got three months.

Prison's a funny place. Not that it would make you laugh. I thought they would all be tough gangsters in there, you know, hard men. But there were only a few like that. The rest were just cracked, like at the home I went to. It wasn't bad there, nowhere near as bad as I thought it was going to be. My cell wasn't very different from my room in Muswell Hill. In fact from the window there was a much better view from my prison room because I was higher up. There was a bed, table, a small book case and a sink. You could cut pictures out of magazines and stick them on the wall, and I wasn't allowed to do that in my room in Muswell Hill. Nor was I locked up in the cell, except for a couple of hours a day. We could wander about and visit the other cells, but only those on your floor. There was an iron gate which stopped you going up or down the stairs out of hours.

There were some strange types in that prison. There was a bloke who used to climb on his chair during meal time and expose himself. I was pretty shocked when it happened first, but everyone went on eating and talking so I did the same. After a while it didn't bother me at all even though he did it quite regular. It's surprising what you can get used to in time. And then there was Jacko. He walked into my cell on the second morning and introduced himself. He said he was in for fraud and he told me how his father was a horse trainer and they were down on their luck. And on and on, a load of things he told me which I've forgotten. Then he walked out. Next time he came up and introduced himself all over again, as if he'd never seen me before in his life. This time he said he was inside for multiple rape and that he'd never been able to satisfy his sexual appetite. I thought he was having me on because I still believed his first story. He was dead serious, though. He had a different story each time he saw me. He never remembered our last conversation or who he was. I don't think he knew who he was himself. Like he didn't have an identity of his own. One of the others told me that Jacko was knocked over the head during an armed robbery. I don't know if that was true or not. You never know what to believe.

Don't get me wrong. They weren't all like that. There were some good blokes and one of the best was Deafy. No one knew his real name, nor could Deafy tell them because he was deaf and dumb. I think he had been inside nearly all his life. His cell was the most comfortable in the whole prison, he was the only one who was allowed to brew up tea for himself. I often sat in his room. Of course, there was no conversation. We just sat there, sometimes we smiled at each other, nothing else. He would make tea – the best I've ever tasted. Some afternoons I would doze in his armchair while he read one of his war comics from a pile he kept in the corner. When I had something on my mind I used to talk to him about it. He couldn't understand a word but he nodded and smiled or looked sad, whatever he thought was needed from the expression on my face. I think he liked to feel that he was taking part in something. Most of the other prisoners ignored him most of the time. He was popular with the guards and they brought him whatever he wanted. Sometimes we'd have chocolate cake with our tea. He could read and write so he wasn't much worse off than I was.

Those three months were the best since I left home. I made my cell comfortable and I fell into a closed routine. I didn't speak to many people apart from Deafy. I didn't want to, I wanted a life without complications. You might be thinking that what I said about being locked in an oven was the same thing as being locked in a cell. No, it wasn't the pain-pleasure of feeling frustrated. It was a deeper pleasure of feeling safe. In fact I remember now wishing sometimes I had less freedom. I enjoyed the time of day we had to keep to our cells. If they had made us stay in them all day I don't think I would have complained, except that I would not have been able to see Deafy. I never had to plan anything. Each day was like the one before it. I didn't have to worry about meals and rent. Time stood still for me, like floating on a lake. I began to worry about coming out. I went to see the assistant governor and asked him if I could stay in. But he said it cost sixteen pounds a week to keep a man inside, and that there were plenty of others waiting to come in. They didn't have room for us all.

I had to come out then. They found me a job in a factory. I moved into this attic room where I've been ever since. In the factory I had to take tins of raspberries off a conveyor belt. I didn't mind that since it was so noisy you didn't have to speak to anyone. Now I'm strange. Not strange to me because I knew it was going to turn out like this. Ever since that oven, I want to be contained. I want to be small. I don't want this noise and these people all

around me. I want to be out of all that, in the dark. Do
you see that wardrobe there, takes up most of this room?
If you look inside you won't find any clothes hanging up.
It's full of cushions and blankets. I go in there, I lock the
door behind me and sit in the darkness for hours. That
must sound pretty stupid to you. I feel all right in there.
I don't get bored or anything, I just sit. Sometimes I wish
the wardrobe would get up and walk around and forget
that I was in there. At first I went in there only very occasionally but then it got more and more frequent till I
started spending whole nights in there. I did not want to
come out in the mornings either so I was late for work.
Then I stopped going to work altogether. It's three months
since I've been. I hate going outside. I prefer it in my
cupboard.

I don't want to be free. That's why I envy these babies
I see in the street being bundled and carried about by their
mothers. I want to be one of them. Why can't it be me?
Why do I have to walk around, go to work, cook my meals
and do all the hundred things you have to do each day to
keep alive? I want to climb in the pram. It's stupid, I'm
six feet tall. But that doesn't make any difference to the
way I feel. The other day I stole a blanket from a pram. I
don't know why, I suppose I had to make contact with
their world, to feel I was not completely irrelevant to it.
I feel excluded. I don't need sex or anything like that. If I
see a pretty girl like the one I was telling you about I get
all bent up inside, and then I come back here and toss
myself off, like I told you. There can't be many like me. I
keep that blanket I stole in the cupboard. I want to fill it
with dozens like it.

I don't go out much now. It's two weeks since I've been
out of this attic. I bought some tins of food last time,
though I am never very hungry. Mostly I sit in the

cupboard thinking about the old times in Staines, wishing it all again. When it rains at night it beats against the roof and I wake up. I think about that girl who lives in our house now, I can hear the wind and the traffic. I want to be one year old again. But it won't happen. I know it won't.

First Love, Last Rites

From the beginning of summer until it seemed pointless, we lifted the thin mattress on to the heavy oak table and made love in front of the large open window. We always had a breeze blowing into the room and smells of the quayside four floors down. I was drawn into fantasies against my will, fantasies of the creature, and afterwards when we lay on our backs on the huge table, in those deep silences I heard it faintly running and clawing. It was new to me, all this, and I worried, I tried to talk to Sissel about it for reassurance. She had nothing to say, she did not make abstractions or discuss situations, she lived inside them. We watched the seagulls wheeling about in our square of sky and wondered if they had been watching us up there, that was the kind of thing we talked about, mildly entertaining hypotheses of the present moment. Sissel did things as they came to her, stirred her coffee, made love, listened to her records, looked out the window. She did not say things like I'm happy, or confused, or I want to make love, or I don't, or I'm tired of the fights in my family, she had no language to split herself in two, so I suffered alone what seemed like crimes in my head while we fucked, and afterwards listened alone to it scrabbling in the silence. Then one afternoon Sissel woke from a doze, raised her head from the mattress and said, 'What's that scratching noise behind the wall?'

My friends were far away in London, they sent me anguished and reflective letters, what would they do now? Who were they, and what was the point of it all? They were my age, seventeen and eighteen, but I pretended not to understand them. I sent back postcards, find a big table and an open window, I told them. I was happy and it seemed easy, I was making eel traps, it was so easy to have a purpose. The summer went on and I no longer heard from them. Only Adrian came to see us, he was Sissel's ten-year-old brother and he came to escape the misery of his disintegrating home, the quick reversals of his mother's moods, the endless competitive piano playing of his sisters, the occasional bitter visits of his father. Adrian and Sissel's parents after twenty-seven years of marriage and six children hated each other with sour resignation, they could no longer bear to live in the same house. The father moved out to a hostel a few streets away to be near his children. He was a businessman who was out of work and looked like Gregory Peck, he was an optimist and had a hundred schemes to make money in an interesting way. I used to meet him in the pub. He did not want to talk about his redundancy or his marriage, he did not mind me living in a room over the quayside with his daughter. Instead he told me about his time in the Korean war, and when he was an international sales-man, and of the legal fraudery of his friends who were now at the top and knighted, and then one day of the eels in the River Ouse, how the river bed swarmed with eels, how there was money to be made catching them and taking them live to London. I told him how I had eighty pounds in the bank, and the next morning we bought netting, twine, wire hoops and an old cistern tank to keep eels in. I spent the next two months making eel traps.

On fine days I took my net, hoops and twine outside and worked on the quay, sitting on a bollard. An eel trap is cylinder-shaped, sealed at one end, and at the other is a long tapering funnel entrance. It lies on the river bed, the eels swim in to eat the bait and in their blindness cannot find their way out. The fishermen were friendly and amused. There's eels down there, they said, and you'll catch a few but you won't make no living on it. The tide'll lose your nets fast as you make them. We're using iron weights, I told them, and they shrugged in a good-natured way and showed me a better way to lash the net to the hoops, they believed it was my right to try it for myself. When the fishermen were out in their boats and I did not feel like working I sat about and watched the tidal water slip across the mud, I felt no urgency about the eel traps but I was certain we would be rich.

I tried to interest Sissel in the eel adventure, I told her about the rowing-boat someone was lending to us for the summer, but she had nothing to say. So instead we lifted the mattress on to the table and lay down with our clothes on. Then she began to talk. We pressed our palms together, she made a careful examination of the size and shape of our hands and gave a running commentary. Exactly the same size, your fingers are thicker, you've got this extra bit here. She measured my eyelashes with the end of her thumb and wished hers were as long, she told me about the dog she had when she was small, it had long white eyelashes. She looked at the sunburn on my nose and talked about that, which of her brothers and sisters went red in the sun, who went brown, what her youngest sister said once. We slowly undressed. She kicked off her plimsolls and talked about her foot rot. I listened with my eyes closed, I could smell mud and seaweed and dust through the open window. Wittering on, she called it, this kind of

talk. Then once I was inside her I was moved, I was inside
my fantasy, there could be no separation now of my mush-
rooming sensations from my knowledge that we could
make a creature grow in Sissel's belly. I had no wish to
be a father, that was not in it at all. It was eggs, sperms,
chromosomes, feathers, gills, claws, inches from my
cock's end the unstoppable chemistry of a creature growing out of a dark red slime, my fantasy was of being helpless before the age and strength of this process and the
thought alone could make me come before I wanted.
When I told Sissel she laughed. Oh, Gawd, she said. To
me Sissel was right inside the process, she *was* the process
and the power of its fascination grew. She was meant to
be on the pill and every month she forgot it at least two or
three times. Without discussion we came to the arrangement that I was to come outside her, but it rarely worked.
As we were swept down the long slopes to our orgasms, in
those last desperate seconds I struggled to find my way out
but I was caught like an eel in my fantasy of the creature
in the dark, waiting, hungry, and I fed it great white gobs.
In those careless fractions of a second I abandoned my life
to feeding the creature, whatever it was, in or out of the
womb, to fucking only Sissel, to feeding more creatures,
my whole life given over to this in a moment's weakness.
I watched out for Sissel's periods, everything about women
was new to me and I could take nothing for granted. We
made love in Sissel's copious, effortless periods, got good
and sticky and brown with the blood and I thought we
were the creatures now in the slime, we were inside fed by
gobs of cloud coming through the window, by gases drawn
from the mudflats by the sun. I worried about my fantasies, I knew I could not come without them. I asked Sissel
what she thought about and she giggled. Not feathers and
gills, anyway. What *do* you think about, then? Nothing

much, nothing really. I pressed my question and she withdrew into silence.

I knew it was my own creature I heard scrabbling, and when Sissel heard it one afternoon and began to worry, I realized her fantasies were involved too, it was a sound which grew out of our lovemaking. We heard it when we were finished and lying quite still on our backs, when we were empty and clear, perfectly quiet. It was the impression of small claws scratching blindly against a wall, such a distant sound it needed two people to hear it. We thought it came from one part of the wall. When I knelt down and put my ear to the skirting-board it stopped, I sensed it on the other side of the wall, frozen in its action, waiting in the dark. As the weeks passed we heard it at other times in the day, and now and then at night. I wanted to ask Adrian what he thought it was. Listen, there it is, Adrian, shut up a moment, what do you think that noise is, Adrian? He strained impatiently to hear what we could hear but he would not be still long enough. There's nothing there, he shouted. Nothing, nothing, nothing. He became very excited, jumped on his sister's back, yelling and yodelling. He did not want whatever it was to be heard, he did not want to be left out. I pulled him off Sissel's back and we rolled about on the bed. Listen again, I said, pinning him down, there it was again. He struggled free and ran out of the room shouting his two-tone police-car siren. We listened to it fade down the stairs and when I could hear him no more I said, Perhaps Adrian is really afraid of mice. Rats, you mean, said his sister, and put her hands between my legs.

By mid-July we were not so happy in our room, there was a growing dishevelment and unease, and it did not seem possible to discuss it with Sissel. Adrian was coming to us every day now because it was the summer holidays and he could not bear to be at home. We would hear him four floors down, shouting and stamping on the stairs on his way up to us. He came in noisily, doing handstands and showing off to us. Frequently he jumped on Sissel's back to impress me, he was anxious, he was worried we might not find him good company and send him away, send him back home. He was worried too because he could no longer understand his sister. At one time she was always ready for a fight, and she was a good fighter, I heard him boast that to his friends, he was proud of her. Now changes had come over his sister, she pushed him off sulkily, she wanted to be left alone to do nothing, she wanted to listen to records. She was angry when he got his shoes on her skirt, and she had breasts now like his mother, she talked to him now like his mother. Get down off there, Adrian. Please, Adrian, please, not now, later. He could not quite believe it all the same, it was a mood of his sister's, a phase, and he went on taunting and attacking her hopefully, he badly wanted things to stay as they were before his father left home. When he locked his forearms round Sissel's neck and pulled her backwards on to the bed his eyes were on me for encouragement, he thought the real bond was between us, the two men against the girl. He did not see there was no encouragement, he wanted it so badly. Sissel never sent Adrian away, she understood why he was here, but it was hard for her. One long afternoon of torment she left the room almost crying with frustration. Adrian turned to me and raised his eyebrows in mock horror. I tried to talk to him then but he was already making his yodelling sound and squaring up for a fight with me. Nor did Sissel have anything to say to me about her brother, she never made general remarks about people because she never made general remarks. Sometimes when we heard Adrian on his way up the stairs she glanced across at me and seemed to betray herself by a slight pursing of her beautiful lips.

There was only one way to persuade Adrian to leave us in peace. He could not bear to see us touch, it pained him, it genuinely disgusted him. When he saw one of us move across the room to the other he pleaded with us silently, he ran between us, pretending playfulness, wanted to decoy us into another game. He imitated us frantically in a desperate last attempt to show us how fatuous we appeared. Then he could stand it no more, he ran out of the room machine-gunning German soldiers and young lovers on the stairs.

But Sissel and I were touching less and less now, in our quiet ways we could not bring ourselves to it. It was not that we were in decline, not that we did not delight in each other, but that our opportunities were faded. It was the room itself. It was no longer four floors up and detached, there was no breeze through the window, only a mushy heat rising off the quayside and dead jellyfish and clouds of flies, fiery grey flies who found our armpits and bit fiercely, houseflies who hung in clouds over our food. Our hair was too long and dank and hung in our eyes. The food we bought melted and tasted like the river. We no longer lifted the mattress on to the table, the coolest place now was the floor and the floor was covered with greasy sand which would not go away. Sissel grew tired of her records, and her foot rot spread from one foot to the other and added to the smell. Our room stank. We did not talk about leaving because we did not talk about anything. Every night now we were woken by the scrabbling behind the wall, louder now and more insistent. When we made love it listened to us behind the wall. We made love less and our rubbish gathered around us, milk bottles we could not bring ourselves to carry away, grey sweating cheese, butter wrappers, yogurt cartons, over-ripe salami. And among it all Adrian cart-wheeling, yodelling, machine-gunning and attacking Sissel. I tried to write poems about my fantasies, about the creature, but I could see no way in and I wrote nothing down, not even a first line. Instead I took long walks along the river dyke into the Norfolk hinterland of dull beet fields, telegraph poles, uniform grey skies. I had two more eel nets to make, I was forcing myself to sit down to them each day. But in my heart I was sick of them, I could not really believe that eels would ever go inside them and I wondered if I wanted them to, if it was not better that the eels should remain undisturbed in the cool mud at the bottom of the river. But I went on with it because Sissel's father was ready to begin, because I had to expiate all the money and hours I had spent so far, because the idea had its own tired, fragile momentum now and I could no more stop it than carry the milk bottles from our room.

Then Sissel found a job and it made me see we were different from no one, they all had rooms, houses, jobs, careers, that's what they all did, they had cleaner rooms, better jobs, we were anywhere's striving couple. It was one of the windowless factories across the river where they canned vegetables and fruit. For ten hours a day she was to sit in the roar of machines by a moving conveyor belt, talk to no one and pick out the rotten carrots before they were canned. At the end of her first day Sissel came home in a pink-and-white nylon raincoat and pink cap. I said, Why don't you take it off? Sissel shrugged. It was all the same to her, sitting around in the room, sitting around in a factory where they relayed Radio One through speakers strung along the steel girders, where four hundred women half listened, half dreamed, while their hands spun backwards and forwards like powered shuttles. On Sissel's second day I took the ferry across the river and waited for her at the factory gates. A few women stepped through a small tin door in a great windowless wall and a wailing siren sounded all across the factory complex. Other small doors opened and they streamed out, converging on the gates, scores of women in pink-and-white nylon coats and pink caps. I stood on a low wall and tried to see Sissel, it was suddenly very important. I thought that if I could not pick her out from this rustling stream of pink nylon then she was lost, we were both lost and our time was worthless. As it approached the factory gates the main body was moving fast. Some were half running in the splayed, hopeless way that women have been taught to run, the others walked as fast as they could. I found out later they were hurrying home to cook suppers for their families, to make an early start on the housework. Latecomers on the next shift tried to push their way through in the opposite direction. I could not see Sissel and I felt on the edge of panic, I shouted her name and my words were trampled underfoot. Two older women who stopped by the wall to light cigarettes grinned up at me. Sizzle yerself. I walked home by the long way, over the bridge, and decided not to tell Sissel I had been to wait for her because I would have to explain my panic and I did not know how. She was sitting on the bed when I came in, she was still wearing her nylon coat. The cap was on the floor. Why don't you take that thing off? I said. She said, Was that you outside the factory? I nodded. Why didn't you speak to me if you saw me standing there? Sissel turned and lay face downwards on the bed. Her coat was stained and smelled of machine oil and earth. I dunno, she said into the pillow, I didn't think. I didn't think of anything after my shift. Her words had a deadening finality, I glanced around our room and fell silent.

Two days later, on Saturday afternoon, I bought pounds of rubbery cows' lungs sodden with blood (lights, they were called) for bait. That same afternoon we filled the traps and rowed out into mid-channel at low tide to lay them on the river bed. Each of the seven traps was marked by a buoy. Four o'clock Sunday morning Sissel's father called for me and we set out in his van to where we kept the borrowed boat. We were rowing out now to find the marker buoys and pull the traps in, it was the testing time, would there be eels in the nets, would it be profitable to make more nets, catch more eels and drive them once a week to Billingsgate market, would we be rich? It was a dull windy morning, I felt no anticipation, only tiredness and a continuous erection. I half dozed in the warmth of the van's heater. I had spent many hours of the night awake listening to the scrabbling noises behind the wall. Once I got out of bed and banged the skirting-board with a spoon. There was a pause, then the digging continued. It seemed certain now that it was digging its way into the room. While Sissel's father rowed I watched over the side for markers. It was not as easy as I thought to find them, they did not show up white against the water but as dark low silhouettes. It was twenty minutes before we found the first. As we pulled it up I was amazed at how soon the clean white rope from the chandlers had become like all other rope near the river, brown and hung about with fine strands of green weed. The net too was old-looking and alien, I could not believe that one of us had made it. Inside were two crabs and a large eel. He untied the closed end of the trap, let the two crabs drop into the water and put the eel in the plastic bucket we had brought with us. We put fresh lights in the trap and dropped it over the side. It took another fifteen minutes to find the next trap and that one had nothing inside. We rowed up and down the channel for half an hour after that without finding another trap, and by this time the tide was coming up and covering the markers. It was then that I took the oars and made for the shore.

We went back to the hostel where Sissel's father was staying and he cooked breakfast. We did not want to discuss the lost traps, we pretended to ourselves and to each other that we would find them when we went out at the next low tide. But we knew they were lost, swept up or downstream by the powerful tides, and I knew I could never make another eel trap in my life. I knew also that my partner was taking Adrian with him on a short holiday, they were leaving that afternoon. They were going to visit military airfields, and hoped to end up at the Imperial War Museum. We ate eggs, bacon and mushrooms and drank coffee. Sissel's father told me of an idea he had, a simple but lucrative idea. Shrimps cost very little on the quayside here and they were very expensive in Brussels. We could drive two vanloads across there each week, he was optimistic in his relaxed, friendly way and for a moment I was sure his scheme would work. I drank the last of my coffee. Well, I said, I suppose that needs some thinking about. I picked up the bucket with the eel in, Sissel and I could eat that one. My partner told me as we shook hands that the surest way of killing an eel was to cover it with salt. I wished him a good holiday and we parted, still maintaining the silent pretence that one of us would be rowing out at the next low tide to search for the traps.

After a week at the factory I did not expect Sissel to be awake when I got home, but she was sitting up in bed, pale and clasping her knees. She was staring into one corner of the room. It's in here, she said. It's behind those books on the floor. I sat down on the bed and took off my wet shoes and socks. The mouse? You mean you heard the mouse? Sissel spoke quietly. It's a rat. I saw it run across the room, and it's a rat. I went over to the books and kicked them, and instantly it was out, I heard its claws on the floorboards and then I saw it run along the wall, the size of a small dog it seemed to me then, a rat, a squat, powerful grey rat dragging its belly along the floor. It ran the whole length of the wall and crept behind a chest of drawers. We've got to get it out of here, Sissel wailed, in a voice which was strange to me. I nodded, but I could not move for the moment, or speak, it was so big, the rat, and it had been with us all summer, scrabbling at the wall in the deep, clear silences after our fucking, and in our sleep, it was our familiar. I was terrified, more afraid than Sissel, I was certain the rat knew us as well as we knew it, it was aware of us in the room now just as we were aware of it behind the chest of drawers. Sissel was about to speak again when we heard a noise outside on the stairs, a familiar stamping, machine-gunning noise. I was relieved to hear it. Adrian came in the way he usually did, he kicked the door and leaped in, crouching low, a machine-gun ready at his hip. He sprayed us with raw noises from the back of his throat, we crossed our lips with our fingers and tried to hush him. You're dead, both of you, he said, and got ready for a cartwheel across the room. Sissel shushed him again, she tried to wave him towards the bed. Why sshh? What's wrong with you? We pointed to the chest of drawers. It's a rat, we told him. He was down on his knees at once, peering. A rat? he gasped. Fantastic, it's a big one, look at it. Fantastic. What are you going to do? Let's catch it. I crossed the room quickly and picked up a poker from the fireplace, I could lose my fear in Adrian's excitement, pretend it was just a fat rat in our room, an adventure to catch it. From the bed Sissel wailed again. What are you going to do with that? For a moment I felt my grip loosen on the poker, it was not just a rat, it was not an adventure, we both knew that. Meanwhile Adrian danced his dance, Yes, that, use that. Adrian helped me carry the books across the room, we built a wall right round the chest of drawers with only one gap in the middle where the rat could get through. Sissel went on asking, What are you doing? What are you going to do with that? but she did not dare leave the bed. We had finished the wall and I was giving Adrian a coat-hanger to drive the rat out with when Sissel jumped across the room and tried to snatch the poker from my hand. Give me that, she cried, and hung on to my lifted arm. At that moment the rat ran out through the gap in the books, it ran straight at us and I thought I saw its teeth bared and ready. We scattered, Adrian jumped on the table, Sissel and I were back on the bed. Now we all had time to see the rat as it paused in the centre of the room and then ran forward again, we had time to see how powerful and fat and fast it was, how its whole body quivered, how its tail slid behind it like an attendant parasite. It knows us, I thought, it wants us. I could not bring myself to look at Sissel. As I stood up on the bed, raised the poker and aimed it, she screamed. I threw it as hard as I could, it struck the floor point first several inches from the rat's narrow head. It turned instantly and ran back between the gap in the books. We heard the scratch of its claws on the floor as it settled itself behind the chest of drawers to wait.

I unwound the wire coat-hanger, straightened it and doubled it over and gave it to Adrian. He was quieter now, slightly more fearful. His sister sat on the bed with her knees drawn up again. I stood several feet from the gap in the books with the poker held tight in both hands. I glanced down and saw my pale bare feet and saw a ghost rat's teeth bared and tearing nail from flesh. I called out,

Wait, I want to get my shoes. But it was too late, Adrian was jabbing the wire behind the chest of drawers and now I dared not move. I crouched a little lower over the poker, like a batsman. Adrian climbed on to the chest and thrust the wire right down into the corner. He was in the middle of shouting something to me, I did not hear what it was. The frenzied rat was running through the gap, it was running at my feet to take its revenge. Like the ghost rat its teeth were bared. With both hands I swung the poker down, caught it clean and whole smack under its belly, and it lifted clear off the ground, sailed across the room, borne up by Sissel's long scream through her hand in her mouth, it dashed against the wall and I thought in an instant, It must have broken its back. It dropped to the ground, legs in the air, split from end to end like a ripe fruit. Sissel did not take her hand from her mouth, Adrian did not move from the chest, I did not shift my weight from where I had struck, and no one breathed out. A faint smell crept across the room, musty and intimate, like the smell of Sissel's monthly blood. Then Adrian farted and giggled from his held-back fear, his human smell mingled with the wide-open rat smell. I stood over the rat and prodded it gently with the poker. It rolled on its side, and from the mighty gash which ran its belly's length there obtruded and slid partially free from the lower abdomen a translucent purple bag, and inside five pale crouching shapes, their knees drawn up around their chins. As the bag touched the floor I saw a movement, the leg of one unborn rat quivered as if in hope, but the mother was hopelessly dead and there was no more for it.

Sissel knelt by the rat, Adrian and I stood behind her like guards, it was as if she had some special right, kneeling there with her long red skirt spilling round her. She parted the gash in the mother rat with her forefinger and thumb, pushed the bag back inside and closed the blood-spiked fur over it. She remained kneeling a little while and we still stood behind her. Then she cleared some dishes from the sink to wash her hands. We all wanted to get outside now, so Sissel wrapped the rat in newspaper and we carried it downstairs. Sissel lifted the lid of the dustbin and I placed it carefully inside. Then I remembered something, I told the other two to wait for me and I ran back up the stairs. It was the eel I came back for, it lay quite still in its few inches of water and for a moment I thought that it too was dead till I saw it stir when I picked up the bucket. The wind had dropped now and the cloud was breaking up, we walked to the quay in alternate light and shade. The tide was coming in fast. We walked down the stone steps to the water's edge and there I tipped the eel back in the river and we watched him flick out of sight, a flash of white underside in the brown water. Adrian said goodbye to us, and I thought he was going to hug his sister. He hesitated and then ran off, calling out something over his shoulder. We shouted after him to have a good holiday. On the way back Sissel and I stopped to look at the factories on the other side of the river. She told me she was going to give up her job there.

We lifted the mattress on to the table and lay down in front of the open window, face to face, the way we did at the beginning of summer. We had a light breeze blowing in, a distant smoky smell of autumn, and I felt calm, very clear. Sissel said, This afternoon let's clean the room up and then go for a long walk, a walk along the river dyke. I pressed the flat of my palm against her warm belly and said, Yes.

Disguises

Mina that Mina. Soft and breathy now and thick glasses too remembers her last appearance on stage. Sour Goneril at the Old Vic, she took no nonsense, though friends said even then the mind of that Mina was slipping. Prompted, they say, in act one, shouting at the guilty A.S.M. in the interval, and scratched him with her long vermilion nail, below the eye and to the right, a little nick across the cheek. King Lear stepped between, knighted the week before, a household venerate among non-theatregoers, and the director stepped between, flapping at Mina with his programme sheet. 'You royal arse-licker' to one, and 'You backstage pimp' to the other, she spat at each and played one more night. And that to give her understudy time. The last night on stage for Mina, what a grande dame she was sweeping here and there, in and out of cue, a train in a tunnel of blank verse, and her proud unpadded bosom lifting with her caterwaul, and brave. She, near the beginning, carelessly tossed a plastic rose into the front row, and when Lear gave forth she had a fancy business with her fan, it raised a titter from time to time. The audience, sophisticated sentients, felt for her and the melodrama of desperation because they knew about Mina and gave a special cheer at curtain call which sent her weeping to her dressing-room and as she went she pressed the back of her hand into her forehead.

Two days later Brianie died, her sister, Henry's mother, so Mina confusing dates persuaded Mina at the funeral tea, and this is what she told her friends, she gave up the stage to tend her sister's child then ten years old and in need, so Mina told her friends, of a real mother, a Real Mother. And Mina was a surreal mother.

In the drawing-room of her Islington house she drew her nephew to her, pressed his blotchy face into the padded now and scented bosom, and the same again that next day in the taxi to Oxford Street where she bought him a bottle of cologne and a Fauntleroy suit with lace trimmings. In the months she let his hair grow down below the collar and the ears, daring for the early 'sixties, and encouraged him to dress for dinner, the motif of this story, showed him how to mix her drink from the cocktail cabinet in the evening, had a violin teacher round, a dancing-master too, on his birthday a shirt-maker, and then a photographer with a voice pitched politely high. He came to take faded and brown-tinted shots of Henry and Mina posing in costume before the mantelpiece and it was all, Mina told Henry, it was all good training.

Good training for what? Henry did not put this question to her or to himself, not an introspect or sensitive, the kind to accept a new life and this narcissism with no opinion either way, all being part of one fact. The fact was his mother had died, her image six months on was elusive like a faint star. There were details, though, and he questioned them. When the photographer flouncing back and across the room packed his tripod and left, Henry asked Mina, returning from the front door, 'Why does that man have a funny voice?' He was satisfied understanding nothing from Mina. 'I think, darling, because he's queer.' The pictures came soon in heavy packets with Mina running through the kitchen and out for her glasses and shrieking and giggling and tearing at the stiff brown paper with her fingers. They were in gilded oval frames, she passed them across the table to Henry. At the edge the brown faded to nothing, like smoke, precious and unreal, Henry there, wan, impassive, and a straight back, and one hand was resting lightly on Mina's shoulder. She was on the piano stool, skirts spilling around, head lifted back a little, attempting a lady's pout and her hair in a black bun down the nape of her neck. Mina was laughing, excited and getting her other glasses to look at the pictures arm's length, and turning knocked the milk jug over, laughed more and leaping back in her chair to escape the white streams which dribbled to the floor between her legs. And between the laughs, 'What do you think, dear? Aren't they super?' 'They're all right,' said Henry, 'I suppose.'

Good training? Mina did not ask herself either what she meant, but it was to do with the stage if she had, everything Mina did was to do with that. Always on stage even when alone an audience watched and her actions were for them, a kind of superego, she dared not displease them or herself, so sinking with a moan to her bed after some exhaustion, that moan had shape and told. And in the morning sitting to make up her face by the bedroom mirror with a small horseshoe of naked light bulbs around, she felt at her back a thousand eyes and was poised and carried each motion through to its end with a mind to its uniqueness. Henry was not the kind to see the unseen, he mistook Mina. Mina singing, or flinging out her arms, pirouetting in the room, buying parasols and costumes, imitating to the milkman the milkman's accent, or just Mina carrying in a dish from the kitchen to the dining-room table, held out high in front of her and she whistling some military march between her teeth and beating time with strange ballet slippers she always wore, it seemed to

Henry to be for him. He was uneasy, a little unhappy –
should he clap, was there something he had to do, join in
or Mina might think he was sulking? There were times,
catching Mina's mood, he did join in, falteringly, in some
celebratory manic around the room. Something then in
Mina's eye warned against, said room for one performer
only, so he let his steps peter to the nearest chair.

Sure she worried him, but for the rest she was not un-
kind, tea was ready in the afternoon when he came in from
school, special treats, some favourite, custard cakes or
toasted buns, and then the talk. Mina sketched out her
day's impressions and confidences, more wife in these than
aunt, talking fast through mouthfuls blowing out crumbs,
and made a crescent moon of grease above the upper lip.

'I saw Julie Frank at lunch Three Tuns she was putting
them away still living with that jockey or horse-trainer or
whatever and not thinking of marriage but she's a spiteful
bitch Henry. "Julie," I said, "now what of these stories
you're putting out about Maxine's abortion?" – I told you
about that, didn't I! – "Abortion?" she said, "Oh, *that*.
All fun and giggles, Mina, nothing more." "Fun and
giggles?" I said. "I felt a complete fool when I went round
there." "Oooo, did you now?" she said.'

Henry ate the eclairs, nodding quietly and liking to sit
down after all day at school to listen to a story, Mina told
them so well. Then on the second cup of tea it was Henry's
turn to tell his day, more linear and slowly, like this. 'First
we had history and then singing and then Mr Carter took
us on a walk up Hampstead Hill because he said we were
all falling asleep and then it was break and after that we
had French and then we had composition.' But it took
longer with Mina breaking in with, 'History was *my* favourite subject, I remember ...' and, 'Hampstead Hill is the
highest point in London, you must be careful not to fall

off, darling,' and the composition, the story, did he have it with him? was he going to read it? wait, she must get comfortable first, now go ahead. Making apologies in his mind and very reluctant, Henry brought the exercise book from his satchel, flattened out the pages, began to read, the monotone of a self-conscious robot, 'No one in the village ever went near the castle on Grey Crag because of the terrible cries they heard at midnight ...' At the end Mina banged the floor with her feet, and clapped, shouted like someone at the back of a hall, lifted high her teacup, 'We must get you an agent, dear.' Now it was her turn, she took the story, reading it back with the right pauses and piping howls and rattling spoons for effects, convinced him it was good, even eerie.

This tea and confession could be two hours; when it was over they went to their rooms, it was dressing for dinner. Later than September Henry found his fire lit a waving glow and writhing furniture shadows on the wall, his suit or costume unfolded on the bed, whichever Mina chose that night for him to wear. Dressing for dinner. It allowed two hours or so for Mrs Simpson to let herself in with her own key, cook the meal and let herself out, Mina to bathe and with black goggles lie beneath her artificial sun, Henry to do his homework, read his old books, play with his old junk. Mina and Henry together found old books and charts in damp bookshops near the British Museum, collected junk from the Portobello Road and Camden market, the we buy and sell everything shops of Kentish Town. A queue of yellow-eyed elephants diminishing, carved in wood, a still working clockwork train of painted tin, puppets with no strings, a scorpion pickled in a jar. And a Victorian children's theatre giving instructions from a polite booklet for two people to play scenes from the *Thousand and One Nights*. For two months they pushed the faded cardboard figures across the variable backdrops, you change them with a flick of your wrist, banging knives on teaspoons for sword fights, and Mina got tense crouching on her knees there, angry sometimes when he missed the cue – he often did – but she missed them too, and then they laughed. Mina could do the voices, the villain's master's prince's heroine's plaintiff's voices, and tried to teach him how, but uselessly and they laughed again for Henry could do two, a high one and a low one. Mina tired of the cardboard theatre, now only Henry took it out before the fire and, shy, let the figures speak in his mind. Twenty minutes before the dinner he took off his school clothes, washed, took up the costume Mina had planned and joined her in the dining-room where she waited in her costume.

Mina collected them, costumes, guises, outfits, old clothes, wherever she could get them and she sewed them into shape, packing three wardrobes. And now for Henry too. A few suits from Oxford Street, but the rest unwanted stock, from amateur theatre groups which were folding up, forgotten pantomimes, seconds from the best costumiers, it was her hobby, you see. To dinner Henry wore a soldier's uniform, and a lift-boy's from an American hotel before the war, he must be an old man now, a kind of monk's habit and a shepherd's smock from the Virgilian Eclogues, performed once and eurhythmically by the girls of the upper sixth, written by or arranged by the head prefect, who Mina was once. Henry was uncurious, obedient, put on each evening what he found at the foot of his bed, and found Mina downstairs in bustle or whalebone hoops, sequined cat suit, or become a Crimean war nurse. But she was not different nor did she play a part to her costume, she made no comment on either's appearance, seemed in fact to want to forget the matter, eat the meal, relax, drink from the glass her nephew passed her, so he was trained. Henry took the routine, enjoyed the ritual of the long tea and structured privacy, beginning to wonder on the way home from school what was ready for him to wear, hope to find something new on his bed. But Mina was mysterious, not warning over tea of something new, let him discover it and smiled to herself while he mixed her drink and poured himself a lemonade, standing there in a toga she found, toasting with their glasses across the large room, silently. She turned him round, making to herself some note of an alteration, then started the meal, the usual chatter and stories of her days on the stage, or other people's stories. All so very strange, somehow to Henry ordinary, homely in winter.

One afternoon retiring after tea, opening the door of his room Henry found a girl lying face down across his bed; stepping a little closer, it was not a girl it was a kind of party frock and a wig of long blonde hair, white tights, black leather slippers. Catching his breath he touched the dress, cold, ominously silky, it rustled when he picked it up, all flounces and frills, layer on layer with white satin and lace edged with pink, a cute bow falling at the back. He let it fall back on the bed, the most girlish thing he ever saw, wiped his hand on his trousers, not daring to touch the wig which seemed alive. Not these, not him, did Mina really want him to? He stared miserably at the bed and picked up the white tights, not these, surely. All right being a soldier, a Roman, a pageboy, something like that, but not a girl, it was wrong to be a girl. Like the best of Henry's friends at school he did not care for girls, avoided their huddles and intrigues, their whispers and giggles and holding hands and passing notes and I love I love, they set his teeth on edge to see. Unhappily Henry paced the room, sat at his desk to work at memorizing French words, *armoire* cupboard *armoire* cupboard *armoire* cupboard *armoire* ...? and glanced across his shoulder every minute to see if they were still there on the bed, and they were. Twenty minutes to dinner, it could not be right, he could not take his own clothes off or put those on, and yet a terrible thing to upset the ritual of the dressing-up, and now he could hear Mina singing as she left the bathroom, she was doing up her face in the next room. Could he ask to wear something else, when she had been out today to buy him this, when yesterday she told him how good wigs cost and were hard to come by? Sitting on that end of the bed farthest from the clothes and wanting to cry, for the first time in months he missed his mother, solid and always the same, typing at the Ministry of Transport. He heard Mina pass the door going downstairs to wait for him and he began to loosen his shoe and then not, he did not want to. Mina called up to him nothing different in her voice, 'Henry, darling, are you coming down?' and he said out loud, 'Just a moment.' But he could not move, could not touch those things, did not want to, even if only for pretend, appear a girl. Now there were her footsteps on the stairs, she was coming to see, he pulled one shoe off in token palliation, there was nothing he could do.

She came into his room dressed, he had not seen her wear it before, an officer's uniform, brisk, straight-lined, thin buckle epaulettes, and a red stripe in the trousers, her hair pinned back, perhaps it was greased, shiny black shoes, and her face with a man's heavy lines, the hint of a moustache. She marched across the room, 'But darling, you haven't started to get ready yet, let me help you, it will need tying at the back anyway,' and she began to loosen his tie. Henry stood too numb to resist, she was so certain, pulling off his shirt, trousers, the other shoe, his socks, and then strangely his underpants. Had he washed yet? She took him by the wrist, steered him to the washbasin, was filling it with warm water and flanneling his face, drying it, sweeping him along in a frenzy of her own, a special momentum. He stood naked in the centre of the room in a horror dream while Mina rummaged on the bed among the clothes and found them, turning from the bed with them in her hand, a pair of white knickers, and Henry said 'No' to himself as they came towards. Bending down by his feet, 'Lift one leg,' she said cheerily and knocked on one foot with the back of her hand, to which he could not stir, just stood, frightened by the edge of impatience in her voice, 'Come on, Henry, or dinner will be spoiled.' He moved his tongue before he spoke, 'No, I don't want to wear those.' For a moment her back held there bent over by his feet, then she straightened, caught his forearm in a pinching mean grip and was looking close in his face, sucking him in with her look. He saw the mask of makeup wadded on, an old man, the lines of frivolous scars and her lower lip stretched with anger across her teeth, first in his legs and then everywhere he began to tremble. She shook his arm, hissed, 'Lift one leg', and waited while he made the beginnings of the movement, but that movement released him, let fall a trickle of urine down his leg. She pushed him to the sink again, wiping him quickly with the towel and said, 'Now', so that too frightened, too humiliated, to refuse Henry lifted one leg and then the other, submitted to the cold layers of the dress against his skin, lowered over his head, laced from behind, then the tights, the leather slippers, and last the close-fitting wig, the gold hair fell past both his eyes, tumbled freely across his shoulders.

In the mirror he saw her, a sickeningly pretty little girl, he glanced away and followed miserably Mina downstairs, rustling sulkily and still shaking in his legs. Mina was gay now, she made conciliatory jokes about his reluctance this evening, spoke of a trip somewhere, Battersea funfair perhaps, and even Henry in his confusion knew she was excited by his presence and appearance, for twice in the meal she got up from her place to come to kiss and hug him where he sat and run her fingers through the fabric, 'All is forgiven, all is forgiven.' Later Mina drank three glasses of port and sprawled herself in the armchair, a drunken soldier calling to his girl, wanted her to come and sit on this officer's knee. Henry stayed out of reach, small panics in his stomach at each thought that Mina – was she very wicked or very mad? he could not decide, but for sure the dressing-up game loses its fun by this, he sensed some compulsion in it for Mina, he dared not contradict it, there was something dark – the way she pushed him, the way she hissed, something he did not understand and he pushed it from his mind. So towards the end of the evening, escaping Mina's hands to pull him on her knee, and catching glimpses of himself in the many mirrors in that room, reflections of the pretty little blonde girl in her party frock, he told himself, 'It's for her, it's nothing to do with anything, it's for her, it's nothing to do with me.'

Afraid of the thing in her he did not understand. Henry for the most part liked her, she was his friend, she wanted to make him laugh, not to tell him what to do. She made him laugh with all her funny voices, and if she told a story and was excited, and that was often, she acted it out for him, telling it up and down the length of the sitting-room. 'The day Deborah left her husband she walked straight down to the bus stop ...' and here Mina danced a little arm-swinging march into the centre of the room ... 'but it was only *then* that she remembered that at lunchtime there were no buses from the village ...' shading her eyes with her hand she scoured the room for a bus, then the other hand flew to her mouth, wide eyes, jaw sagging, remembrance came all over her face, like the sun from behind a cloud ... 'so she went back home to have her lunch ...' again the little walk ... 'and there was her husband sitting in front of two empty plates, belching away and saying, "Well, I didn't expect you home so I ate yours"' ... hands on her hips Mina bulged her eyes at Henry who was now the husband sitting at the table, and he wondering if he should join in, lean back in his chair and belch. But he laughed instead because Mina was laughing now, she always did when she came to the end of her story. Mina was on television now and then, he admired her for that, even though it was only the commercials, she was usually the housewife with the right soap powder, curlers, and knotted scarf in her hair gabbling over a garden wall, some neighbour leaned over and asked about her sheets, what was her secret, and Mina told her in her Souf Lunnun accent. She hired the set just for the ads, they sat there with the schedule sheet waiting for it to come on and when it did they laughed. When it was over she turned it off, only sometimes did they watch a programme, and then it was the actors, they made her angry in advance, 'Christ! that's Paul Cook, I knew him when he swept the floor at the Ipswich rep,' she jumped up from her chair, unplugged the set on the way to the kitchen, Henry sat in his chair watching the white dot recede in the centre of the screen.

One afternoon nearing a Christmas, coming cold and late from school, there was a pile near his plate at tea, arranged by Mina and he was bound to find them, of smooth white cards, reading in elaborate copperplate, lean and decorous, Mina and Henry invite you to their party. Come disguised. RSVP. Henry read several, his own unfamiliar name in print, and looked across at Mina watching him, some kind of pursed-up smile hovering in the space between them, all ready to break out and she was waiting for him. Excited but unable to show it because he was waited for, so lamely he said, 'That's very nice,' and that was wrong, that was not how he felt it at all, never been to a party and never been on an invitation card. Still something in Mina made it hard to say, more was required, 'Disguises though, what kind of disguises?' But too late because Mina was laughing and rising while he said it, and making a strutting ballerina walk across the room and chanting in time to her steps, '*That's* nice? Ni-ice? Ni-ice? Ni-ice?' and so round the room back to the table and the chair where he sat watching her and very unsure. She stood behind his chair tousling his hair for pretend affection, but pulling it, and stung his eyes. 'Henry, dear, it will be formidable, fantastical, awful, but never nice, nothing we ever do will be nice,' speaking this all the while she ran her hands in his hair, twined it through her fingers. He turned to look upwards and escape her, and she was caught in the sudden wild upward stare in the large white of his eyes, relented now, squeezed him with real affection, 'We'll have the time of our lives, aren't you excited? What do you think of the cards?' He took the cards again, saying seriously, 'No one will dare not come.' The edge of the vicious gone from her tone she told him, pouring the tea, that the disguises must be impenetrable, and made jokes and anecdotes about the friends she was going to invite.

After dinner they sat by the coal fire talking, Mina wearing a New Look of the rationing days and Henry in his Fauntleroy suit, Mina said suddenly after a long silence, 'And you? Who are you going to invite?' He did not reply for several minutes, thinking of his friends at school. At school he was different, it was different, he played chasing games and loud football against the wall, and in class borrowed some of Mina's words and anecdotes to make his own; the teachers considered him mildly precocious. He had many friends, but he wandered and did not have a best friend like some of them. And then at home sitting quietly through the drama spectacles and Mina's moods, attending so not to miss a cue, he had not thought of the two things together, one large and free with big windows, lino floors, long rows of pegs to hang your coat on, the other was dense, the things in his room, two cups of tea and Mina's games. Telling his day to Mina was like telling a dream over breakfast, true and not true, at last he said, 'I don't know, I can't think of anyone.' Could the ones he played football with be in the same room as Mina? 'Have you not made any friends at school worth bringing home?' Henry did not make an answer. How could they be in disguises, costumes and things like that, he was sure it would not fit.

She did not ask him again the next day, but unwound the details, ideas which flooded to her, all day thinking of nothing else. To help the disguises along the rooms shall be dimly lit. 'Even best friends won't be able to recognize each other,' and disguises must stay a secret, no one will know who Mina is, she can move around, have a good time, let them get their own drinks, do their own introducing – false names of course – and they are all theatre people, masters of disguise, masters at the art of creating character, because that is the art of acting as Mina sees it, creating a self, in other words a disguise. And breathlessly on and on with the details, it came to her in the bath, of course red light bulbs, a special recipe for punch, arrange the music from somewhere and perhaps we will burn some joss sticks. Then the invitations were sent away, all the

arrangements made that could be made and it was still
two weeks, so Mina and therefore Henry spoke of the
thing no more. Since she knew his costumes, had bought
them all herself and did not want to know him on the day,
she gave him money for his disguise, he must get it himself
and promise to hold it to himself. Walking all one Saturday he found it in a junk shop near the Highbury and
Islington tube station, among the cameras, broken shavers,
and yellow books, a kind of monstrous Boris Karloff face
of cloth with holes for the eyes and mouth, and in the
shape of a hood you pulled it over your head. It had wiry
hair in all directions, it was funny and surprised, not
frightening, though, cost thirty shillings, the man said.
And not having his money with him that day he told the
man he would be along to collect it Monday when he
came from school.

But that day he was not there, that day he met Linda, it
was the way the desks were arranged, in pairs, four by
four and a gangway to walk down. Henry was the newest
to the class, proud to have a desk to himself, that was the
way it worked out when all the others had to share. His
charts and books and two puppets took both sides of it,
good to sit at the back all spread out. The teacher explaining twenty-five feet said that it was about from here to
Henry's desk, and they turned round to look at everyone
in the class, of course it was his desk. On Monday there
was a girl, a new girl, and sitting at his desk, setting out
her coloured pencils as if she belonged. Seeing him stare
she turned her look down, said quietly but with no sub-
mission, 'Teacher told me to sit here,' and Henry scowled,
sat down, his space violated was bad, and this was a girl.
Through the first three lessons she sat, a no presence, by
his side, and Henry stared ahead, for looking round was to

admit her, these seeking girls who meet your eye. At break he rose before the others, stood under the stairs drinking milk, avoiding his friends, and waited till the classroom was empty to go back in there to clear one half of his table for her, sulkily, packing the bits, the tender off the clockwork train, some old clothes and things, into two carrier bags, and feeling obscurely martyred put them behind her chair, he wanted her to know how the inconvenience was. She made a nervous little smile coming in to sit down but he was brisk, a pretender, dismissive, looking away and rubbing his hands.

But bad temper fades and he became curious, stole some glances and then again some more, the striking things about her moved something, like the long fine sun-yellow hair all over her shoulders on the soft wool about her back, and bloodless skin like this paper but almost transparent, and then her nose, very stretched, tight and taut, flared like a horse, her scared large grey eyes. Knowing him watching her again she made the beginnings of a smile with the corner of her lips, gave Henry a little uneasy thrill, that movement, in the pit of his stomach, so he moved his eyes to the front of the classroom, understanding vaguely what it was when they said this or that girl was beautiful, when it always seemed before an exaggeration Mina might make.

Growing up you fell in love, Henry knew that, with some girl you met, and that was when you got married, but only if you met a girl you liked, and how for him when most girls could not be understood? This one, though, he could see her elbow almost on to his part of the desk, this one was frail and different, he wanted to touch her neck or put his foot near hers, or did Henry feel guilty with all this new, this confusion and feeling? A history lesson and all drawing a map of Norway and colouring Viking ships with their bows pointing south. He touched her elbow, 'Can I borrow a blue pencil?' 'Blue for the sea or blue for the sky?' 'Blue for the sea.' She found a pencil for him, told him her name was Linda, and holding it still warm from her own hand he bent over his own map with extra care, scratched a blue halo for his coastline making it sound *linda linda* as he worked it up and down three inches from his eyes. Then he remembered, 'I'm Henry' he whispered, the grey eyes opened wider to take it in, 'Henry?' 'Yes.' Frightened by himself he steered round her at lunch, made sure of another table to eat his meal and noisily sought out his friends across the playground who taunted, 'See you got a girl,' for which he pantomimed a tremor of real disgust to make them laugh and take him in. They played football against the playground wall and Henry shouted most, swung his elbows and fists, but when the ball went over the wall and they hung about waiting, then his mind was gone on in advance into the classroom sitting next to a girl. And returning himself he found her already there and let her see by the slightest incline of his head he saw her smile. The afternoon trickled out bored and slow, he shifted around in his seat not wanting it to end or continue, knowing she was sitting there.

He knelt behind her chair when school was over, making as if to look for something in the bags, certain he would not see her till the morning. She was still sitting at the desk, completing something and not noticing, so Henry rustled the bags some more, standing up cleared his throat, said roughly, 'See you, then,' echoing his voice in the empty classroom. She stood up, closing her book, 'I can carry one.' Taking one of the bags from him she led the way out of the room and they crossed the silent playground, Henry looking round to see if his friends were still about. There was a woman by the school gates with a leather coat and her hair was tied in a ponytail, young and old at the same time, who bent down to Linda and kissed her on the lips. She said, 'Have you made a friend already?' looking at Henry, he stood a few paces off. Linda said simply, 'His name is Henry,' and called to him, 'She's my mother,' and her mother stretched out her hand towards Henry who came over and shook it, very grown-up. 'Hello, Henry, can we give you a ride home with your bags?' described with a vague tossing of her wrist joint the big black car parked behind her. She put his bags in the back seat, suggested they all sit in the front, which they did, and Linda pressed close up against him to let her mother change the gears. He was not expected home straight away because of the mask, he had told Mina he would be late, he accepted then the invitation to tea and sat pressed along the car door, listened to Linda tell her mother of her first day at the new school. Down a gravel curving driveway they stopped by a large house of red brick and trees all round and through the trees the Heath dropping down in one long sweep towards a lake, which Linda pointed to when they walked round the side of the house. 'The mansion there, you can just make it out in the trees, that's Kenwood House, it's got lots of old pictures you can see for free. They have Rembrandt's "Self-Portrait" in there, the most famous picture in the world.' Henry wondered what about the Mona Lisa, but he was very impressed.

Her mother made the tea, Linda took Henry to show him her room, along a corridor with thick carpets which muffled their steps, it opened into the hallway at the foot of a wide stairway, split half way up in two directions on to the great landing, a horseshoe expanse with a grandfather clock at one end, at the other a massive chest covered in brass with figures stamped upon it. It was a trousseau chest, Linda told him, where they put gifts for the bride, it was four hundred years old. They went up another staircase, did all the house belong to them? 'It used to be Daddy's but he went away so now it's Mummy's.' 'Where did he go?' 'He wanted to marry someone else instead of Mummy so they had a divorce.' 'And so he gave your m-mother this house to make up for it.' He could not bring himself to say 'mummy'. It was a junk heap with a bed, Linda's room, covered the floor and blocked the doorway, toy prams, dolls, their clothes, games and bits of games, a big blackboard on the wall and the bed unmade, the sheets trailing into the centre of the room, beyond that the pillow, bottles and brushes in front of a dressing mirror and all the walls pink, alien girlish, it excited him. 'Don't you have to tidy it up?' 'This morning we had a pillow fight. I like it untidy, don't you.' Henry followed Linda down the stairs, it is always much better to do just what you want if you can find a place to do it.

She said at tea, Linda's mother, to call her Claire, and later asking him if there was something else and he said, 'No thank you, Claire,' it made Linda choke on a mouthful of drink and Henry and Claire pounded her back, they went on after that laughing at nothing at all, Linda clutched at Henry to keep herself from falling on the floor. A tall man, in the middle of all this, put his head round the kitchen door, he had thick black eyebrows, he smiled, 'Enjoying yourselves,' and disappeared. When Henry put on his coat to leave and asked Linda who that man was, she told him it was Theo who sometimes came to stay with them, and whispered, 'He sleeps in Mummy's bed.' As he spoke them, wishing the words back, he asked, 'What for?' and made Linda giggle into the wall of coats. They all three sat in the front again, squashed up close, and after a little way Linda wanted them to sing *Frère Jacques* which they did all the distance to Islington so loud the people in their cars could hear them when they stopped at the traffic lights, smiling at them through their car windows. The singing broke off when Claire pulled up at Henry's house, it was suddenly very quiet. He reached over to the back seat for his bags, muttering thanks for having ... but Claire interrupted would he like to come on Sunday, and Linda shouted that it must be for the whole day, till they were all talking at once, Claire, if he wanted she could pick him up in the car, Linda, promised to take him to see the pictures in Kenwood House, Henry, that he must ask Mina first but he was sure it was all right. Linda squeezed his hand, 'See you at school,' shouting, waving, the beginnings of another chorus lost in the roar of a passing lorry, they left him there on the pavement with his bags, waiting a while before he went inside.

Mina was sitting at the table, her head was in her hands, the tea things were all around her. She did not look round at his hello, he lingered uneasily in the doorway, taking off his coat, fussing with the bags. Mina said quietly, 'Where have you been?' He looked at the clock, it was ten to six, he was an hour and thirty-five minutes late. 'I told you I was going to be an hour late.' 'An hour?' she drawled slowly, 'it's almost two hours now.' There was something familiar in Mina's strangeness, he felt his legs begin to go weak. At the table he began to play with a teaspoon, squeezing it into a tunnel made by his knuckles, till Mina drew air sharply through her nostrils. 'Put that down,' she snapped, 'I asked you where have you been?' Trembling in his voice, he explained, the mother of a school friend invited him home for tea and – 'I thought you were picking up your costume,' she spoke very softly. 'Well, I was but ...' Henry stared down at his fingers spread out on the table. 'And if you were going to someone's house why couldn't you let me know?' Now she yelled at the top of her voice, 'We got a bloody telephone.' Neither spoke, Mina's echo lasted five minutes in the room, still chiming in his head, and then she said quietly, 'You don't give a damn anyway. Go up and get changed.' There were things he knew he could say and make it all right, but none of the words was in his head, all that was were the things he could see, his knuckles, the pattern of the cloth beneath them filled his attention, nothing to say. Walking behind Mina's chair to the door, she turned to hold him by the elbow, 'And this time no fuss,' and then pushed him away. At the top of the stairs he thought of what she had said, no fuss, some new costume for humiliation, for being late and breaking with the afternoon ritual. He approached the girl laid neatly on the bed, the same girl as before. Without thought he took his clothes off, could not bring to the open again Mina's frenzy, the vicious compulsion to make a stranger of her, then he was frightened of her, feared it now and shivered, pulling the cold material over his skin, and the white tights, hurrying in case she thought he was hesitating. He fumbled with the thin leather laces, his fingers were pursued, and took up the wig, standing in front of the mirror to adjust it, standing there he glanced up, his motions froze, again that movement in his belly's pit, for there she was in his bedroom now, the hair falling freely about the back, her pale taut skin, her nose. He took the hand mirror from the basin, watched his face from all sides, the eyes were coloured different, his were bluer and his nose a little larger. But it was the first glance, the shock of the first glance was still with him. He removed the wig, it was clownish, his short black hair with the party frock, it made him laugh. He put the wig back on, did a short dance across the room, Henry and Linda at once, closer than in the car, inside her now and she was in him. It was no longer an oppression, he was free of Mina's anger, invisible inside this girl. He began to brush out the wig, the way he saw Linda do it when she came in from school, starting from the end and downwards, so not to split the ends she told him.

He was in front of the mirror still when she came into the room suddenly, the same officer's uniform, her face even harder than last time, she turned him by the shoulders so he faced away from her, then she tied the dress from behind, humming softly beneath her breath. She too combed out the wig, ran her hand up the inside of his leg to feel his underwear, and, satisfied, spun him round to face her so he felt the same immobile fear seeing close to the black heavy lines of her made-up face, the straight rods of greased hair. She leaned over him, pulled him in close, kissing his forehead, 'You'll do,' and led him by the hand downstairs in silence, and this time it was she who poured the drinks, two full glasses of red wine. She bowed, delivered the glass to his hand and clicking her heels and saying in a mock gruff voice, 'There you are, my dear.' He held the unusual glass, its long tinted stem was too short for his whole fist, he held it in both hands. On special occasions Mina mixed him shandy, and the rest was always lemonade. Now Mina stood with her back to the fire, shoulders well back, the glass level with her flattened chest, 'Cheers,' and swallowed two large mouthfuls, 'drink up.' He wet the end of his tongue, held down the shudder of bittersweet, then closing his eyes took in a mouthful, pushing it to the back of his throat quickly with his tongue and this way avoided all the taste but for something furry left behind in his mouth as aftertaste. Mina finished her wine, was waiting now for him to finish his, and took his empty glass to fill at the cabinet, set the wine on the table, and began to fetch the dishes. Dizzy and

unreal he helped carry a dish from the hotplate, wondering at Mina's silence. They sat down, Linda and Henry,
Henry and Linda. Through the meal Mina lifted her
glass saying, 'Cheers,' waiting for him to lift his before
drinking, and once she got up to pour more wine. It was
sliding from him now, all the things he looked at drifting
away from themselves and yet staying at the same time,
the space between objects undulated, Mina's face splin-
tered moved and merged with its images, so he gripped
the edge of the table to steady the room and saw Mina see
him do this, saw her jagged smile meant to be encouragement, saw her drift heavily away to fetch the coffee pot
against the movement of the room haled on its three
axes, and if he closed his eyes if you close your eyes you
might fall off the edge of the world, it tilts upwards beginning somewhere near your feet. And through all this
Mina was saying, Mina was wanting to know something,
what about his afternoon, what had he done in the other
house, so that to tell her he gathered his tongue from
whatever it was, heard his own voice come faintly in on
him from the next room, the glue on the roof of his mouth,
'We and ... we took out, she took us ...' till he gave up,
submitting to Mina's braying and barking and laughing,
'Oh my poor little girl's had a little too much,' and as she
was saying this was lurching toward him, lifted him under
the armpits half carried him half dragged him to the armchair pulling him there on to her lap and turned his body
to make his legs hang over the chair's side, cradled his head
in her arms pressed tight hot and all over him like a
wrestler, he could not move his arms and legs together to
free himself, she had him tight she pressed his face hard
between the gap of her unbuttoned tunic, so spinning
there in her arms he knew to move suddenly was to be
suddenly sick. She seemed to want this girl and pushed his

face closer to her breast, for there was nothing beneath the
tunic, nothing but Henry's face against the faintly scented
corrugated skin of her limp old dugs and her hand was
cupped by the back of his neck, he could not move out of
the brown tissue, dared not jerk suddenly, he knew what
was in his stomach, could not stir even when she began to
sing and her other hand began to wander in the layers of
his dress in and around his thigh, she half said, she half
sang, 'A soldier needs a girl, a soldier needs a girl,' trailing
off to the rhythm of her breathing becoming ever sharper
ever deeper and Henry rose and fell with it, felt himself
pulled closer, opened his eyes into the grey-blue pallor of
Mina's breasts, grey and blue the way he imagined a
dead person's face. 'Sick,' he murmured into her body and
out of his mouth slid noiselessly a brown-red mess of dinner
and wine, colour for the death pallor inside the tunic. He
rolled off her no longer held, on to the floor with the wig
slipping from his head, red and brown stains streaked the
fresh white and pink all tawdry now, he pulled the wig
completely clear, 'I'm Henry,' said thickly. Mina did not
move for a while, sat staring at the wig where it lay on the
floor, then getting up she stepped over Henry, upstairs,
and from his spinning room he could hear her run the
bath water, and just sat where he landed, watched the
moving carpet patterns between his fingers, he felt better
for being sick, he could not move.

Mina returned from her bath in an everyday dress,
herself now, and helped him to his feet, led him by the
fire where she untied the dress, taking it in the kitchen to
soak in a bucket. She gathered up the wig, took his hand,
and taught him how to walk the stairs, singsonging each
one as for a child, 'One and two and three and ...' In his
bedroom he swayed against her shoulder while she took the
rest of his clothes, found his pyjamas while she was talking

all the time, the time *she* got drunk for the first ... well the next day she couldn't remember a *thing*, and Henry, not sure of what she was saying but the tone was fine, recognized it like her dress, he lay on his back in bed her hand on his forehead to stay the room a little, while Mina sang and spoke the song from downstairs, 'A soldier needs a girl like a lion needs a mane, To murmur in his ear and kiss away the pain.' She stroked his hair, and when he woke up the following day the wig was beside him on the pillow, it must have fallen off in the night.

Waking up he thought of Linda, and the pain behind his eyes, and how there was some ling in the room it was no longer morning. Downstairs Mina said, 'Do you want some lunch, I let you sleep it off,' but he was dressed for school, taking his satchel from its hook, out the door and across the street with Mina calling after him to come back, the damp wind was free in his hair, the night before a confusion but, he was certain, Mina had forfeited something by it that made it easy now to run from her fading voice. To Linda. At the school he made his excuses, a sickness and that was not untrue, he was still white enough this afternoon to be believed. To his desk for the beginning of the afternoon classes, where she was waiting smiling as he came towards, ready to press a note in his hand, a scrap reading, 'Are you coming Sunday?' He turned it and wrote yes, in the same spirit he had run free this morning, held it under the table for her to take it with her fingers which came locking into his and did not let go a moment or two, gripped and slid away. In his stomach the pit, in his groin a little blood stirring in a pre-pubertal skin, pushed up like spring flowers, into the folds of his clothes and the note fell unnoticed to the floor.

Could he tell her of glancing in the mirror, Henry and Linda fused by appearances, how they were one at once and he felt free and did a dance before Mina came in, he wanted to tell her, but all the other explaining too, about Mina; where could you begin, how are games which are not really games explained? Instead he told her of the mask he was to buy that afternoon, a kind of monster, 'But more to make you laugh than run away,' and that meant he told her of the party, his name was on the invitation card with Mina's, all disguised and no one knows who you are, anyone can do what they want because it doesn't matter. They were in the playground, empty after everyone had left, they made stories about the things you can do when no one knows who you are. Did she want to come? she did, she wanted to very much. Her mother was crossing the playground towards them, she kissed Linda, put her hand on Henry's shoulder, and they all walked to the car. Linda told her mother of Henry's mask and Henry's party, Claire told her she could go, it sounded fun. They said goodbye.

He was at the shop out of breath, not wanting to be late home again for Mina. The man behind the counter, he had a way with little boys, a jovial unfunny way, 'Where's the fire?' he said when Henry came in his shop, and trying to put over his urgency, Henry told him quickly, 'I've come about the mask.' The shop man leaned slowly across the counter, his joke quivering about the corner of his lips, he could hardly wait to say it. 'S'funny, I thought you had it on,' and watched Henry's face, waiting for his laugh to fall in with his own. Henry smiled for him, 'You said you would keep it for me.' 'Let's see,' making a great show of tracing the figures on the calendar, 'if I'm not mistaken,' he held his breath and drawled out, 'if I'm not mistaaaken today is Tuesday.' He beamed at Henry his customer, arched his eyebrows, watching his customer fidget, 'Have you still got it?' and still with his eyebrows raised he was pointing one finger in the air, a goon amusing no one, 'Now that's the point, have I still got it?' While Henry began to understand how violence was done he was reaching under the counter, 'Let me see, what have we here,' and brought the mask out, Henry's mask. 'Can you wrap it for me, you see it has to be kept a secret.' The man, Henry saw for the first time, was an old man and he felt a little sorry. The man carefully wrapped his mask in two layers of stiff brown paper and found him an old string bag to carry it in. He was silent now, Henry wished he would go on with the bad jokes, at least he could understand those. The only other word he said was 'There,' handing the bag to Henry across the counter. Henry called goodbye as he left the shop but the man had gone into the back room, he did not hear him.

Mina said nothing of the evening before, she cut slices of cake for him instead and talked a lot and fast, made a quick humorous reference to the way he left the house, she was back to herself. In the kitchen Henry saw the dress in a bucket of water, like a rare dead fish. He spoke with hesitation, 'This friend of mine, the family has asked me to spend the day with them on Sunday,' and Mina was distant, 'Really, have I met your friend, why don't you ask him to the party?' 'I already have and they want me to go there on Sunday,' why was it important not to mention the sex of his friend? Mina was vague, 'We'll see,' but he was there behind her, following her out to the kitchen, 'You see I have to let them know tomorrow,' and by the turn of his voice demanded of the silence which followed, an answer. She smiled, she brushed the hair from his eyes with her hand, friendly and resigned she said, 'I think not, darling. Now what about the homework you missed last night,' propelling him gently to the foot of the stairs where he stepped to one side, 'But they asked me to go, I want to go.' Mina was cheery, 'I don't think so really, darling.' 'I want to go.' She took her hand off his shoulder, she sat on the bottom step, chin on her hands, and she was thinking for a long time, and then, 'And what am I meant to do on Sunday when you're off with all your friends?' This sudden change, he was the giver when before he was the asker, he was standing and she was sitting by his feet, there was nothing to say, he was numb. After a while she said, 'Well?' stretching her hands towards him, he moved a little closer till he was where she could take both his hands in hers, and she looked at him over her glasses, she took them off, and he saw then the moisture collecting in her eyes' rims. That was wrong, that was a terrible thing, a terrible weight on him now he felt, can people be so important? She squeezed his hands tighter, 'All right,' he said, 'I'll stay.'

By his arms she tried to bring him closer but he shook his hands free, stepping round her to run upstairs. He took the brown suit from his bed and hung it on the chair, lay on the bed on his back, pushed the image of Linda away, guiltily. Mina came in, she sat by his shoulder staring into his face while he avoided hers, he did not want to see her eyes again, and she just sat playing with the corner of the blanket, pinching it between her finger and thumb. Mina combed his hair with her fingers, he went stiff inside waiting for her to stop, he did not like her fingers near his face, not now. 'Are you angry with me, dear?' He shook his head, still not looking in her face. 'You are angry with me, I can tell.' She stood by the table picking up from it a piece of rough wood, he was carving it now for months, intended as a swordfish, he could not give it power or sinuosity to its trunk, it was still a piece of wood only, a child's representation of Fish. Mina turned and turned it in her hand, looking at it, not seeing it. In the ceiling, there was the big stairway which split in two ways half way up and Linda and Claire pillow-fighting in the bedroom, probably Claire wanted to cheer Linda up because it was her first day at school, and the tall man with thick eyebrows, he slept in the same bed as Claire. Mina said, 'You really want to go, don't you?' Henry said, 'It doesn't matter, really it's not that important.' Mina turned the wood in her hand, 'You want to go, so you go.' Henry sat up, he was not quite old enough to know the special games that people might like to play, he was not old enough so he said, 'All right then, I'll go.' Mina left the room, the powerless swordfish in her hand still.

Henry lifted the heavy knocker and let it fall against the white door. Claire led him down the dark corridor to the kitchen, 'Linda spends most of Sunday mornings in bed,' they emerged in the fluorescent light of the kitchen, 'you can go up and play with her but first you can talk to me and have a hot drink.' He let her take his coat, he turned round for her to admire his new suit, 'We must find you some clothes to play in.' She made him a chocolate drink, she carried him along with her talk, he was not on his guard against sudden surprises. She was pleased he was a friend of Linda's, she said so, and said how Linda talked about him all the time, 'She's made a painting of you and a drawing, but she won't show them to you, I know.' She wanted to know about him so he told her about the things he collected from junk shops, the cardboard theatre and all the old books, and then about Mina, how she was good at telling stories because she used to be on the stage, he had never spoken so much in one go before and he was going to tell her everything, the dressing up and the getting drunk, but he held back, he was not sure how to say it and he wanted her to like him, perhaps she wouldn't if he told her how drunk he was and sick over Mina. She brought him some play clothes, a light-blue sweater and a faded pair of jeans which belonged to Linda, did he mind wearing them, she asked him, and he smiled and said no. She left the kitchen to answer the phone, calling behind her that he should find his own way up to Linda's room, back down the dark corridor leading to the foot of the stairs, he could not understand why there were no lights except at either end. On the landing he stopped by the massive chest, traced with his finger the figures in the brass, a procession with the rich people up front, perhaps relatives of the married couple, all filling out the street and the pavements with their costumes billowing out behind, all with their backs straight and proud, and then after them the townspeople, just a rabble, each with a wine cup in his hand, tottering and grabbing at his neighbour, drunk and laughing at the ones in front. Near him there was a door open and he looked in, a bedroom, the biggest he had ever seen, a large double bed in the middle not against any wall. Taking a few paces into the room, the bed was unmade, bunched up in the middle, and he could see now there was a man asleep face downwards, he froze, then walked backwards quickly out into the landing closing the door quietly behind. He remembered Linda's clothes left on the trunk, found them, and ran up the second stair-case to Linda's room.

She was sitting up in bed making a drawing in black crayon on to white cardboard, she was talking to him as he was coming into the room, 'Why are you so out of breath?' Henry sat on the bed, 'I ran up the stairs, I saw a man asleep in one of the bedrooms, looked as though he was dead.' Linda let the drawing fall to the floor, she laughed, 'That's Theo, didn't I tell you about him?' She pulled the sheet up round her chin, 'I wake up early on Sunday but I don't get up till it's lunch.' He showed her the clothes, 'Your mother gave me these, where can I get changed?' 'In here, of course, there's a hanger by your foot and you can put your suit in the cupboard.' She pulled the sheet up farther so that now just her eyes were visible, watching him hang his suit up, come to sit down by her again without his trousers or jacket where he could feel against his bare legs the warmth of her body through the thick rugs, let his weight rest on her feet, stared at the yellow hair spread on the pillow like a fan. They both laughed suddenly at nothing, Linda slipped her hand out of the bed, pulled at his elbow. 'Why don't you get inside too?' Henry stood up, 'All right.' She ducked under the covers giggling, calling out in a muffled way, 'But you have to take all your clothes off first.' He did that, climbed in beside her, his body cooler than Linda's and making her shiver when he lay down, his chest into her back. She rolled over to face him, in the pink gloom she smelled animal and milky, this was the beginning and end of his Sunday when he came to recall it to himself, his heart thumping from the pillow to his ear, lifting his head once to let her free her hair, and talking, mostly about school, her first week there, the friends they knew and the teachers, it did not seem possible the day was taken with other things, that he put on Linda's jeans and sweater, ate his lunch and walked with the thousands milling without direction on Hampstead Heath, and let Linda show him the pictures in Kenwood House, cold superior ladies, their unlikely children, and standing a long time in front of the Rembrandt agreeing it was the best there and maybe the best in the world, though Linda did not like the darkness around the figure, she wanted to see his room, then they sat in Samuel Johnson's summerhouse, sure he was a famous writer but of what and when? and back

across the Heath with the hundreds in the winter gloom,
he came out of the blankets for air and she leaned her
face against his chest then came out herself, lay there with
their foreheads touching and dozed for half an hour, did it
happen in the half hour he slept, all a kind of extended
dream. The real thing was lying down for half an hour or
more, that's how it seemed that night when he was in his
own bed, at home.

It was not quite how he thought, things are never as you
think they are going to be, not exactly, for on the day she
forgot the red light bulbs and it was too late now because
the shops were closed, and the recipe for punch was in an
envelope, no time to look for it now, instead Mina bought
a crate of bottles, mostly wine, she said, because nearly
everybody likes wine, and two flagons of cider for those
who did not. It was not a tape recorder, Henry had never
seen one of those, it was the old record player borrowed
from Mrs Simpson's son and the old records borrowed
from Mrs Simpson. In anticipation, acting out the party
in his mind, the house was bigger, the rooms were halls, the
guests dwarfed by the height of the ceilings, music pounding at them from all sides, the disguises exotic, foreign
princes, ghouls, sea captains and the like, and him with the
mask. But now it was near the time for the first guest to
arrive, the rooms were the same size as always, and why
not, the music was from one corner, scratchy and dull, and
here were the first guests, Henry opening the door to them
in his thirty-shilling face with a startled look, here were
the guests disguised as ordinary people, was it a disguise at
all? had they read the card closely? He stood by the door
holding it open, silent, as they streamed past him, nodded,
seemed to think there was nothing special about his mask,
just someone's little boy holding open the door, they

streamed in in twos and fours, laughing and talking with restraint, poured their own drinks and laughed and talked with less restraint, men in grey suits and black suits and their hands deep in their pockets swaying towards and away from their neighbour as they talked, the women with grey hair piled up, fingering their glasses, they all looked the same. Mina was upstairs planning to drift down, fuse unnoticed and disguised with her guests, he looked about, she could be here already, there was no woman here who looked like her, or man. He wandered between the talking groups, there was something about the men, something about the women, the hips of one, the shoulders of the others, a short man, bald and scented, his neck was too thin for his shirt, the tie knot the size of his fist, he leaned over Henry as he passed by looking for Mina, 'You must be Henry,' his voice was thin and rasped, 'you must be, I can tell by the look on your face.' He straightened out to laugh, turning to see if any of the others had heard his good joke, Henry waited, it was like this in the shop waiting on other people's jokes. The bald short man turned back to him, wanted to reconcile him, in a lower voice, 'I knew it was you of course by your height, dear. Do you know who I am?' Henry shook his head, watching the man place his fingers on his pate, lift the skin between forefinger and thumb to show not brain or bone but hair, frizzy black hair in waves, which he covered back now with the skin of his head, 'Can you guess now? No?' He was pleased, obviously pleased, he bent lower to whisper in Henry's ear, 'It's your Aunt Lucy,' and then walked away. Lucy, one of those aunts not an aunt, a friend of Mina's who came to coffee in the mornings and wanted Henry in her small theatre company, always wanted him to join and was not put off by his refusals, Mina, jealous perhaps, did not want him to join, there was no danger. But Mina, which of these wide-hipped men, which of these stout women was she? or was she still waiting for them all to drink more wine? He drank wine through his mask, remembering his last first time, his dress soaking in a bucket afterwards, where was it now? He pushed the wine quickly down his throat, avoiding the taste, the furriness on his teeth unmoved by his tongue, looking for Mina, waiting for Linda who was to come soon, undisguised, he told her there was no need because she was not known, she was a stranger and all strangers are in disguise. But was this a party, where they all stood around, talked, made jokes, moved from one group to another, no one listening to the record player which could not be heard above the voices, no one changed the record, was this how it was at parties? He changed the record himself, reached out for the record cover, a peeling remnant of shredded cardboard, when a hand took his wrist, an old hand, and looking up he saw an old man, a very old man, stooped over one shoulder, cocked round a hump bulging just slightly under his jacket and a scrub of beard about his face with the hairs far apart, and above his lips an oily patch where it did not grow at all, this man took his wrist, gripped it then let his hand fall, 'Wouldn't bother, no one can hear it anyway.' Henry faced the man, picked up for his defence his wine glass, 'Are you someone in disguise, is everyone in disguise?' The man pointed over his shoulder, he was not hurt, 'How do you get to disguise this?' 'It could be all part of it, I mean padding or something ...' Henry trailed away, lost his voice in the din, the man was turning his back to him and calling out, 'Feel it, go on you feel it and tell me if that's padding or not.' Like the wine these things can be done if done quickly, push it quickly down your stomach, he reached out and touched the man's back, withdrew his hand, and again when the

man said that was not enough to tell if it was padding or
not, this time he fingered the hump, Henry in his smiling
horror face, the hair in all directions, the coloured lips
drenched in wine, this small grinning monster fingered the
old man's hump at once hard and yielding, till the man
was satisfied and turned round, 'You can't hide a thing
like that,' and walked to the other side of the room,
standing there alone grinning at the people and drinking
from his glass. Henry filled his glass and drank from it too,
wandering between the circles of talkers, their voices rose
and fell about him, wailing organ stops that made him
dizzy, needed to lean by the table for support, waiting,
where was Mina, where was Linda? They were none of
them baffled by each other, these talkers and drinkers,
assuming they were in some disguise they knew who they
were, found it easy to talk, there was no question of being
able to do what you want, when you are not yourself you
are still someone, and someone has to take the blame,
blame, blame for what? Henry held the table tighter by
the edge with both hands, what blame? what was he
thinking just now? More wine more wine, something
nervous made him bring the glass to his mouth every ten
seconds, for not being noticed, for being no one at a grown-
ups' party, some small boy who held the door open when
they came in, for it not being crisp, as he had imagined it,
for all this he took in four glasses of wine. On the far side
of the room a man came away from a group, tottering
backwards with a glass in his hand, he fell into the large
chair behind him, and lay there laughing up at his friends
laughing down at him. Henry's words staggered on in his
head like big numbers on a board, occurring to him slowly,
if he left the table he would fall on the ground. Was it the
monster who fell to the ground or Henry, who was to
blame? it came back to him now, dressed like somebody

else and pretending to be them you took their blame for
what they did, or what you as them do ... did? the big
numbers were so slow, there was something in all this,
when Mina dressed for dinner who did she think she was
when she did what she did? The dress in the bucket like
a rare sea animal, they stood in the deserted playground
and made a joke about what you could do in disguise and
Claire was walking towards them looking old and young,
and the military officer who wiped his leg with a towel, the
man in the bed, the black behind Rembrandt's head,
Linda over there said she preferred, Linda over there,
there was Linda on the other side of the room, her back to
him, her waterfall of hair like Alice in Wonderland, there
were too many other voices for her to hear him calling, he
could not let go of the table. And she was talking to the
man who fell in the chair, the man in the chair, the man
in the chair, these big numbers, the man in the chair was
pulling Linda on to his lap, Linda and Henry, he stood in
front of his bedroom mirror feeling free, made a little
dance as Henry and Linda, was pulling Linda on to his
lap held her tight there behind her head, she was too
frightened to move, terrified and could not make her
tongue move and who would hear her in all these voices?
was unbuttoning his shirt with one hand the man in the
chair, the voices made a crescendo this dissonant choir,
no one could see, the man in the chair pressed her face
tight against him, would not let her go, Henry thought
who was to blame? letting go of the table he began, but
unsteadily and very slowly and the wine rising from his
stomach, began to move towards them across the crowded
room.

In Between the Sheets

To Vic Sage

Acknowledgments

The author and publishers wish to thank the following for permission to reproduce copyright material: *The New Review* for 'Pornography', 'Reflections of a Kept Ape', 'To and Fro' and 'In Between the Sheets'; *Encounter* for 'Saturday, March 199–' (published as 'Without Blood'); *Harpers/Queen* for 'Sunday, March 199–'; *Bananas* for 'Dead As They Come'; *American Review* for 'Psychopolis'; and Mick Jagger, Keith Richard and Essex Music International for the song extracts on pp. 252 and 253.

Pornography

O'Byrne walked through Soho market to his brother's shop in Brewer Street. A handful of customers leafing through the magazines and Harold watching them through pebble-thick lenses from his raised platform in the corner. Harold was barely five foot and wore built-up shoes. Before becoming his employee O'Byrne used to call him Little Runt. At Harold's elbow a miniature radio rasped details of race meetings for the afternoon. 'So,' said Harold with thin contempt, 'the prodigal brother … ' His magnified eyes fluttered at every consonant. He looked past O'Byrne's shoulder. 'All the magazines are for sale, gentlemen.' The readers stirred uneasily like troubled dreamers. One replaced a magazine and walked quickly from the shop. 'Where d'you get to?' Harold said in a quieter voice. He stepped from the dais, put on his coat and glared up at O'Byrne, waiting for an answer. Little Runt. O'Byrne was ten years younger than his brother, detested him and his success but now, strangely, wanted his approbation. 'I had an appointment, didn't I,' he said quietly. 'I got the clap.' Harold was pleased. He reached up and punched O'Byrne's shoulder playfully. 'Serves you,' he said and cackled theatrically. Another customer edged out of the shop. From the doorway Harold called, 'I'll be back at five.' O'Byrne smiled as his brother left. He hooked his thumbs into his jeans and sauntered towards the tight knot of customers. 'Can I help you gentlemen, the magazines are all for sale.' They scattered before him like frightened fowl, and suddenly he was alone in the shop.

A plump woman of fifty or more stood in front of a plastic shower curtain, naked but for panties and gasmask. Her hands hung limply at her sides and in one of them a cigarette smouldered. Wife of the Month. Since gasmasks and a thick rubber sheet on the bed, wrote JN of Andover, we've never looked back. O'Byrne played with the radio for a while then switched it off. Rhythmically he turned the pages of the magazine, and stopped to read the letters. An uncircumcised male virgin, without hygiene, forty-two next May, dared not peel back his foreskin now for fear of what he might see. I get these nightmares of worms. O'Byrne laughed and crossed his legs. He replaced the magazine, returned to the radio, switched it on and off rapidly and caught the unintelligible middle of a word. He walked about the shop straightening the magazines in the racks. He stood by the door and stared at the wet street intersected by the coloured strips of the plastic walk-thro. He whistled over and over a tune whose end immediately suggested its beginning. Then he returned to Harold's raised platform and made two telephone calls, both to the hospital, the first to Lucy. But Sister Drew was busy in the ward and could not come to the phone. O'Byrne left a message that he would not be able to see her that evening after all and would phone again tomorrow. He dialled the hospital switchboard and this time asked for trainee Nurse Shepherd in the children's ward. 'Hi,' O'Byrne said when Pauline picked up the phone. 'It's me.' And he stretched and leaned against the wall. Pauline was a silent girl who once wept in a film about the effects of pesticides on butterflies, who wanted to redeem O'Byrne with her love. Now she laughed, 'I've been phoning you all morning,' she said. 'Didn't your brother tell you?'

'Listen,' said O'Byrne, 'I'll be at your place about eight,' and replaced the receiver.

Harold did not return till after six, and O'Byrne was almost asleep, his head pillowed on his forearm. There were no customers. O'Byrne's only sale was *American Bitch*. 'Those American mags,' said Harold as he emptied the till of £15 and a handful of silver, 'are *good*.' Harold's new leather jacket. O'Byrne fingered it appreciatively. 'Seventy-eight quid,' said Harold and braced himself in front of the fish-eye mirror. His glasses flashed. 'It's all right,' said O'Byrne. 'Fucking right it is,' said Harold, and began to close up shop. 'Never take much on Wednesdays,' he said wistfully as he reached up and switched on the burglar alarm. 'Wednesday's a cunt of a day.' Now O'Byrne was in front of the mirror, examining a small trail of acne that led from the corner of his mouth. 'You're not fucking kidding,' he agreed.

Harold's house lay at the foot of the Post Office Tower and O'Byrne rented a room from him. They walked along together without speaking. From time to time Harold glanced sideways into a dark shop window to catch the reflection of himself and his new leather jacket. Little Runt. O'Byrne said, 'Cold, innit?' and Harold said nothing. Minutes later, when they were passing a pub, Harold steered O'Byrne into the dank, deserted public saying, 'Since you got the clap I'll buy you a drink.' The publican heard the remark and regarded O'Byrne with interest. They drank three scotches apiece, and as O'Byrne was paying for the fourth round Harold said, 'Oh yeah, one of those two nurses you've been knocking around with phoned.' O'Byrne nodded and wiped his lips. After a pause Harold said, 'You're well in there ... ' O'Byrne nodded again. 'Yep.' Harold's jacket shone. When he reached for his drink it creaked. O'Byrne was not going to tell him anything. He banged his hands together. 'Yep,' he said once more, and stared over his brother's head at the empty bar. Harold tried again. 'She wanted to know where you'd been … ' 'I bet she did,' O'Byrne muttered, and then smiled.

Pauline, short and untalkative, her face bloodlessly pale, intersected by a heavy black fringe, her eyes large, green and watchful, her flat small, damp and shared with a secretary who was never there. O'Byrne arrived after ten, a little drunk and in need of a bath to purge the faint purulent scent that lately had hung about his fingers. She sat on a small wooden stool to watch him luxuriate. Once she leaned forwards and touched his body where it broke the surface. O'Byrne's eyes were closed, his hands floating at his side, the only sound the diminishing hiss of the cistern. Pauline rose quietly to bring a clean white towel from her bedroom, and O'Byrne did not hear her leave or return. She sat down again and ruffled, as far as it was possible, O'Byrne's damp, matted hair. 'The food is ruined,' she said without accusation. Beads of perspiration collected in the corners of O'Byrne's eyes and rolled down the line of his nose like tears. Pauline rested her hand on O'Byrne's knee where it jutted through the grey water. Steam turned to water on the cold walls, senseless minutes passed. 'Never mind, love,' said O'Byrne, and stood up.

Pauline went out to buy beer and pizzas, and O'Byrne lay down in her tiny bedroom to wait. Ten minutes passed. He dressed after cursory examination of his clean but swelling meatus, and wandered listlessly about the sitting room. Nothing interested him in Pauline's small collection of books. There were no magazines. He entered the kitchen in search of a drink. There was nothing but an overcooked meat pie. He picked round the burnt bits and

as he ate turned the pages of a picture calendar. When he
finished he remembered again he was waiting for Pauline.
He looked at his watch. She had been gone now almost
half an hour. He stood up quickly, tipping the kitchen
chair behind him to the floor. He paused in the sitting
room and then walked decisively out of the flat and
slammed the front door on his way. He hurried down the
stairs, anxious not to meet her now he had decided to get
out. But she was there. Halfway up the second flight, a
little out of breath, her arms full of bottles and tinfoil
parcels. 'Where d'you get to?' said O'Byrne. Pauline
stopped several steps down from him, her face tilted up
awkwardly over her goods, the whites of her eyes and the
tinfoil vivid in the dark. 'The usual place was closed. I
had to walk miles . . . sorry.' They stood. O'Byrne was not
hungry. He wanted to go. He hitched his thumbs into the
waist of his jeans and cocked his head towards the invisible
ceiling, then he looked down at Pauline who waited.
'Well,' he said at last, 'I was thinking of going.' Pauline
came up, and as she pushed past whispered, 'Silly.'
O'Byrne turned and followed her, obscurely cheated.

He leaned in the doorway, she righted the chair. With
a movement of his head O'Byrne indicated that he wanted
none of the food Pauline was setting out on plates. She
poured him a beer and knelt to gather a few black pastry
droppings from the floor. They sat in the sitting room.
O'Byrne drank, Pauline ate slowly, neither spoke. O'Byrne
finished all the beer and placed his hand on Pauline's
knee. She did not turn. He said cheerily, 'What's wrong
with you?' and she said, 'Nothing.' Alive with irritation
O'Byrne moved closer and placed his arm protectively
across her shoulders. 'Tell you what,' he half whispered.
'Let's go to bed.' Suddenly Pauline rose and went into the
bedroom. O'Byrne sat with his hands clasped behind his
head. He listened to Pauline undress, and he heard the

creak of the bed. He got to his feet and, still without desire, entered the bedroom.

Pauline lay on her back and O'Byrne, having undressed quickly, lay beside her. She did not acknowledge him in her usual way, she did not move. O'Byrne raised his arm to stroke her shoulder, but instead let his hand fall back heavily against the sheet. They both lay on their backs in mounting silence, until O'Byrne decided to give her one last chance and with naked grunts hauled himself on to his elbow and arranged his face over hers. Her eyes, thick with tears, stared past him. 'What's the matter?' he said in resignatory sing-song. The eyes budged a fraction and fixed on his own. 'You,' she said simply. O'Byrne returned to his side of the bed, and after a moment said threateningly. 'I see.' Then he was up, and on top of her, and then past her and on the far side of the room. 'All right then ... ' he said. He wrenched his laces into a knot, and searched for his shirt. Pauline's back was to him. But as he crossed the sitting room her rising, accelerating wail of denial made him stop and turn. All white, in a cotton nightdress, she was there in the bedroom doorway and in the air, simultaneously at every point of arc in the intervening space, like the trick photographer's diver, she was on the far side of the room and she was at his lapels, knuckles in her mouth and shaking her head. O'Byrne smiled, and put his arms around her shoulders. Forgiveness swept through him. Clinging to each other they returned to the bedroom. O'Byrne undressed and they lay down again, O'Byrne on his back, Pauline with her head pillowed on his shoulder.

O'Byrne said, 'I never know what's going on in your mind,' and deeply comforted by this thought, he fell asleep. Half an hour later he woke. Pauline, exhausted by a week of twelve-hour shifts, slept deeply on his arm. He shook her gently. 'Hey,' he said. He shook her firmly, and as the rhythm of her breathing broke and she began to stir, he said in a laconic parody of some unremembered film, 'Hey, there's something we ain't done yet ... '

Harold was excited. When O'Byrne walked into the shop towards noon the following day Harold took hold of his arms and waved in the air a sheet of paper. He was almost shouting. 'I've worked it all out. I know what I want to do with the shop.' 'Oh yeah,' said O'Byrne dully, and put his fingers in his eyes and scratched till the intolerable itch there became a bearable pain. Harold rubbed his small pink hands together and explained rapidly. 'I'm going All American. I spoke to their rep on the phone this morning and he'll be here in half an hour. I'm getting rid of all the quid a time piss-in-her-cunt letters. I'm gonna carry the whole of the House of Florence range at £4·50 a time.'

O'Byrne walked across the shop to where Harold's jacket was spread across a chair. He tried it on. It was of course too small. 'And I'm going to call it Transatlantic Books,' Harold was saying. O'Byrne tossed the jacket on to the chair. It slid to the floor and deflated there like some reptilian air sac. Harold picked it up, and did not cease talking. 'If I carry Florence exclusive I get a special discount *and*,' he giggled, 'they pay for the fucking neon sign.'

O'Byrne sat down and interrupted his brother. 'How many of those soddin' inflatable women did you unload? There's still twenty-five of the fuckers in the cellar.' But Harold was pouring out scotch into two glasses. 'He'll be here in half an hour,' he repeated, and offered one glass to O'Byrne. 'Big deal,' said O'Byrne, and sipped. 'I want you to take the van over to Norbury and collect the order this afternoon. I want to get into this straight away.'

O'Byrne sat moodily with his drink while his brother whistled and was busy about the shop. A man came in and bought a magazine. 'See,' said O'Byrne sourly while the customer was still lingering over the tentacled condoms, 'he bought English, didn't he?' The man turned guiltily and left. Harold came and crouched by O'Byrne's chair and spoke as one who explains copulation to an infant. 'And what do I make? Forty per cent of 75p. Thirty p. Thirty fucking p. On House of Florence I'll make fifty per cent of £4·50. And that,' he rested his hand briefly on O'Byrne's knee, 'is what I call business.'

O'Byrne wriggled his empty glass in front of Harold's face, and waited patiently for his brother to fill it ... Little Runt.

The House of Florence warehouse was a disused church in a narrow terraced street on the Brixton side of Norbury. O'Byrne entered by the main porch. A crude plasterboard office and waiting room had been set up in the west end. The font was a large ash-tray in the waiting room. An elderly woman with a blue rinse sat alone in the office typing. When O'Byrne tapped on the sliding window she ignored him, then she rose and slid aside the glass panel. She took the order form he pushed towards her, glancing at him with unconcealed distaste. She spoke primly. 'You better wait there.' O'Byrne tap-danced abstractedly about the font, and combed his hair, and whistled the tune that went in a circle. Suddenly a shrivelled man with a brown coat and clipboard was at his side. 'Transatlantic Books?' he said. O'Byrne shrugged and followed him. They moved together slowly down long aisles of bolted steel shelves, the old man pushing a large trolley and O'Byrne walking a little in front with his hands clasped behind his back. Every few yards the warehouseman stopped, and with bad-tempered gasps lifted a thick pile of magazines from the shelves. The load on the trolley grew. The old man's breath echoed hoarsely around the church. At the end of the first aisle he sat down on the trolley, between his neat piles, and coughed and hawked for a minute or so into a paper handkerchief. Then, carefully folding the tissue and its ponderous green contents back into his pocket, he said to O'Byrne. 'Here, you're young. You push this thing.' And O'Byrne said, 'Push the fucker yourself. It's your job,' and offered the man a cigarette and lit it for him.

O'Byrne nodded at the shelves. 'You get some reading done here.' The old man exhaled irritably. 'It's all rubbish. It ought to be banned.' They moved on. At the end, as he was signing the invoice, O'Byrne said, 'Who you got lined up for tonight? Madam in the office there?' The warehouseman was pleased. His cackles rang out like bells, then tailed into another coughing fit. He leaned feebly against the wall, and when he had recovered sufficiently he raised his head and meaningfully winked his watery eye. But O'Byrne had turned and was wheeling the magazines out to the van.

Lucy was ten years older than Pauline, and a little plump. But her flat was large and comfortable. She was a sister and Pauline no more than a trainee nurse. They knew nothing of each other. At the underground station O'Byrne bought flowers for Lucy, and when she opened the door to him he presented them with a mock bow and the clicking of heels. 'A peace offering?' she said contemptuously and took the daffodils away. She had led him into the bedroom. They sat down side by side on the bed. O'Byrne ran his hand up her leg in a perfunctory kind of way. She pushed away his arm and said, 'Come on then. Where have you been the past three days?' O'Byrne could barely remember. Two nights with Pauline, one night in the pub with friends of his brother.

He stretched back luxuriously on the pink candlewick. 'You know ... working late for Harold. Changing the shop around. That kind of thing.'

'Those dirty books,' said Lucy with a little high-pitched laugh.

O'Byrne stood up and kicked off his shoes. 'Don't start that,' he said, glad to be off the defensive. Lucy leaned forwards and gathered up his shoes. 'You're going to ruin the backs of these,' she said busily, 'kicking them off like that.'

They both undressed. Lucy hung her clothes neatly in the wardrobe. When O'Byrne stood almost naked before her she wrinkled her nose in disgust. 'Is that you smelling?' O'Byrne was hurt. 'I'll have a bath,' he offered curtly.

Lucy stirred the bathwater with her hand, and spoke loudly over the thunder of the taps. 'You should have brought me some clothes to wash.' She hooked her fingers into the elastic of his pants. 'Give me these now and they'll be dry by the morning.' O'Byrne laced his fingers into hers in a decoy of affection. 'No, no,' he shouted rapidly. 'They were clean on this morning, they were.' Playfully Lucy tried to get them off. They wrestled across the bathroom floor, Lucy shrieking with laughter, O'Byrne excited but determined.

Finally Lucy put on her dressing gown and went away. O'Byrne heard her in the kitchen. He sat in the bath and washed away the bright green stains. When Lucy returned his pants were drying on the radiator. 'Women's Lib, innit?' said O'Byrne from the bath. Lucy said, 'I'm getting in too,' and took off her dressing gown. O'Byrne made room for her. 'Please yourself,' he said with a smile as she settled herself in the grey water.

O'Byrne lay on his back on the clean white sheets, and Lucy eased herself on to his belly like a vast nesting bird. She would have it no other way, from the beginning she had said, 'I'm in charge.' O'Byrne had replied, 'We'll see about that.' He was horrified, sickened, that he could enjoy being overwhelmed, like one of those cripples in his brother's magazines. Lucy had spoken briskly, the kind of voice she used for difficult patients. 'If you don't like it then don't come back.' Imperceptibly O'Byrne was initiated into Lucy's wants. It was not simply that she wished to squat on him. She did not want him to move. 'If you move again,' she warned him once, 'you've had it.' From mere habit O'Byrne thrust upwards and deeper, and quick as the tongue of a snake she lashed his face several times with her open palm. On the instant she came, and afterwards lay across the bed, half sobbing, half laughing. O'Byrne, one side of his face swollen and pink, departed sulking. You're a bloody pervert,' he had shouted from the door.

Next day he was back, and Lucy agreed not to hit him again. Instead she abused him. 'You pathetic helpless little shit,' she would scream at the peak of her excitement. And she seemed to intuit O'Byrne's guilty thrill of pleasure, and wish to push it further. One time she had suddenly lifted herself clear of him and, with a far-away smile, urinated on his head and chest. O'Byrne had struggled to get clear, but Lucy held him down and seemed deeply satisfied by his unsought orgasm. This time O'Byrne left the flat enraged. Lucy's strong, chemical smell was with him for days, and it was during this time that he met Pauline. But within the week he was back at Lucy's to collect, so he insisted, his razor, and Lucy was persuading him to try on her underwear. O'Byrne resisted with horror and excitement. 'The trouble with you,' said Lucy, 'is that you're scared of what you like.'

Now Lucy gripped his throat in one hand. 'You dare move,' she hissed, and closed her eyes. O'Byrne lay still. Above him Lucy swayed like a giant tree. Her lips were forming a word, but there was no sound. Many minutes later she opened her eyes and stared down, frowning a little as though struggling to place him. And all the while she eased backwards and forwards. Finally she spoke, more to herself than to him. 'Worm ... ' O'Byrne moaned. Lucy's legs and thighs tightened and trembled. 'Worm ... worm ... you little worm. I'm going to tread on you ... dirty little worm.' Once more her hand was closed about his throat. His eyes were sunk deep, and his word travelled a long way before it left his lips. 'Yes,' he whispered.

The following day O'Byrne attended the clinic. The doctor and his male assistant were matter-of-fact, unimpressed. The assistant filled out a form and wanted details of O'Byrne's recent sexual history. O'Byrne invented a whore at Ipswich bus station. For many days after that he kept to himself. Attending the clinic mornings and evenings, for injections, he was sapped of desire. When Pauline or Lucy phoned, Harold told them he did not know where O'Byrne was. 'Probably taken off for somewhere,' he said, winking across the shop at his brother. Both women phoned each day for three or four days, and then suddenly there were no calls from either.

O'Byrne paid no attention. The shop was taking good money now. In the evenings he drank with his brother and his brother's friends. He felt himself to be both busy and ill. Ten days passed. With the extra cash Harold was giving him, he bought a leather jacket, like Harold's, but somehow better, sharper, lined with red imitation silk. It both shone and creaked. He spent many minutes in front of the fish-eye mirror, standing sideways on, admiring the manner in which his shoulders and biceps pulled the leather to a tight sheen. He wore his jacket between the shop and the clinic and sensed the glances of women in the street. He thought of Pauline and Lucy. He passed a day considering which to phone first. He chose Pauline, and phoned her from the shop.

Trainee Nurse Shepherd was not available, O'Byrne

was told after many minutes of waiting. She was sitting an examination. O'Byrne had his call transferred to the other side of the hospital. 'Hi,' he said when Lucy picked up the phone. 'It's me.' Lucy was delighted. 'When did you get back? Where have you been? When are you coming round?' He sat down. 'How about tonight?' he said. Lucy whispered in sex-kitten French, 'I can 'ardly wait ... ' O'Byrne laughed and pressed his thumb and forefinger against his forehead and heard other distant voices on the line. He heard Lucy giving instructions. Then she spoke rapidly to him. 'I've got to go. They've just brought a case in. About eight tonight then ... ' and she was gone.

O'Byrne prepared his story, but Lucy did not ask him where he had been. She was too happy. She laughed when she opened the door to him, she hugged him and laughed again. She looked different. O'Byrne could not remember her so beautiful. Her hair was shorter and a deeper brown, her nails were pale orange, she wore a short black dress with orange dots. There were candles and wine glasses on the dining table, music on the record player. She stood back, her eyes bright, almost wild, and admired his leather jacket. She ran her hands up the red lining. She pressed herself against it. 'Very smooth,' she said. 'Reduced to sixty quid,' O'Byrne said proudly, and tried to kiss her. But she laughed again and pushed him into a chair. 'You wait there and I'll get something to drink.'

O'Byrne lay back. From the record player a man sang of love in a restaurant with clean white tablecloths. Lucy brought an icy bottle of white wine. She sat on the arm of his chair and they drank and talked. Lucy told him recent stories of the ward, of nurses who fell in and out of love, patients who recovered or died. As she spoke she undid the top buttons of his shirt and pushed her hand down to his belly. And when O'Byrne turned in his chair and reached up for her she pushed him away, leaned down and kissed him on the nose. 'Now now,' she said primly. O'Byrne exerted himself. He recounted anecdotes he had heard in the pub. Lucy laughed crazily at the end of each, and as he was beginning the third she let her hand drop lightly between his legs and rest there. O'Byrne closed his eyes. The hand was gone and Lucy was nudging him. 'Go on,' she said. 'It was getting interesting.' He caught her wrist and wanted to pull her on to his lap. With a little sigh she slipped away and returned with a second bottle. 'We should have wine more often,' she said, 'if it makes you tell such funny stories.'

Encouraged, O'Byrne told his story, something about a car and what a garage mechanic said to a vicar. Once again Lucy was fishing round his fly and laughing, laughing. It was a funnier story than he thought. The floor rose and fell beneath his feet. And Lucy so beautiful, scented, warm ... her eyes glowed. He was paralysed by her teasing. He loved her, and she laughed and robbed him of his will. Now he saw, he had come to live with her, and each night she teased him to the edge of madness. He pressed his face into her breasts. 'I love you,' he mumbled, and again Lucy was laughing, shaking, wiping the tears from her eyes. 'Do you ... do you ... ' she kept trying to say. She emptied the bottle into his glass. 'Here's a toast ... ' 'Yeah,' said O'Byrne, 'To us.' Lucy was holding down her laughter. 'No, no,' she squealed. 'To *you*.' 'All right,' he said, and downed his wine in one. Then Lucy was standing in front of him pulling his arm. 'C'mon,' she said. 'C'mon.' O'Byrne struggled out of the chair. 'What about dinner then?' he said. 'You're the dinner,' she said, and they giggled as they tottered towards the bedroom.

As they undressed Lucy said, 'I've got a special little surprise for you so ... no fuss.' O'Byrne sat on the edge of

Lucy's large bed and shivered. 'I'm ready for anything,' he said. 'Good ... good,' and for the first time she kissed him deeply, and pushed him gently backwards on to the bed. She climbed forward and sat astride his chest. O'Byrne closed his eyes. Months ago he would have resisted furiously. Lucy lifted his left hand to her mouth and kissed each finger. 'Hmmm ... the first course.' O'Byrne laughed. The bed and the room undulated softly about him. Lucy was pushing his hand towards the top corner of the bed. O'Byrne heard a distant jingle, like bells. Lucy knelt by his shoulder, holding down his wrist, buckling it to a leather strap. She had always said she would tie him up one day and fuck him. She bent low over his face and they kissed again. She was licking his eyes and whispering, 'You're not going anywhere,' O'Byrne gasped for air. He could not move his face to smile. Now she was tugging at his right arm, pulling it, stretching it to the far corner of the bed. With a dread thrill of compliance O'Byrne felt his arm die. Now that was secure and Lucy was running her hands along the inside of his thigh, and on down to his feet ... he lay stretched almost to breaking, splitting, fixed to each corner, spread out against the white sheet. Lucy knelt at the apex of his legs. She stared down at him with a faint, objective smile, and fingered herself delicately. O'Byrne lay waiting for her to settle on him like a vast white nesting bird. She was tracing with the tip of one finger the curve of his excitement, and then with thumb and forefinger making a tight ring about its base. A sigh fled between his teeth. Lucy leaned forwards. Her eyes were wild. She whispered, 'We're going to get you, me and Pauline are ... '

Pauline. For an instant, syllables hollow of meaning. 'What?' said O'Byrne, and as he spoke the word he remembered, and understood a threat. 'Untie me,' he said quickly. But Lucy's finger curled under her crotch and her eyes half closed. Her breathing was slow and deep. 'Untie me,' he shouted, and struggled hopelessly with his straps. Lucy's breath came now in light little gasps. As he struggled, so they accelerated. She was saying something ... moaning something. What was she saying? He could not hear. 'Lucy,' he said, 'please untie me.' Suddenly she was silent, her eyes wide open and clear. She climbed off the bed. 'Your friend Pauline will be here, soon,' she said, and began to get dressed. She was different, her movements brisk and efficient, she no longer looked at him. O'Byrne tried to sound casual. His voice was a little high. 'What's going on?' Lucy stood at the foot of the bed buttoning her dress. Her lip curled. 'You're a bastard,' she said. The doorbell rang and she smiled. 'Now that's good timing, isn't it?'

'Yes, he went down very quietly,' Lucy was saying as she showed Pauline into the bedroom. Pauline said nothing. She avoided looking at either O'Byrne or Lucy. And O'Byrne's eyes were fixed on the object she carried in her arms. It was large and silver, like an outsized electric toaster. 'It can plug in just here,' said Lucy. Pauline set it down on the bedside table. Lucy sat down at her dressing table and began to comb her hair. 'I'll get some water for it in a minute,' she said.

Pauline went and stood by the window. There was silence. Then O'Byrne said hoarsely, 'What's that thing?' Lucy turned in her seat. 'It's a steriliser,' she said breezily. 'Steriliser?' 'You know, for sterilising surgical instruments.' The next question O'Byrne did not dare ask. He felt sick and dizzy. Lucy left the room. Pauline continued to stare out the window into the dark. O'Byrne felt the need to whisper. 'Hey, Pauline, what's going on?' She turned to face him, and said nothing. O'Byrne discovered that the strap round his right wrist was slackening a little, the leather was stretching. His hand was concealed by pillows. He worked it backwards and forwards, and spoke urgently. 'Look, let's get out of here. Undo these things.'

For a moment she hesitated, then she walked round the side of the bed and stared down at him. She shook her head. 'We're going to get you.' The repetition terrified him. He thrashed from side to side. 'It's not my idea of a fucking joke,' he shouted. Pauline turned away. 'I hate you,' he heard her say. The right-hand strap gave a little more. 'I hate you. I hate you.' He pulled till he thought his arm would break. His hand was too large still for the noose around his wrist. He gave up.

Now Lucy was at the bedside pouring water into the steriliser. 'This is a sick joke,' said O'Byrne. Lucy lifted a flat, black case on to the table. She snapped it open and began to take out long-handled scissors, scalpels and other bright, tapering, silver objects. She lowered them carefully into the water. O'Byrne started to work his right hand again. Lucy removed the black case and set on the table two white kidney bowls with blue rims. In one lay two hypodermic needles, one large, one small. In the other was cotton wool. O'Byrne's voice shook. 'What is all this?' Lucy rested her cool hand on his forehead. She enunciated with precision. 'This is what they should have done for you at the clinic.' 'The clinic ... ?' he echoed. He could see now that Pauline was leaning against the wall drinking from a bottle of scotch. 'Yes,' said Lucy, reaching down to take his pulse. 'Stop you spreading round your secret little diseases.' 'And telling lies,' said Pauline, her voice strained with indignation.

O'Byrne laughed uncontrollably. 'Telling lies ... telling lies,' he spluttered. Lucy took the scotch from Pauline and raised it to her lips. O'Byrne recovered. His legs were shaking. 'You're both out of your minds.' Lucy tapped the steriliser and said to Pauline, 'This will take a few minutes yet. We'll scrub down in the kitchen.' O'Byrne tried to raise his head. 'Where are you going?' he called after them. 'Pauline … Pauline.'

But Pauline had nothing more to say. Lucy stopped in the bedroom doorway and smiled at him. 'We'll leave you a pretty little stump to remember us by,' and she closed the door.

On the bedside table the steriliser began to hiss. Shortly after it gave out the low rumble of boiling water, and inside the instruments clinked together gently. In terror he pumped his hand. The leather was flaying the skin off his wrist. The noose was riding now round the base of his thumb. Timeless minutes passed. He whimpered and pulled, and the edge of the leather cut deep into his hand. He was almost free.

The door opened, and Lucy and Pauline carried in a small, low table. Through his fear O'Byrne felt excitement once more, horrified excitement. They arranged the table close to the bed. Lucy bent low over his erection. 'Oh dear … oh dear,' she murmured. With tongs Pauline lifted instruments from the boiling water and laid them out in neat silver rows on the starched white tablecloth she had spread across the table. The leather noose slipped forwards fractionally. Lucy sat on the edge of the bed and took the large hypodermic from the bowl. 'This will make you a little sleepy,' she promised. She held it upright and expelled a small jet of liquid. And as she reached for the cotton wool O'Byrne's arm pulled clear. Lucy smiled. She set aside the hypodermic. She leaned forwards once more … warm, scented … she was fixing him with wild red eyes … her fingers played over his tip … she held him still between her fingers. 'Lie back, Michael, my sweet.' She nodded briskly at Pauline. 'If you'll secure that strap, Nurse Shepherd, then I think we can begin.'

Reflections of a Kept Ape

Eaters of asparagus know the scent it lends the urine. It has been described as reptilian, or as a repulsive inorganic stench, or again as a sharp, womanly odour ... exciting. Certainly it suggests sexual activity of some kind between exotic creatures, perhaps from a distant land, another planet. This unworldly smell is a matter for poets and I challenge them to face their responsibilities. All this ... a preamble that you may discover me as the curtain rises, standing, urinating, reflecting in a small overheated closet which adjoins the kitchen. The three walls which fill my vision are painted a bright and cloying red, decorated by Sally Klee when she cared for such things, a time of remote and singular optimism. The meal, which passed in total silence and from which I have just risen, consisted of a variety of tinned foods, compressed meat, potatoes, asparagus, served at room temperature. It was Sally Klee who opened the tins and set their contents on paper plates. Now I linger at my toilet washing my hands, climbing on to the sink to regard my face in the mirror, yawning. Do I deserve to be ignored?

I find Sally Klee as I left her. She is in her dining room playing with used matches in a musty pool of light. We were lovers once, living almost as man and wife, happier than most wives and men. Then she wearying of my ways and I daily exacerbating her displeasure with my persistence, we now inhabit different rooms. Sally Klee does not look up as I enter the room, and I hover between her chair and mine, the plates and tins arranged before me. Perhaps I am a little too squat to be taken seriously, my arms a little too long. With them I reach out and stroke gently Sally Klee's gleaming black hair. I feel the warmth of her skull beneath her hair and it touches me, so alive, so sad.

Perhaps you will have heard of Sally Klee. Two and a half years ago she published a short novel and it was an instant success. The novel describes the attempts and bitter failures of a young woman to have a baby. Medically there appears to be nothing wrong with her, nor with her husband, nor his brother. In the words of *The Times Literary Supplement*, it is a tale told with 'wan deliberation'. Other serious reviews were less kind, but in its first year it sold thirty thousand copies in hardback, and so far a quarter of a million in paperback. If you have not read the book you will have seen the cover of the paperback edition as you buy your morning paper at the railway station. A naked woman kneels, face buried in hands, amidst a barren desert. Since that time Sally Klee has written nothing. Every day for months on end she sits at her typewriter, waiting. But for a sudden flurry of activity at the end of each day her machine is silent. She cannot remember how she wrote her first book, she does not dare depart from what she knows, she does not dare repeat herself. She has money and time and a comfortable house in which she languishes, bored and perplexed, waiting.

Sally Klee places her hand on mine as it moves across her head, either to forestall or acknowledge tenderness — her head is still bowed and I cannot see her face. Knowing nothing, I compromise and hold her hand and seconds later our hands drop limply to our sides. I say nothing and, like the perfect friend, begin to clear away the plates and cutlery, tins and tin opener. In order to assure Sally Klee that I am not at all piqued by or sulking at her silence I whistle Lillibulero cheerfully through my teeth, rather in the manner of Sterne's Uncle Toby in times of stress.

Exactly so. I am stacking the plates in the kitchen and sulking, almost to the point of forgetting to whistle. Despite my negative sentiments I set about preparing the coffee. Sally Klee will have a blend of no less than four different kinds of bean in emulation of Balzac whose life she read in a lavishly illustrated volume while attending to the proofs of her first novel. We always call it her *first* novel. The beans must be measured out carefully and ground by hand – a task to which my physique is well suited. Secretly, I suspect, Sally Klee believes that good coffee is the essence of authorship. Look at Balzac (I believe she says to herself), who wrote several thousand novels and whose coffee bills present themselves to the well-wisher from behind glass cases in tranquil suburban museums. After the grinding I must add a little salt and pour the mixture into the silver cavity of a compact, stainless-steel machine sent here by post from Grenoble. While this warms on the stove I peer in at Sally Klee from behind the dining-room door. She has folded her arms now and is resting them on the table in front of her. I advance a few paces into the room, hoping to catch her eye.

Perhaps from the very beginning the arrangement was certain to fail. On the other hand, the pleasures it afforded – particularly to Sally Klee – were remarkable. And while she believes that in my behaviour towards her I was a little too persistent, too manic, too 'eager', and while I for my part still feel she delighted more in my unfamiliarity ('funny little black leathery penis' and 'your saliva tastes like weak tea') than in my essential self, I would like to think there are no profound regrets on either side. As

Moira Sillito, the heroine of Sally Klee's first novel, says to herself at her husband's funeral, 'Everything changes.' Is the quiet, assertive yet ultimately tragic Moira consciously misquoting Yeats? So, no lasting regrets, I hope, when, this afternoon, I carried my few personal effects from Sally Klee's spacious bedroom to my own small room at the top of the house. Yes, I rather like to climb stairs, and I left without a murmur. In effect (why deny it?) I was dismissed, but I had my own reasons for quitting those sheets. This liaison, for all its delights, was involving me too deeply in Sally Klee's creative problems and only a final act of good-natured voyeurism could show me how far out of my depth I was. Artistic gestation is a private matter and my proximity was, and perhaps is still, obscene. Sally Klee's gaze lifts clear of the table and for an immeasurable moment meets my own. With a slight affirmative motion of the head she indicates she is ready to take coffee.

Sally Klee and I sip our coffee 'in pregnant silence'. This at least is how Moira and her husband Daniel, a rising young executive at a local bottling factory, sip their tea and digest the news that there are no medical reasons why between them they should be incapable of producing a child. Later the same day they decide to try (a good word, I thought) yet again for a baby. Personally speaking, sipping is something at which I rather excel, but silence, of whatever kind, makes me uncomfortable. I hold the cup several inches away from my face and propel my lips towards the rim in a winsome, tapering pout. Simultaneously I roll my eyes into my skull. There was a time — I remember the first occasion particularly — when the whole performance brought a smile to the less flexible lips of Sally Klee. Now I excel uncomfortably and when my eyeballs are facing outwards into the world once more I see no smile but Sally Klee's pale, hairless fingers drumming on the polished surface of the dining table. She refills her cup, stands and leaves the room, leaves me to listen to her footsteps on the stairs.

Though I remain below I am with her every inch of the way — I have said my proximity is obscene. She ascends the stairs, enters her bedroom, sits at her table. From where I sit I hear her thread into her typewriter a single sheet of paper, off-white, A4, 61 mg per square metre, the very same paper on which she effortlessly composed her first novel. She will ensure the machine is set at double space. Only letters to her friends, agent and publisher go at single space. Decisively she punches the red key which will provide, when there are words to surround it, a neat, off-white emptiness to precede her first sentence. An awesome silence settles over the house, I commence to writhe in my chair, an involuntary high-pitched sound escapes my throat. For two and a half years Sally Klee has grappled not with words and sentences, nor with ideas, but with form, or rather, with tactics. Should she, for instance, break silence with a short story, work a single idea with brittle elegance and total control? But what single idea, what sentence, what word? Moreover, good short stories are notoriously hard to write, harder perhaps than novels, and mediocre stories lie thick on the ground. Perhaps then another novel about Moira Sillito. Sally Klee closes her eyes and looks hard at her heroine and discovers yet again that everything she knows about her she has already written down. No, a second novel must break free of the first. What about a novel set (my tentative suggestion) in the jungles of South America? How ridiculous! What then? Moira Sillito stares up at Sally Klee from the empty page. Write about me, she says simply. But I can't, Sally Klee cries out loud, I know nothing more about you. Please, says Moira. Leave me alone, Sally Klee cries out louder than before. Me, me,

says Moira. No, no, Sally Klee shouts, I know nothing, I
hate you. Leave me alone!

Sally Klee's cries pierce many hours of tense silence and
bring me to my feet trembling. When will I ever accustom
myself to these terrible sounds which cause the very air to
bend and warp with strain? In calmer retrospection I will
be reminded of Edvard Munch's famous woodcut, but
now I scamper about the dining room, unable to stifle the
agitated squeals which well from me in moments of panic
or excitement and which, to Sally Klee's ears, diminish
my romantic credibility. And at night when Sally Klee
shouts in her sleep, my own pathetic squeals render me
dismally incapable of giving comfort. Moira has nightmares too, as is established with chilling economy in the
first line of Sally Klee's first novel: 'That night pale Moira
Sillito rose screaming from her bed ... ' *The Yorkshire Post*
was one of the few papers to take notice of this opening
but, sadly, found it 'too energetic by half'. Moira of
course has a husband to soothe her and by the foot of
page two she is 'sleeping like a little child in the young
man's strong arms'. In a surprise review the feminist
magazine *Refractory Girl* quotes this line to evidence the
redundance of both 'little' and the novel's 'banal sexism'.
However, I found the line poignant, more so when it
describes the very solace I yearn to bring in the dead of
night to its begetter.

I am silenced by the scrape of a chair. Sally Klee will
come downstairs now, enter the kitchen to fill her cup with
cold, black coffee and then return to her desk. I climb on
to the chaise longue and arrange myself there in an attitude
of simian preoccupation in case she should look in. Tonight
she passes by, her form framed briefly in the open doorway, while her cup, rattling harshly in its saucer, an-
nounced her nervous wretchedness. Upstairs again I hear
her remove the sheet of paper from her typewriter and

replace it with a fresh piece. She sighs and presses the red key, pushes her hair clear of her eyes and begins to type at her steady, efficient forty words per minute. Music fills the house. I stretch my limbs on the chaise longue and drift into an after-dinner sleep.

I familiarised myself with Sally Klee's ritual ordeals during my brief residence in her bedroom. I lay on her bed, she sat at the desk, in our separate ways doing nothing. I luxuriated in, I congratulated myself hourly on, my recent elevation from pet to lover and, stretched out on my back, arms folded behind my head, legs crossed, I speculated upon further promotion, from lover to husband. Yes, I saw myself, expensive fountain pen in hand, signing hire purchase agreements for my pretty wife. I would teach myself to hold a pen. I would be man-about-the-house, scaling drainpipes with uxorious ease to investigate the roof gutters, suspending myself from light fittings to re-decorate the ceiling. Down to the pub in the evening with my husband credentials to make new friends, invent a name for myself in order to bestow it on my wife, take up wearing slippers about the house, and perhaps even socks and shoes outside. Of genetic rules and regulations I knew too little to reflect on the possibility of progeny, but I was determined to consult medical authorities who would in turn inform Sally Klee of her fate. She meanwhile sat before her empty page, pale as screaming, rising Moira Sillito, but silent and still, progressing ineluctably towards the crisis which would bring her to her feet and propel her downstairs for unwarmed coffee. In the early days she cast in my direction nervous encouraging smiles and we were happy. But as I came to know of the agony behind her silence my empathic squeals — so she was to insinuate — made it harder to concentrate and the smiles in my direction ceased.

They ceased and, therefore, likewise my speculations.
I am not, as you may have gathered, one to seek confrontations. Think of me rather as one who would suck
yolks from eggs without damage to the shells, remember
my dextrous sipping. Beyond my silly noises, which were
more evolutionary than personal, I said nothing. Late one
evening, overwhelmed by a sudden intuition, I scampered
into the bathroom minutes after Sally Klee had left it. I
locked the door, stood on the edge of the bath, opened the
small, scented cupboard in which she kept her most
private, womanly things and confirmed what I already
knew. Her intriguing cap still lay inside its plastic oyster,
dusted and somehow disapproving of me. I passed rapidly
then, in the long afternoons and evenings on the bed,
from speculation to nostalgia. The long prelude of mutual
exploration, she counting my teeth with her ballpoint pen,
I searching in vain for nits in her copious hair. Her playful
observations on the length, colour, texture of my member,
my fascination with her endearingly useless toes and coyly
concealed anus. Our first 'time' (Moira Sillito's word) was
a little dogged by misunderstanding largely due to my
assumption that we were to proceed *a posteriori*. That
matter was soon resolved and we adopted Sally Klee's
unique 'face to face', an arrangement I found at first, as
I tried to convey to my lover, too fraught with communica-
tion, a little too 'intellectual'. However, I rapidly made
myself comfortable, and not two afternoons later was
bringing to mind:

> And pictures in our eyes to get
> Was all our propagation.

Fortunately it was not, at this stage, quite all. 'The experience of falling in love is common but nevertheless
ineffable.' These sentiments are offered to Moira Sillito
by her brother-in-law, the only one of a large family to

have been to a university. I should add that Moira, though familiar with the word from the hymns of her schooldays, does not know what 'ineffable' means. After a suitable silence she excuses herself, runs upstairs to the bedroom, finds the word in a pocket dictionary there, runs downstairs to the living room and says cosily as she comes through the door, 'No, it is not. Falling in love is like floating on clouds.' Like Moira Sillito's brother-in-law, I was in love and, as will happen, it was not long before my tirelessness began to oppress Sally Klee, nor was it long before she complained that the friction of our bodies brought her out in a rash, and that my 'alien seed' (alien corn, I quipped fruitlessly at the time) was aggravating her thrush. This and my 'bloody gibbering on the bed' precipitated the end of the affair, the happiest eight days of my life. I will be two and a half next April.

After speculation, after nostalgia, and before my removal to the room upstairs, I had leisure to pose myself certain questions concerning Sally Klee's creative ordeals. Why, after a long day of inactivity before one blank sheet of paper, did she return to the room in the evening with her unwarmed coffee and replace that sheet with another? What was it she then began to type so fluently that each day took up only one sheet of paper and was afterwards filed with a thick bank of other such sheets? And why did this sudden activity not offer her relief from her quiet suffering, why did she rise from her table each night still pained, preoccupied with the emptiness of the other sheet? Certainly the sound of the keys was release for me, and invariably at the very first stroke I fell into a grateful sleep. Have I not left myself dozing in the crystalline present on the chaise longue downstairs? Once, instead of falling asleep I sidled up to Sally Klee's chair on the pretext of affection and glimpsed the words 'in which case the whole thing could be considered from' before my lover – as she still was then—kissed me gently on the ear and shoved me tenderly in the direction of the bed. This rather pedestrian construction dulled my curiosity, but only for a day or two. What whole thing? What whole thing could be considered from what? A few days later the plastic oyster had ceased to yield up its rubber pearl and I began to feel that I, as Sally Klee's rejected lover, had the right to know the contents of what I had come to regard as a private diary. Between them curiosity and vanity concocted a balm to ease my prying conscience, and like an out-of-work actor I longed to see a favourable notice of myself, even one relating—as it were—to a past production.

While Sally Klee sat at her table I had lain in luxury, planning her future and mine, I then had lain there in remorse and now, as our incommunicativeness became firmly established, I lay in wait. I stayed awake late into the evening in order to watch her as she opened a drawer in her desk, removed from it a faded, blue clasp file, peeled from her typewriter the completed sheet, placed it face downwards in the file to ensure (I surmised through half closed eyes) that the earliest entries were on top, closed the file and returned it to its drawer, closed the drawer and stood, eyes dulled by exhaustion and defeat, jaw slack, spirit oblivious to the lover-turned-spy feigning sleep on her bed, making his silent calculations. Though not remotely altruistic, my intentions were not purely selfish either. Naturally I hoped that by gaining access to Sally Klee's most intimate secrets and sorrows I might, by pitting my strength against selected locales of her clandestine frailty, persuade her that itch, thrush and gibbering were small prices to pay for my boundless affection. On the other hand I did not think only of myself. I ran and re-ran fantasy footage which show me poring over the journal while its author was out of the house, me confessing

to Sally Klee on her return my slight treachery and con-
gratulating her with passionate embrace before she can
draw breath on having written a masterpiece, a colossal
and devastating psychic journey, she sinking into the chair
I deftly proffer, eyes widening and glowing with the dawn-
ing realisation of the truth of what I say, us, shot here in
tight close-up, studying the journal long into the night,
me advising, guiding, editing, the publisher's rapturous
reception of the manuscript outdone by that of the critics
and that in turn by the reading, buying public, the
renewal of Sally Klee's writing confidence, the renewal,
through our co-operative endeavours, of our mutual
understanding and love ... yes, renewal, renewal, my film
was all about renewal.

It was not until today that an opportunity finally
offered itself. Sally Klee was obliged to visit her accountant
in town. In order to sublimate my near-hysterical excitement I performed kind services at high speed. While she
retired to the bathroom to arrange her hair before the
mirror there, I searched the house for bus and train timetables and pushed them under the bathroom door. I
climbed the hat tree and plucked from its highest branch
Sally Klee's red silk scarf and ran to her with it. After she
had left the house, however, I noticed the scarf back in its
position. Had I not offered it, I conjectured sulkily as I
watched her at the bus stop from the attic window, she
would most likely have worn it. Her bus was a long time
coming (she should have consulted the timetables) and I
watched her pace round the concrete post and finally
engage in conversation with a woman who also waited
and who carried a child on her back, a sight which communicated to me across the suburban gables a chemical
pang of generic longing. I was determined to wait until
I had seen the bus carry Sally Klee away. Like Moira
Sillito gazing, in the long days that followed her husband's

funeral, at a snapshot of his brother, I did not wish to appear, even to myself, precipitate. The bus came and the pavement was suddenly and conspicuously vacant. Touched by a momentary sense of loss I turned away from the window.

Sally Klee's desk is unpretentious, standard office equipment of the kind used by middle-stratum administrators of hospitals and zoos, its essential constituent being plywood. The design is simplicity itself. A plain writing surface rests on two parallel banks of drawers, and the whole is backed by one lacquered sheet of wood. I had long ago noted that the typed sheets were filed in the top left side drawer, and my initial reaction on descending from the attic and finding it locked was one of anger rather than despair. Was I not to be trusted then after so long an intimacy, was this how one species in its arrogance treated another? As an insult of omission, all the other drawers slid out like mocking tongues and displayed their dull stationery contents. In the face of this betrayal (what else had she locked? The fridge? The greenhouse?) of our shared past I felt my claim to the faded blue clasp file utterly vindicated. From the kitchen I fetched a screwdriver and with it set about prising loose the sheet of flimsy wood that bound the back of the desk. With a sound like the crack of a whip a large piece detached itself along a line of weakness, and left in its place an ugly rectangular hole. I was not concerned with appearances however. I thrust my hand deep inside, found the back of the drawer, insinuated my fingers farther, finding the file began to lift it clear and, had not its leading edge caught on a nail and tipped its contents in a white swarm on to the splinter-strewn floor, could have congratulated myself on an impeccable appropriation. Instead I gathered as many sheets as my left foot could convey to my right hand in one continuous movement, and retired to the bed.

I closed my eyes and, in the manner of those who, poised above the pan, fleetingly hug their faeces to their bowels, retained the moment. For the sake of future recollection, I concentrated on the precise nature of my expectations. I was well aware of the universal law which pre-ordains a discrepancy between the imagined and the real—I even prepared myself for a disappointment. When I opened my eyes a number filled my vision—54. Page 54. Below that I found myself halfway through a sentence which had its origins on page fifty-three, a sentence sinister in its familiarity. 'said Dave, carefully wiping his lips with it and crumpling it on to his plate.' I turned my face into the pillow, sickened and stunned by an apprehension of the complexity and sophistication of Sally Klee's species and the brutish ignorance of my own. 'Dave stared intently through the candlelight at his sister-in-law and her husband, his brother. He spoke quietly. "Or again some think of it as a sharp, womanly odour (he glanced at Moira) ... exciting. Certainly it suggests sexual activity of some ... " ' I threw the sheet aside and clutched at another, page 196: 'of earth struck the coffin lid, the rain ceased as suddenly as it had begun. Moira detached herself from the main group and wandered across the cemetery, reading without real comprehension the inscriptions on the stones. She felt mellow, as if she had seen a depressing but ultimately good film. She stopped under a yew tree and stood there a long time, abstractedly picking at the bark with her long orange finger nails. She thought, Everything changes. A sparrow, its feathers fluffed against the cold, hopped forlornly at her feet.' Not one phrase, not one word modified, everything unaltered. Page 230: '-ing on clouds?" Dave repeated peevishly. "What exactly does that mean?" Moira let her gaze fall on a flaw in the Bokhara design and said nothing. Dave crossed the room and took her hand. "What I mean when I ask that," he said hurriedly, "is that I have so many things to learn from you. You've suffered so much. You know so much." Moira released her hand to pick up her cup of barely warm, weak tea. She thought listlessly, Why do men despise women?'

I could read no more. I squatted on the bed post picking at my chest, listening to the ponderous tick of the clock in the hallway downstairs. Was art then nothing more than a wish to appear busy? Was it nothing more than a fear of silence, of boredom, which the merely reiterative rattle of the typewriter's keys was enough to allay? In short, having crafted one novel, would it suffice to write it again, type it out with care, page by page? (Gloomily I recycled nits from torso to mouth.) Deep in my heart I knew it would suffice and, knowing that, seemed to know less than I had ever known before. Two and a half next April indeed! I could have been born the day before yesterday.

It was growing dark when I finally set about arranging the papers and returning them to the file. I worked quickly, turning pages with all four limbs, driven less by the fear of Sally Klee returning home early than by an obscure hope that by restoring order I could erase the afternoon from my mind. I eased the file through the back of the desk and into its drawer. I secured the jagged segment of wood with drawing pins hammered down with the heel of a shoe. I threw the splinters of wood out the window and pushed the desk against the wall. I crouched in the centre of the room, knuckles barely brushing the carpet, questioning the semi-darkness and the frightful hiss of total silence about my head ... now everything was as it had been and as Sally Klee would expect it to be – typewriter, pens, blotting paper, a single withering daffodil – and still I knew what I knew and understood nothing at all. Simply, I was unworthy. I did not wish to turn on the light and illuminate my memories of the happiest eight days of my life. I groped, therefore, in the gloom unique to bedrooms until, vibrant with self-pity, I had located all of my few possessions—hairbrush, nail file, stainless-steel mirror and toothpicks. My resolve to leave the room without once looking back failed me when I reached the bedroom door. I turned and peered, but I could see nothing. I closed the door softly behind me and, even as I set my hand on the first step of the narrow attic staircase, I heard Sally Klee's key scratching for leverage in the front door lock.

I wake from my after-dinner sleep into silence. Perhaps silence, the sudden cessation of Sally Klee's typewriter, has woken me. My empty coffee cup still hangs by its handle from my finger, a viscous residue of tinned foods coats my tongue, whereas a trickle of saliva from my sleeping mouth has stained the paisley pattern of the chaise longue. Sleep after all solves nothing. I rise scratching and long for my toothpicks (fishbone in chamois pouch) but now they are at the very top of the house and to fetch them I should have to pass Sally Klee's open door. And why should I not pass her open door? Why should I not be seen and be taken account of in this household? Am I invisible? Do I not deserve for my quiet, self-effacing removal to another room a simple acknowledgment, the curt exchange of nods and sighs and smiles between two who have known both suffering and loss? I find myself standing before the hallway clock, watching the small hand edge toward ten. The truth is that I do not pass her door because I smart from being ignored, because I *am* invisible and of no account. Because I long to pass her door. My eyes stray to the front door and fix there. To leave, yes, regain my independence and dignity, to set out on the City Ring Road, my possessions clasped to my chest, the infinite stars towering above me and the songs of nightingales ringing in my ears. Sally Klee receding ever farther behind me, she caring nothing for me, no, nor I for her, to lope carefree towards the orange dawn and on into the next day and again into the following night, crossing rivers and penetrating woods, to search for and find a new love, a new post, a new function, a new life. A new life. The very words are deadweight on my lips, for what new life could be more exalted than the old, what new function rival that of Sally Klee's ex-lover? No future can equal my past. I turn towards the stairs and almost immediately begin to wonder if I could not convince myself of alternative descriptions of the situation. This afternoon, blighted by my own inadequacy, I acted for the best, it was in both our interests. Sally Klee returning home from a troubled day must have entered her room to discover it bereft of a certain few familiar articles and she must have felt then that her only source of comfort had left her side without a word. Without one word! My hands and feet are on the fourth stair. Surely it is she, not I, who is hurt. And what are explanations but silent, invisible things in your head? I have appropriated more than my fair share of damage and she is silent because she is sulking. It is she who longs for explanations and reassurance. She who longs to be esteemed, stroked, breathed on. Of course! How could I have failed to understand that during our silent meal. She needs *me*. I gain this realisation like a mountaineer a virgin summit and arrive at Sally Klee's open door a little out of breath, less from exertion than from triumph.

Wreathed by the light from her writing lamp she sits with her back to me, elbows resting on the desk, head supported under the chin by her cupped hands. The sheet of paper in her typewriter is crowded with words. It has yet to be pulled clear and laid in the blue clasp file. Standing here directly behind Sally Klee I am struck by a vivid memory from my earliest infancy. I am staring at my mother who squats with her back to me and then, for the first time in my life, I see past her shoulder as through a mist pale, spectral figures beyond the plate glass, pointing and mouthing silently. I advance noiselessly into the room and squat down a few feet behind Sally Klee's chair. Now I am here, it seems an impossible idea she will ever turn in her chair and notice me.

Two Fragments: March 199-

Saturday

Towards dawn Henry woke, but did not open his eyes. He saw a luminous white mass fold in upon itself, the residue of a dream he could not recall. Superimposed black shapes with arms and legs drifted upwards and away like crows against a blank sky. When he opened his eyes the room was sunk in deep blue light and he was staring into the eyes of his daughter. She stood close to the bed, her head level with his. Pigeons grunted and stirred on the window-ledge. Father and daughter, they stared and neither spoke. Footsteps receded on the street outside. Henry's eyes narrowed. Marie's grew larger, she moved her lips faintly, her tiny body shivered under the white nightgown. She watched her father drift into sleep.

Presently she said, 'I've got a vagina.'

Henry moved his legs and woke again. 'Yes,' he said.

'So I'm a girl, aren't I?'

Henry supported himself on his elbow. 'Go back to bed now, Marie. You're cold.'

She moved away from the bed, out of his reach, and stood facing the window, facing the grey light. 'Are pigeons boys or girls?'

Henry lay on his back and said, 'Boys *and* girls.'

Marie moved closer to the sound of the pigeons and listened. 'Do girl pigeons have a vagina?'

'Yes.'

'Where do they?'

'Where do you think?'

She considered, she listened. She looked back at him over her shoulder. 'Under their feathers?'

'Yes.' She laughed delightedly. The grey light was brightening.

'Into bed now,' Henry said with faked urgency.

She walked towards him. 'In *your* bed, Henry,' she demanded. He moved over for her and pulled back the covers. She climbed in and he watched her fall asleep.

An hour later Henry slipped from the bed without waking the child. He stood beneath the dribbling shower and afterwards paused for a moment in front of a large mirror and regarded his naked dripping body. Lit from one side only by the watery light of first day he appeared to himself sculpted, monumental, capable of superhuman feats.

He dressed hurriedly. When he was pouring coffee in the kitchen he heard loud voices and footsteps on the stairs outside his flat. Automatically he glanced out the window. A light rain was falling and the light was dropping. Henry went to the bedroom to watch out the window. Behind him Marie still slept. The sky was thick and angry.

As far as he could see in either direction the street was filling with people preparing to collect rain-water. They were unrolling canvas tarpaulins, working in twos, in families. It grew darker. They stretched the canvases across the road and secured the ends to drain-pipes and railings. They rolled barrels into the centre of the street to collect water from the tarpaulins. For all this activity there was silence, jealous, competitive silence. As usual fights were breaking out. Space was limited. Beneath Henry's window two figures wrestled. It was hard to make them out at first. Now he saw that one was a heavily built woman, the other a man of slight build in his early twenties. With their arms locked about each other's neck they edged sideways like a monstrous crab. The rain fell in a continuous sheet and the wrestlers were ignored. Their tarpaulins lay in piles at their feet, the disputed space was taken by others. Now they fought for pride alone and a few children gathered round to watch. They rolled to the ground. The woman was suddenly on top, pinning the man to the ground with her knee pressed against his throat. His legs kicked uselessly. A small dog, its pink member erect and vivid in the gloom, threw itself into the struggle. It clasped the man's head between its front paws. Its haunches quivered like plucked strings and its pink tongue flashed from the root. The children laughed and pulled it away.

Marie was out of bed when he turned away from the window. 'What are you doing, Henry?'

'Watching the rain,' he said, and gathered her up in his arms and carried her to the bathroom.

It took an hour to walk to work. They stopped once, half-way across Chelsea bridge. Marie climbed from her push-chair and Henry held her up so she could look down at the river. It was a daily ritual. She gazed in silence and struggled a little when she'd had enough. Thousands walked in the same direction each morning. Henry rarely recognised a friend but if he did they walked together in silence.

The Ministry rose from a vast plain of pavement. The pushchair bumped over green wedges of weed. The stones were cracking and subsiding. Human refuse littered the plain. Vegetables, rotten and trodden down, cardboard boxes flattened into beds, the remains of fires and the carcasses of roasted dogs and cats, rusted tin, vomit, worn tyres, animal excrement. An old dream of horizontal lines converging on the thrusting steel and glass perpendicular was now beyond recall.

The air above the fountain was grey with flies. Men and boys came there daily to squat on the wide concrete rim and defecate. In the distance, along one edge of the plain, several hundred men and women still slept. They were wrapped in striped, brightly coloured blankets which in day time marked out shop space. From that group came the sound of a child crying, carried on the wind. No one stirred. 'Why is that baby crying?' Marie shouted suddenly, and her own voice was lost in that big, miserable place. They hurried on, they were late. They were tiny, the only moving figures on the great expanse.

To save time Henry ran down the stairs to the basement with Marie in his arms. Even before he was through the swing doors someone was saying to him, 'We like them to be on time.' He turned and set Marie down. The playgroup leader rested her hand on Marie's head. She was over six feet tall and emaciated, her eyes were sunk deep and broken blood vessels danced on her cheeks. When she spoke again she stretched her lips tightly round her teeth and rose on her toes. 'And if you don't mind ... the subscriptions. Would you care to settle now?' Henry was three months behind. He promised to bring money the next day. She shrugged and took Marie's hand. He watched them pass through a door and caught a glimpse of two black children in a violent embrace. The noise was shrill and deafening, and cut off dead when the door closed behind them.

When, thirty minutes later, Henry began to type the second letter of the morning, he could no longer remember the contents of the first. He worked from the long-hand scrawl of some higher official. When he came to the end of the fifteenth letter, shortly before lunch, he could not remember its beginning. And he did not care to move his eyes up the page to see. He carried the letters into a smaller office and gave them to someone without seeing who it was who took them. Henry returned to his desk, with only minutes now to waste before lunch. All the typists were smoking as they worked and the air was thick and sharp with smoke, not of this day alone but of ten thousand previous days and ten thousand days to come. There seemed no way forward. Henry lit a cigarette and waited.

He descended the sixteen floors to the basement and joined a long queue of parents, mostly mothers, who came in their lunch hour to see their children. It was a murmuring queue of supplicants. They came out of need not duty. They spoke to each other in soft voices about their children while the line shuffled towards the swing doors. Each child had to be signed for. The playgroup leader stood by the doors, by her presence alone conveying a need for silence and order. The parents complied, and signed. Marie was waiting for him just beyond the doors, and when she saw him she raised two clenched fists above her head and made an innocent little dance. Henry signed and took her hand.

The sky had cleared and a sickly warmth rose from the flagstones. The vast plain teemed now like a colony of ants. Above it hung a pale sickle moon, clear against the blue sky. Marie climbed in the pushchair and Henry wheeled her through the crowds.

All those with something to sell crammed on to the plain and spread their goods on coloured blankets. An old woman was selling half-used cakes of soap arranged across a bright yellow rug like precious stones. Marie chose a green piece the size and shape of a chicken's egg. Henry bargained with the woman and brought her down to half her first price. As they exchanged money for soap she made a show of scowls and Marie recoiled from her in surprise. The old woman smiled, reached into her bag and brought out a small present. But Marie climbed back into her pushchair and would not take it. 'Go away,' Marie shouted at the old woman, 'Go away.' They walked on. Henry headed for a far corner of the plain where there was space to sit and eat lunch. He made a wide detour round the fountain, on the rim of which men perched like featherless birds.

They sat on a parapet which ran along one side of the plain and ate bread and cheese. Below them stretched the deserted buildings of Whitehall. Henry asked Marie questions about the playgroup. There were rumours of indoctrination but his questions were casual and unpressing. 'What did you play with today?'

She told him excitedly of a game with water and a boy who had cried, a boy who always cried. He took from his pocket a small treat, cold, bright yellow, mysteriously curved and laid it in her hands. 'What is it, Henry?'

'It's a banana. You can eat it.' He showed her how to peel the skin away, and told her how they grew in bunches in a far-off country. Later he asked, 'Did the lady read you a story, Marie?'

She turned and stared over the parapet. 'Yes,' she said after a while.

'What was it about?'

She giggled. 'It was about bananas ... bananas ... bananas.' They began the half-mile walk back to the Ministry and Marie chanted her new word quietly to herself.

Far ahead the crowd was collecting round a point of interest. Some people were running past them to join it and were forming a circle around a compulsive beat, around a man with a drum. By the time Henry and Marie arrived the circle was ten deep and the cries of the man were muffled. Henry lifted Marie on to his shoulders and pushed deeper into the crowd. By his clothes the people recognised him as a Ministry worker and indifferently stood aside. Now it was possible to see. In the centre of the ring was a squat, black oil drum. Animal skin was stretched over one end and the man beside it, a man the size of a great lumbering bear, banged it with his bare fist. Sacking doused in red paint wound round his body like a toga. His hair was red and coarse and reached almost to his waist. The hair on his bare arms was thick and matted like animal fur. Even his eyes were red.

He was not shouting words. With each pulse of the drum he gave out a deep loud growl. He was watching something closely in the crowd and Henry, following his eyeline, saw a large rusty tin passing from hand to hand and heard the clink of coins. Then he saw in the crowd a dull flash of reflected sunlight. It was a long sword, slightly curved with an ornamental handle. The crowd reached out to hold it, touch it, assure themselves of its substantiality. It moved in counter-motion to the biscuit tin. Marie tugged at Henry's ear and demanded explanations. He pushed deeper towards the circle till they were second from the front. The tin came close. Henry felt the man's fierce red eyes on him and threw in three small coins. The man beat the drum and roared and the tin passed on.

Marie shivered on Henry's shoulders and he stroked her bare knees for comfort. Suddenly the man broke into words, a crude chant on two notes. His words were ponderous and slurred. Henry made them out, and at the same time saw the girl for the first time. 'Without blood ... without blood ... without blood ... ' She was standing far to one side, a girl of about sixteen, naked from the waist up and barefoot. She stood perfectly still, hands at her side, feet together, staring at the ground a few feet in front of her. Her hair too was red, but fine and cropped short.

Round her waist she wore a piece of sacking. She was so pale it was quite possible to believe that she was without blood.

Now the drum took on a steady arterial pulse and the sword was returned to the man. He held it high above his head and glowered at the crowd. Someone from the crowd brought him the biscuit tin. He peered inside and shook his great head. The tin was returned to the crowd and the drum beat accelerated. 'Without blood,' the man shouted. 'Through her belly, out her back, without blood.' The tin appeared in his hands again, and again he refused it. The crowd was desperate. Those at the back pushed forward to throw in money, those who had given shouted at those who had not. Quarrels broke out, but the tin was filling. When it returned the third time it was accepted and the crowd sighed with relief. The drum beat ceased.

By a movement of his head the man ordered the girl, surely his daughter, into the centre of the circle. She stood with the oil drum between her and her father. Henry saw her legs shaking. The crowd was silent, anxious to miss nothing. The cries of vendors reached them across the plain as though from another world. Marie shouted out suddenly, her voice thin with fear, 'What's she going to do?' Henry shushed her, the man was putting the sword into his daughter's hands. He did not take his eyes off her and she seemed powerless to look anywhere but into his face. He hissed something in her ear and she raised the point of the sword to her belly. Her father bent down and emptied the biscuit tin into a leather bag which he slung across his shoulder. The sword shook in the girl's hands and the crowd stirred impatiently.

Henry felt sudden warmth spread across his neck and down his back. Marie had urinated. He lifted her to the ground and at that moment, urged on by her father, the

girl pushed the tip of the sword half an inch into her belly.
Marie screamed with rage. She beat her fists against
Henry's legs. 'Lift me up,' she sobbed. A small coin of
crimson, brilliant in the sunlight, spread outwards round
the shaft of the sword. Someone in the crowd sneered,
'Without blood.' The father secured the leather bag beneath his toga. He made towards the sword as if to plunge
it through his daughter. She collapsed at his feet and the
sword clattered on to the pavement. The gigantic man
picked it up and shook it at the angry crowd. 'Pigs,' he
shouted. 'Greedy pigs.' The crowd was enraged and
shouted back. 'Cheat ... murderer ... he's got our money
... '

But they were afraid, for when he pulled his daughter to
her feet and dragged her off they scattered to make a path
for him. He swung the sword about his head. 'Pigs,' he
kept on shouting. 'Get back, you pigs.' A stone was
thrown hard and caught him high on the shoulder. He
spun round, dropped his daughter and went for the crowd
like a madman, sweeping the sword in huge vicious arcs.
Henry picked up Marie and ran with the rest of them.
When he turned back to look the man was far away,
urging his daughter along. The crowd had left him alone
with his money. Henry and Marie walked back and
found the pushchair on its side. One of the handles was
bent.

That evening, on the long walk home, Marie sat quietly
and asked no questions. Henry felt anxious for her, but he
was too tired to be of use. After the first mile she was
asleep. He crossed the river by Vauxhall bridge and
stopped halfway across, this time for himself. The Thames
was lower than he had ever seen it. Some said that one day
the river would dry up and giant bridges would uselessly
span fresh meadows. He remained on the bridge ten

minutes smoking a cigarette. It was difficult to know what to believe. Many people said that tap water was slow poison.

At home he lit all the candles in the house to dispel Marie's fears. She followed him about closely. He cooked a fish on the paraffin stove and they ate in the bedroom. He talked to Marie about the sea which she had never seen and later he read her a story till she fell asleep on his lap. She woke as he was carrying her to her bed and said, 'What did that lady do with her sword?'

Henry said, 'She danced. She danced with it in her hands.' Marie's clear blue eyes looked deep into his own. He sensed her disbelief and regretted his lie.

He worked late into the night. Towards two o'clock he went to the window in his bedroom and opened it. The moon had sunk and clouds had moved in and covered the stars. He heard a pack of dogs down by the river. To the north he could see the fires burning on the Ministry plain. He wondered if things would change much in his lifetime. Behind him Marie called out in her sleep and laughed.

Sunday

I left Marie with a neighbour and walked northwards across London – a distance of six miles – to a reunion with an old lover. We knew each other from the old times, and it was in their memory rather than for passion that we continued to meet occasionally. On this day our love-making was long and poignantly unsuccessful. After, in a room of dusty sunshine and torn plastic furniture, we spoke of the old times. In a low voice Diane complained of emptiness and foreboding. She wondered which government and which set of illusions were to blame and how it could have been otherwise. Politically Diane was more sophisticated than I was. 'We'll see what happens,' I said. 'But now roll on to your belly.' She told me about her new job, helping an old man with his fish. He was a friend of her uncle's. Each day at dawn she was down at the river to meet his rowing-boat. They loaded a handcart with fish and eels and pushed it to a small street market where the old man had a stall. He went home to sleep and prepare for the night's work, she sold his fish. In the early evening she took the money to his house and perhaps because she was pretty, he insisted they divide the takings evenly. While she spoke I massaged her neck and back. 'Now everything smells of fish,' she cried. I had taken it for the lingering genital smell of another lover – she had many – but I did not say. Her fears and complaints were no different from mine, and yet – or rather, consequently – I said only bland, comfortless things. I worked my thumbs into the thick folds of skin in the small of her back. She sighed. I said, 'It's a job at least.'

I rose from the bed. In the bathroom I gazed into an ancient-looking mirror. My bag of skin lay against the cool rim of the sink. Orgasm, however desultory, brought on the illusion of clarity. The unvarying buzz of an insect sustained my inaction. Making a guess at my silence Diane called out, 'How's your little girl?'

'All right, coming on,' I said. However, I was thinking of my birthday, thirty in ten days' time, and that in turn brought to mind my mother. I stooped to wash. Two years ago there had reached me, through a friend, a letter written on a coarse sheet of pink paper folded tightly and sealed inside a used envelope. My mother named a village in Kent. She was working in the fields, she had milk, cheese, butter and a little meat from the farm. She sent wistful love to her son and grandchild. Since then, in moments of clarity or restlessness – I could not tell – I had made and retracted plans to leave the city with Marie. I calculated the village to be a week's walk away. But each time I made excuses, I forgot my plans. I forgot even the recurrence of my plans and each occasion was freshly determined. Fresh milk, eggs, cheese ... occasional meat. And yet more than the destination, it was the journey itself which excited me. With an odd sense of making my first preparations I washed my feet in the sink.

I returned to the bedroom transformed – as was usual when I made these plans – and was faintly impatient to find it unchanged. Diane's clothes and mine littered the furniture, dust and sunshine and objects packed the room. Diane had not moved since I left the room. She lay on her back on the bed, legs apart, right knee a little crooked, hand resting on her belly, mouth slack with a buried complaint. We failed to please each other, but we did talk. We were sentimentalists. She smiled and said, 'What was that you were singing?' When I told her of my plans she said, 'But I thought you were going to wait until Marie was older.' I remembered that now as merely an excuse for delay. 'She *is* older,' I insisted.

By Diane's bed there stood a low table with a thick glass top within which there was trapped a still cloud of delicate black smoke. On the table there was a telephone, its wire severed at four inches, and beyond that, propped against the wall, a cathode ray tube. The wooden casing, the glass screen and control buttons had long ago been ripped away and now bunches of bright wire curled about the dull metal. There were innumerable breakable objects — vases, ashtrays, glass bowls, Victorian or what Diane called Art Deco. I was never certain of the difference. We all scavenge for serviceable items, but like many others in her minimally privileged part of the city, Diane amassed items without function. She believed in interior decor, in style. We argued about these objects, once even bitterly. 'We no longer craft things,' she had said. 'Nor do we manufacture or mass-produce them. We make nothing, and I like things that are made, by craftsmen or by processes' (she had indicated the telephone), 'it doesn't matter, because they're still the products of human inventiveness and design. And not caring for objects is one step away from not caring for people.'

I had said, 'Collecting these things and setting them out like this amounts to self-love. Without a telephone system telephones are worthless junk.' Diane was eight years older than I. She had insisted that you cannot love other people or accept their love for you unless you love yourself. I thought that was trite, and the discussion ended in silence.

It was growing colder. We got between the sheets, me with my plans and clean feet, she with her fish. 'The point is,' I said referring to Marie's age, 'that you cannot survive now without a plan.' I lay with my head on Diane's arm and she drew me towards her breast. 'I know someone,' she began, and I knew she was introducing a lover, 'who wants to start a radio station. He doesn't know how to generate electricity. He doesn't know anyone who could build a transmitter or repair an old one. And even if he did, he knows there are no radios to pick up his signal. He talks vaguely about repairing old ones, of finding a book that will tell him how to do it. I say to him, "Radio stations cannot exist without an industrial society." And he says, "We'll see about that." You see, it's the pro-grammes he's interested in. He gets other people interested and they sit around talking about programmes. He wants only *live* music. He wants eighteenth-century chamber music in the early morning, but he knows there are no orchestras. In the evenings he meets his Marxist friends and they plan talks, courses, they discuss which line to take. There's a historian who has written a book and wants to read it aloud in twenty-six half-hour instalments.'

'It's no good trying to have the past all over again,' I said after a while. 'I don't care about the past, I want to make a future for Marie and myself.' I stopped and we both laughed, for as I denied the past I lay on Diane's breasts and spoke of living with my mother. It was an old joke between us. We drifted into reminiscences. Surrounded by Diane's mementoes it was easy enough to imagine the world outside the room as it once was, ordered and cala-mitous. We talked about one of the first days we spent together. I was eighteen, Diane twenty-six. We walked from Camden Town across Regent's Park, along an avenue of bare plane-trees. It was February, cold and bright. We bought tickets to the zoo because we had heard that it was soon to shut down. It was a disappointment, we wandered despondently from one cage, one moated folly of an environment to the next. The cold muted the animals' smell, the brightness illuminated their futility. We regretted the money spent on tickets. After all, the animals simply looked like their names, tigers, lions, penguins, elephants, no more, no less. We passed a better hour in the warm talking and drinking tea, the only customers in a vast café of infinite municipal sadness.

On our way out of the zoo we were drawn by the shouts of schoolchildren towards the chimpanzees. It was a cage in the style of an enormous aviary, a mean parody of the animals forgotten past. Between rhododendron bushes a jungle track curved, an irregular system of bars for swinging spanned the cage and there were two stunted trees. The shouts were for a powerful, bad-tempered male, the cage patriarch, who was terrorising the other chimpanzees. They scattered before him, and were disappearing through a small hole in the wall. Now all that remained was what looked like an elderly mother, perhaps she was a grandmother, round whose belly clung a baby chimpanzee. The male was after her. Screaming, she ran along the track and swung on to the bars. They flew round the cage. He was inches behind her. As her trailing hand left one bar, so his forward hand reached it.

The delighted children danced and screamed as she climbed higher and went faster. The baby clung, its small pink face, half-buried in tit and fur, described wide trajectories in the air. Now the two raced across the ceiling of the cage, the female jabbering as she flew and spattering the bars below with her bright green excrement. Suddenly the male lost interest and permitted his victims to escape through the hole in the wall. The schoolchildren moaned in disappointment. The cage was silent and still, chimpanzees appeared comically at the hole and looked out. The patriarch sat high in one corner gazing with bright, abstracted eyes over his shoulder. Slowly the cage filled and the mother returned with her baby. Glancing warily at her pursuer, she gathered up as much of her excrement as she could find and withdrew to a treetop where she could eat in comfort. From the end of her finger she fed small amounts to the baby. She looked down at the human spectators and stuck out her bright green tongue. The infant huddled against its protectress, the schoolchildren dispersed.

We lay in silence for many minutes after our reminiscences. The bed was small but comfortable and I felt drowsy. My eyes were already closed when Diane said, 'Memories like that don't bother me any more. Everything has changed so much I can hardly believe it was us who were there.' I heard her clearly but I could do no more than grunt in assent. I believed myself to be saying goodbye to Diane. Outside the day was sunny and warm. I leaned out of my car and waved to her where she stood at the window. I found I knew the controls perfectly, of course, I had always known. The car moved forward silently. I felt hungry and drove past restaurants and cafés but I did not stop. I had a destination, a friend in some distant suburb, but I did not know who. What I was driving along was called the Circle Road. The afternoon was warm, the traffic around me swift and agile, the landscape dehumanised and utterly comprehensible. Place names were illuminated on clinical road signs. A glaring tunnel tiled like a urinal swung from left to right through parabolic curves and pitched violently upwards into daylight. Men and women gunned their engines at traffic lights, faulty machines or incompetent drivers would not be tolerated. Through an open window ringed fingers drummed against the side of a car. Before a towering bra advertisement a man scrutinised his watch. Behind him the colossus tugged at her straps with frozen insouciance. The lights changed and we all leapt forward, content and contempt pressed into the set of our lips. I saw a sad boy astride a supermarket horse while his father stood by and smiled.

It was bitterly cold and growing dark. Diane was on the other side of the room lighting a candle. I lay in her bed watching her search for warmer clothes to put on. I felt sorry for her, living alone with all her antiques. We had such easy intimacy but my visits were rare, it was a long walk from south to north and back again, and a little dangerous.

I did not mention my dream. Diane pined for the age of machines and manufacture, for automobiles were once part of the texture of her life. She often spoke of the pleasure of driving a car, of travelling within a set of rules. Stop … Go … Fog Ahead. I was an indifferent passenger as a child and in my teens I watched their dwindling numbers from the pavement. Diane longed for rules. I said, 'I suppose I'd better go,' and began to get dressed. We stood shivering by the door.

'Promise me something,' said Diane.

'What is that?'

'That you won't leave for the country without coming to say goodbye.' I promised. We kissed and Diane said, 'I couldn't bear you both to leave without me knowing.'

As usual in the early evening there were a lot of people about. It was cold enough for street-corner fires to be lit and people stood around them and talked. Behind them their children played in the darkness. To make quicker progress I walked in the middle of the street, down long avenues of rusted, broken cars. It was downhill all the way into central London. I crossed the canal and entered Camden Town. I walked to Euston and turned up the Tottenham Court Road. Everywhere it was the same, people came out of their cold houses and huddled round fires. Some groups I passed stood in silence, staring into the flames; it was too early yet to go to sleep. I turned right at Cambridge Circus into Soho. At the corner of Frith Street and Old Compton Street there was a fire and

I stopped to rest and get warm. Two middle-aged men on either side of the fire were arguing passionately through the flames while the rest listened or stood dreaming on their feet. League football was a fading memory. Men like these would beat their brains out, or each other's, attempting to recall details that once came easily to mind. 'I was there, mate. They scored before half-time.' Without moving his feet the other pretended to walk away in disgust. 'Don't talk like daft,' he said. 'It was a goal-less draw.' They began to talk at the same time and it became difficult to listen.

Someone behind and to my right made a movement towards me and I turned. A small Chinaman stood just within the circle of light. His head was onion-shaped, he was smiling and beckoning with large sweeps of his arm, as though I stood on a distant hill-top. I took a couple of paces towards him and said. 'What do you want?' He wore the upper part of an old grey suit, and bright new drainpipe jeans. Where did he get new jeans? 'What do you want?' I said again. The little man breathed and sang at me. 'Come! You come!' Then he stepped out of the ring of light and disappeared.

The Chinaman walked several feet ahead and was barely visible. We crossed Shaftesbury Avenue into Gerrard Street and here I slowed to a shuffle and stretched my hands in front of my face. A few upper-storey windows gleamed dully, they gave a sense of the direction of the street but they shone no light into it. For several minutes I edged forwards, then the Chinaman lit a lamp. He was fifty yards ahead and stood holding the lamp level with his head, waiting. When I reached him he showed me a low doorway blocked by something square and black. It was a cupboard and as the man squeezed past it I saw by his lamp that beyond it there was a steep flight of stairs. The Chinaman hung the lamp inside the doorway. He lifted his end of the cupboard. I lifted mine. It was unnaturally heavy and we had to take it up one step at a time. To co-ordinate our efforts the Chinaman exhorted 'You come' in his breathing, singing voice. We developed a rhythm and left the lamp far below. A long time passed and the stairs seemed to be without end. 'You come … you come,' the Chinaman sang to me from inside his cupboard. At last a door opened ahead and yellow light and kitchen smells trickled down the stairwell. A taut, tenor voice of indeterminate sex spoke Chinese and somewhere further beyond a child cried.

I sat at a table scattered with biscuit crumbs and salt grains. At the other end of this crowded room the Chinaman was arguing with his wife, a tiny, strained woman with a face of tendons and twisting muscles. Behind them was a boarded-up window and beyond the door was a pile of mattresses and blankets. A few feet from where I sat two male infants, naked but for yellowish vests, stood bow-legged and drooling, watching me, their elbows extended for balance. A girl of about twelve years watched over them. Her face was a creamier version of her mother's, and her dress was her mother's too, far too large and gathered about the waist with a thin plastic belt. From a pot which simmered on a small wood fire came a thin, salty smell, mingling with the milk and urine smell of small children. I was uneasy, I regretted the lost privacy of my walk home in the dark, the contemplation of my plans, but an obscure sense of politeness prevented me from leaving.

I was developing my own version of the argument between man and wife. I knew of Chinese decorum. He was wanting to reward the guest for his help, it was a matter of honour. 'That's nonsense,' she was insisting. 'Look at that thick coat he's wearing. He has more than we do. It would be foolish and sentimental, when we have so little, to make gifts to such a man, however kind.'

'But he helped us,' her husband seemed to counter. 'We can't send him away with nothing. At least let's give him some supper.'

'No, no. There isn't enough.' The discussion was formal and restrained, barely rising above a whisper. Dissent was expressed by monologues which overlapped, the undulating tendons in the woman's neck, the man's left hand which clenched and unclenched. Silently I urged the woman on. I wished to be dismissed with gentle, courteous handshakes, never to return. I would walk southwards home and climb into bed. One of the infants, eyes fixed on mine, began to stagger towards me. I looked to the girl to intercept, who complied, but sullenly, and I suspected she held back longer than was necessary.

The argument was over, the woman was bending over a pile of mattresses preparing a bed for the babies, and her husband was watching her from a chair next to mine. The girl leaned against the wall and made a melancholy examination of her fingers. I played with the crumbs and grains. The Chinaman turned and smiled faintly at me. Then he addressed to his daughter an unbroken sentence of apparent complexity, the final section of which rose steadily in pitch while the expression on his face remained fixed. The girl looked at me and said dully, 'Dad says you gotta eat wiv us.' To clarify this her father pointed at my mouth and then to the pot. 'You come,' he said with enthusiasm. In the corner the mother spoke sharply to her children who lay at either end of a small mattress crying sleepily. I looked steadily in her direction hoping to catch her eye and have her approbation. Bored, the girl resumed her position against the wall, her father sat with folded arms and filmy, vacant eyes. I said, 'What does your mother think?' The girl shrugged and did not look up from her fingernails. Against hers my voice sounded hollow and cultivated, suggestive of laconic manipulation. 'What were your parents talking about just now?' She looked at the black cupboard. 'Mum says Dad paid too much for it.'

I decided to leave. To the Chinaman I pantomimed by making a sick face and pointing to my stomach that I was not hungry. My host seemed to take this to mean that I was too hungry to wait till suppertime. He spoke rapidly to his daughter, and when she answered he cut her off angrily. She shrugged and crossed to the fire. The room filled with a thin, hot, animal smell which resembled the taste of blood. I twisted round in my chair to speak to the girl. 'I don't want to offend your parents, but tell your Dad I'm not hungry and I've got to go.'

'I told him that already,' she said, and ladled something into a large white bowl which she set before me. She seemed to relish my situation. 'Neither of 'em listen,' she said, and returned to her part of the wall.

In a large quantity of clear hot water several dun-coloured globes, partially submerged, drifted and collided noiselessly. The Chinaman's face puckered in encouragement. 'You come.' I was aware of the woman watching me from her side of the room. 'What is it?' I asked the girl.

'It's muck,' she said vaguely. Then she changed her mind and hissed vehemently. 'It's *piss*.' With a low chuckle and small flourish of his dry hands the Chinaman appeared to celebrate his daughter's mastery of a difficult language. Watched by all the family I picked up the spoon. The babies were quiet in their corner. I took two rapid sips and smiled up at the parents through the unswallowed liquid. 'Good,' I said at last, and then to the girl. 'Tell them it's good.' Once again not looking up from her fingernails she said, 'I'd leave it if I was you.' I manoeuvred one of the globes on to my spoon, it was surprisingly heavy. I did not ask the girl what it was, for I knew what she would say.

I swallowed it and stood up. I offered my hand to the Chinaman in farewell, but he and his wife stared and did not move. 'G'wan, just go,' the girl said with resignation. I moved slowly round the table, fearful of vomiting. As I reached the door something the girl said caused the mother to become suddenly angry. She was shouting at her husband and pointing at my bowl from which there still rose, as if in accusation, a fine white trace of steam. The Chinaman sat quietly, apparently indifferent. Now the furious woman lay into her daughter, who abruptly turned her back and would not listen. Father and daughter seemed to wait for silence for a cord to snap in the tiny woman's neck, and I too waited, half-concealed by the cupboard, hoping to go forward and ease the situation and my conscience with friendly goodbyes. But the room and its people were an unmoving tableau. Only the shouting carried forward so I slipped away unnoticed down the stairs.

The lamp still burned above the doorway. Knowing the difficulty of finding paraffin I turned it out, then stepped into the black street.

Dead As They Come

I do not care for posturing women. But she *struck* me. I had to stop and look at her. The legs were well apart, the right foot boldly advanced, the left trailing with studied casualness. She held her right hand before her, almost touching the window, the fingers thrusting up like a beautiful flower. The left hand she held a little behind her and seemed to push down playful lapdogs. Head well back, a faint smile, eyes half-closed with boredom or pleasure. I could not tell. Very artificial the whole thing, but then I am not a simple man. She was a beautiful woman. I saw her most days, sometimes two or three times. And of course she struck other postures as the mood took her. Sometimes as I hurried by (I am a man in a hurry) I allowed myself a quick glance and she seemed to beckon me, to welcome me out of the cold. Other days I remember seeing her in that tired, dejected passivity which fools mistake for femininity.

I began to take notice of the clothes she wore. She was a fashionable woman, naturally. In a sense it was her job. But she had none of the sexless, mincing stiffness of those barely animated clothes-hangers who display *haute couture* in stuffy salons to the sound of execrable musak. No, she was another class of being. She did not exist merely to present a style, a current mode. She was above that, she was *beyond* that. Her clothes were peripheral to her beauty. She would have looked good dressed in old paper bags.

She disdained her clothes, she discarded them every day for others. Her beauty shone through those clothes . . . and yet they were beautiful clothes. It was autumn. She wore capes of deep russet browns, or twirling peasant skirts of orange and green, or harsh trouser suits of burnt ochre. It was spring. She wore skirts of passion-fruit gingham, white calico shirts or lavish dresses of cerulean green and blue. Yes, I noticed her clothes, for she understood, as only the great portrait painters of the eighteenth century understood, the sumptuous possibilities of fabric, the subtleties of folds, the nuance of crease and hem. Her body in its rippling changes of posture, adapted itself to the unique demands of each creation; with breathless grace the lines of her perfect body played tender counterpoint with the shifting arabesques of sartorial artifice.

But I digress. I bore you with lyricism. The days came and passed. I saw her this day and not that, and perhaps twice on another day. Imperceptibly seeing her and not seeing her became a factor in my life, and then before I knew it, it passed from factor to structure. Would I see her today? Would all my hours and minutes be redeemed? Would she look at me? Did she remember me from one time to another? Was there a future for us together . . . would I ever have the courage to approach her? Courage! What did all my millions mean now, what now of my wisdom matured by the ravages of three marriages? I loved her . . . I wished to possess her. And to possess her it seemed I would have to buy her.

I must tell you something about myself. I am wealthy. Possibly there are ten men resident in London with more money than I. Probably there are only five or six. Who cares? I am rich and I made my money on the telephone. I shall be forty-five on Christmas Day. I have been married three times, each marriage lasting, in chrono-logical order, eight, five and two years. These last three years I have not been married and yet I have not been idle. I have not paused. A man of forty-four has no time to pause. I am a man in a hurry. Each throb of jism from the seminal vesicles, or wherever it originates, lessens the total allowance of my lifespan by one. I have no time for the analysis, the self-searching of frenzied relationships, the unspoken accusation, the silent defence. I do not wish to be with women who have an urge to talk when we've finished our coupling. I want to lie still in peace and clarity. Then I want to put my shoes and socks on and comb my hair and go about my business. I prefer silent women who take their pleasure with apparent indifference. All day long there are voices around me, on the telephone, at lunches, at business conferences. I do not want voices in my bed. I am not a simple man, I repeat, and this is not a simple world. But in this respect at least my requisites are simple, perhaps even facile. My predilection is for pleasure unmitigated by the yappings and whinings of the soul.

Or rather it was, for that was all before … before I loved *her*, before I knew the sickening elation of total self-destruction for a meaningless cause. What do I, now, forty-five on Christmas Day, care for meaning? Most days I passed by her shop and looked in at her. Those early days when a glance was sufficient and I hurried on to meet this business friend or that lover … I can pick out no time when I knew myself to be in love. I have described how a factor in my life became a structure, it merged as orange to red in the rainbow. Once I was a man hurrying by a shop window and glancing carelessly in. Then I was a man in love with … simply, I was a man in love. It happened over many months. I began to linger by the window. The others … the other women in the shop window display meant nothing to me. Wherever my Helen stood I could pick her out at a glance. They were mere dummies (oh my love) beneath contempt. Life was generated in her by the sheer charge of her beauty. The delicate mould of her eyebrow, the perfect line of her nose, the smile, the eyes half-closed with boredom or pleasure (how could I tell?). For a long time I was content to look at her through the glass, happy to be within a few feet of her. In my madness I wrote her letters, yes, I even did that and I still have them. I called her Helen ('Dear Helen, give me a sign. I know you know' etc.). But soon I loved her completely and wished to possess her, own her, absorb her, eat her. I wanted her in my arms and in my bed, I longed that she should open her legs to me. I could not rest till I was between her pale thighs, till my tongue had prised those lips. I knew that soon I would have to enter the shop and ask to buy her.

Simple, I hear you say. You're a rich man. You could buy the shop if you wanted. You could buy the street. Of course I could buy the street, and many other streets too. But listen. This was no mere business transaction. I was not about to acquire a site for redevelopment. In business you make offers, you take risks. But in this matter I could not risk failure, for I wanted my Helen, I *needed* my Helen. My profound fear was that my desperation would give me away. I could not be sure that in negotiating the sale I could keep a steady hand. If I blurted out too high a price the shop manager would want to know why. If it was valuable to me, why then, he would naturally conclude (for was he not a business man too?) it must be valuable to someone else. Helen had been in that shop many months. Perhaps, and this thought began to torment my every waking minute, they would take her away and destroy her.

I knew I must act soon and I was afraid.

I chose Monday, a quiet day in any shop. I was not sure whether quietness was on my side. I could have had Saturday, a busy day, but then, a quiet day ... a busy day ... my decisions countered each other like parallel mirrors. I had lost many hours of sleep, I was rude to my friends, virtually impotent with my lovers, my business skills were beginning to deteriorate, I had to choose and I chose Monday. It was October, raining a fine, bitter drizzle. I dismissed my chauffeur for the day and drove to the shop. Shall I slavishly follow the foolish conventions and describe it to you, the first home of my tender Helen? I do not really care to. It was a large shop, a store, a department store and it dealt seriously and solely in clothes and related items for women. It had moving staircases and a muffled air of boredom. Enough. I had a plan. I walked in.

How many details of this negotiation must be set down before that moment when I held my precious in my arms? A few and quickly. I spoke to an assistant. She consulted with another. They fetched a third, and the third sent a fourth for a fifth who turned out to be the under-manageress in charge of window design. They clustered round me like inquisitive children, sensing my wealth and power but not my anxiety. I warned them all I had a strange request and they shifted uneasily from one foot to the other and avoided my eye. I addressed these five women urgently. I wanted to buy one of the coats in the window display, I told them. It was for my wife, I told them, and I also wanted the boots and scarf that went with the coat. It was my wife's birthday, I said. I wanted the dummy (ah my Helen) on which these clothes were displayed in order to show off the clothes to their best advantage. I confided in them my little birthday trick. My wife would open the bedroom door lured there by some trivial domestic matter invented by myself, and there would stand ... could they not see it? I recreated the scene vividly for them. I watched them closely. I brought them on. They lived through the thrill of a birthday surprise.

They smiled, they glanced at each other. They risked glancing into my eyes. What a kind husband was this! They became, each one, my wife. And of course I was willing to pay a little extra ... but no, the under-manageress would not hear of it. Please accept it with the compliments of the shop. The under-manageress led me towards the window display. She led, and I followed through a blood-red mist. Perspiration dribbled from the palms of my hands. My eloquence had drained away, my tongue glued to my teeth and all I could do was feebly lift my hand in the direction of Helen. 'That one,' I whispered.

Once I was a man hurrying by a shop window and glancing carelessly in ... then I was a man in love, a man carrying his love in his arms through the rain to a waiting car. True, they had offered in the shop to fold and pack the clothes to save them from creasing. But show me the man who will carry his true love naked through the streets in an October rain. How I blabbered with joy as I bore Helen through the streets. And how she hung close to me, clinging tightly to my lapels like a newborn monkey. Oh, my sweetness. Gently I laid her across the back seat of my car and gently drove her home.

At home I had everything prepared. I knew she would want to rest as soon as we came in. I brought her into the bedroom, removed her boots and settled her down between the crisp white bed linen. I kissed her softly on the cheek and before my eyes she fell into a deep slumber. For a couple of hours I busied myself in the library, catching up on important business. I felt serene now, I was illuminated by a steady inner glow. I was capable of intense concentration. I tiptoed into the bedroom where she lay. In sleep her features dissolved into an expression of great tenderness and understanding. Her lips were slightly apart. I knelt down and kissed them. Back in the library

I sat in front of a log fire with a glass of port in my hand. I reflected on my life, my marriages, my recent desperation. All the unhappiness of the past seemed now to have been necessary to make the present possible. I had my Helen now. She lay sleeping in my bed, in my house. She cared for no one else. She was mine.

Ten o'clock came and I slipped into bed beside her. I did it quietly, but I knew she was awake. It is touching now to recall that we did not immediately make love. No, we lay side by side (how warm she was) and we talked. I told her of the time I had first seen her, of how my love for her had grown and of how I had schemed to secure her release from the shop. I told her of my three marriages, my business and my love affairs. I was determined to keep no secrets from her. I told her of the things I had been thinking about as I sat in front of the fire with my glass of port. I spoke of the future, our future together. I told her I loved her, yes I think I told her that many times. She listened with the quiet intensity I was to learn to respect in her. She stroked my hand, she gazed wonderingly into my eyes. I undressed her. Poor girl. She had no clothes on under her coat, she had nothing in the world but me. I drew her close to me, her naked body against mine, and as I did so I saw her wide-eyed look of fear ... she was a virgin. I murmured in her ear. I assured her of my gentleness, my expertise, my control. Between her thighs I caressed with my tongue the fetid warmth of her virgin lust. I took her hand and set her pliant fingers about my throbbing manhood (oh her cool hands). 'Do not be afraid,' I whispered, 'do not be afraid.' I slid into her easily, quietly like a giant ship into night berth. The quick flame of pain I saw in her eyes was snuffed by long agile fingers of pleasure. I have never known such pleasure, such total accord ... almost total, for I must confess there was a shadow I could not dispel. She had been a virgin, now she was a demanding lover. She demanded the orgasm I could not give her, she would not let me go, she would not permit me to rest. On and on through the night, she forever teetering on the edge of that cliff, release in that most gentle death ... but nothing I did, and I did everything, I gave everything, could bring her to it. At last, it must have been five o'clock in the morning, I broke away from her, delirious with fatigue, anguished and hurt by my failure. Once again we lay side by side, and this time I felt in her silence inarticulate rebuke. Had I not brought her from the shop where she had lived in relative peace, had I not brought her to this bed and boasted to her of my expertise? I took her hand. It was stiff and unfriendly. It came to me in a panic-filled moment that Helen might leave me. It was a fear that was to return much later. There was nothing to stop her. She had no money, virtually no skills. No clothes. But she could leave me all the same. There were other men. She could go back and work in the shop. 'Helen,' I said urgently. 'Helen ... ' She lay perfectly still, seeming to hold her breath. 'It will come, you see, it will come,' and with that I was inside her again, moving slowly, imperceptibly, bringing her with me every step of the way. It took an hour of slow acceleration, and as the grey October dawn pierced the brooding London clouds she died, she came, she left this sublunary world ... her first orgasm. Her limbs went rigid, her eyes stared into nowhere and a deep inner spasm swept through her like an ocean wave. Then she slept in my arms.

I woke late the following morning. Helen still lay across my arm but I managed to slip out of bed without waking her. I put on a particularly resplendent dressing-gown, a present from my second wife, and went into the kitchen to make myself coffee. I felt myself to be a different man. I looked at the objects around me, the Utrillo on the kitchen wall, a famous forgery of a Rodin statuette, yesterday's newspapers. They radiated originality, unfamiliarity. I wanted to touch things. I ran my hands over the grain of the kitchen table top. I took delight in pouring my coffee beans into the grinder and in taking from the fridge a ripe grapefruit. I was in love with the world, for I had found my perfect mate. I loved Helen and I knew myself to be loved. I felt free. I read the morning paper at great speed and later in the same day could still remember names of foreign ministers and the countries they represented. I dictated half a dozen letters over the phone, shaved, showered and dressed. When I looked in on Helen she was still asleep, exhausted by pleasure. Even when she woke she would not want to get up till she had some clothes to wear. I had my chauffeur drive me to the West End and I spent the afternoon there buying clothes. It would be crude of me to mention how much I spent, but let me say that few men earn as much in a year. However, I did not buy her a bra. I have always despised them as objects, and yet only student girls and New Guinea natives seem to do without them. Furthermore my Helen did not like them either, which was fortunate.

She was awake when I returned. I had my chauffeur carry the parcels into the dining room and then I dismissed him. I myself carried the parcels from the dining room to the bedroom. Helen was delighted. Her eyes gleamed and she was breathless for joy. Together we chose what she was to wear that evening, a long, pure silk evening dress of pale blue. Leaving her to contemplate what amounted to over two hundred separate items, I hurried into the kitchen to prepare a lavish meal. As soon as I had a spare few minutes I returned to help Helen dress. She stood quite still, quite relaxed while I stood back to admire her. It was of course a perfect fit. But more than

that I saw once more her genius for *wearing* clothes, I was
beauty in another being as no man has ever seen it, I saw
... it was art, it was the total consummation of line and
form that art alone can realise. She seemed luminescent.
We stood in silence and gazed into one another's eyes.
Then I asked her if she would like me to show her round
the house.

I brought her into the kitchen first. I demonstrated its
many gadgets. I pointed out the Utrillo on the wall (she
was not very fond, I found out later, of painting). I showed
her the Rodin forgery and I even offered to let her hold it
in her hand but she demurred. Next I took her into the
bathroom and showed her the sunken marble bath and
how to operate the taps that made the water spew from
the mouths of alabaster lions. I wondered if she thought
that a little vulgar. She said nothing. I ushered her into
the dining room ... once again paintings which I rather
bored her with. I showed her my study, my first folio
Shakespeares, assorted rarities and many telephones. Then
the conference room. There was no need for her to see it
really. Perhaps by this time I was beginning to show off a
little. Finally the vast living space I simply call the room.
Here I spend my leisure hours. I shall not hurl more
details at you like so many over-ripe tomatoes ... it is
comfortable and not a little exotic.

I sensed immediately that Helen liked the room. She
stood in the doorway, hands by her side taking it all in.
I brought her over to a large soft chair, sat her down and
poured her the drink she so much needed, a dry martini.
Then I left her and for the next hour devoted my full
attention to the cooking of our meal. What passed that
evening was quite certainly the most civilised few hours I
have ever shared with a woman or, for that matter, with
another person. I have cooked many meals in my home
for lady friends. Without hesitation I describe myself as an

excellent cook. One of the very best. But until this particular occasion these evenings have always been dogged by my guest's conditioned guilt that it was I in the kitchen and not she, that it was I who carried in the dishes and carried them away at the end. And throughout my guest would express continual surprise that I, thrice divorced and a man to boot, was capable of such triumphs of cuisine. Not so Helen. She was my guest and that was the end of it. She did not attempt to invade my kitchen, she did not perpetually coo, 'Is there something I can *do*?' She sat back as a guest should and let herself be served by me. Yes, and the conversation. With those other guests of mine I always felt conversation to be an obstacle course over ditches and fences of contradiction, competition, misunderstanding and so on. My ideal conversation is one which allows both participants to develop their thoughts to their fullest extent, uninhibitedly, without endlessly defining and refining premises and defending conclusions. Without ever reaching conclusions. With Helen I could converse ideally, I could *talk* to her. She sat quite still, her eyes fixed at a point several inches in front of her plate, and listened. I told her many things I had never spoken out loud before. Of my childhood, my father's death rattle, my mother's terror of sexuality, my own sexual initiation with an elder cousin; I spoke of the state of the world, of the nation, of decadence, liberalism, contemporary novels, of marriage, ecstasy and disease. Before we knew it five hours had passed and we had drunk four bottles of wine and half a bottle of port. Poor Helen. I had to carry her to bed and undress her. We lay down, our limbs entwined and we could do nothing more than fall into the deepest, most contented sleep.

So ended our first day together, and thus was the pattern set for many happy months to follow. I was a happy man. I divided my time between Helen and making money. The latter I carried through with effortless success. In fact so rich did I become over this period that the government of the day felt it was dangerous for me not to have an influential post. I accepted the knighthood, of course, and Helen and I celebrated in grand style. But I refused to serve the government in any capacity, so thoroughly did I associate it with my second wife, who appeared to wield great influence among its front bench. Autumn turned to winter and then soon there was blossom on the almond trees in my garden, soon the first tender green leaves were appearing on my avenue of oaks. Helen and I lived in perfect harmony which nothing could disturb. I made money, I made love, I talked, Helen listened.

But I was a fool. Nothing lasts. Everyone knows that, but no one believes there are not exemptions. The time has come, I regret, to tell you of my chauffeur, Brian.

Brian was the perfect chauffeur. He did not speak unless spoken to, and then only to concur. He kept his past, his ambitions, his character a secret, and I was glad because I did not wish to know where he came from, where he was going or who he thought he was. He drove competently and outrageously fast. He always knew where to park. He was always at the front of any queue of traffic, and he was rarely in a queue. He knew every short cut, every street in London. He was tireless. He would wait up for me all night at an address, without recourse to cigarettes or pornographic literature. He kept the car, his boots and his uniform spotless. He was pale, thin and neat and I guessed his age to be somewhere between eighteen and thirty-five.

Now it might surprise you to know that, proud as I was of her, I did not introduce Helen to my friends. I introduced her to no one. She did not seem to need any company other than mine and I was content to let matters rest. Why should I begin to drag her round the tedious

social circuit of wealthy London? And, furthermore, she
was rather shy, even of me at first. Brian was not made an
exception of. Without making too obvious a secret of it,
I did not let him enter a room if Helen was in there. And
if I wanted Helen to travel with me then I dismissed Brian
for the day (he lived over the garage) and drove the car
myself.

All very clear and simple. But things began to go wrong
and I can remember vividly the day it all began. Towards
the middle of May I came home from a uniquely tiring
and exasperating day. I did not know it then (I suspected it) but I had lost almost half a million pounds due
to an error that was completely my own. Helen was
sitting in her favourite chair doing nothing in particular,
and there was something in her look as I came through the
door, something so elusive, so indefinably cool that I had
to pretend to ignore it. I drank a couple of scotches and
felt better. I sat down beside her and began to tell her of
my day, of what had gone wrong, how it had been my
fault, how I had impulsively blamed someone else and had
to apologise later ... and so on, the caries of a bad day
which one has the right to display only to one's mate. But
I had been speaking for a little less than thirty-five
minutes when I realised that Helen was not listening at all.
She was gazing woodenly at her hands which lay across
her knees. She was far, far away. It was such a dreadful
realisation that I could do nothing for the moment (I was
paralysed) but carry on talking. And then I could stand
it no more. I stopped mid-sentence and stood up. I walked
out the room, slamming the door behind me. At no point
did Helen look up from her hands. I was furious, too
furious to talk to her. I sat out in the kitchen drinking from
the bottle of scotch I had remembered to bring with me.
Then I had a shower.

By the time I went back into the room I felt considerably better. I was relaxed, a little drunk and ready to forget the whole matter. Helen too seemed more amenable. At first I was going to ask her what the trouble had been, but we started talking about my day again and in no time we were our old selves again. It seemed pointless going back over things when we were getting on so well. But an hour after dinner the front door bell rang — a rare occurrence in the evening. As I got up from my chair I happened to glance across at Helen and I saw pass across her face that same look of fear she had the night we first made love. It was Brian at the door. He had in his hand a piece of paper for me to sign. Something in connection with the car, something that could have waited till the morning. As I glanced over what it was I was supposed to sign, I saw out of the corner of my eye that Brian was surreptitiously peering over my shoulder into the hallway. 'Looking for something?' I said sharply. 'No sir,' he said. I signed and closed the door. I remembered that because the car was at the garage for servicing Brian had been at home all day. I had taken a taxi to my offices. This fact and Helen's strangeness ... such a sickness came over me when I associated the two that I thought for a moment I was going to vomit and I hurried into the bathroom.

However, I did not vomit. Instead I looked into the mirror. I saw there a man who in less than seven months would be forty-five, a man with three marriages etched about his eyes, the corner of whose mouth drooped downwards from a lifetime talking on the phone. I splashed cold water on my face and joined Helen in the room. 'That was Brian,' I said. She said nothing, she could not look at me. My own voice sounded nasal and toneless. 'He doesn't usually call in the evenings ... ' And still she said nothing. What did I expect? That she suddenly be of a mind to confess an affair with my chauffeur? Helen was a silent woman, she did not find it hard to conceal her feelings.

Nor could I confess what I felt. I was too afraid of being right. I could not bear to hear her confirm the very idea that threatened again to make me vomit. I merely threw out my remarks to make her shore up her pretence ... I so badly wanted to hear it all denied even while knowing the denial to be false. In short, I understood myself to be in Helen's power.

That night we did not sleep together. I made myself up a bed in one of the guest rooms. I did not want to sleep alone, in fact the idea was hateful to me. I suppose (I was so confused) that I wanted to go through the motions so that Helen would ask me what I was doing. I wanted to hear her express surprise that after all these happy months together I was suddenly, without one word being said, making my bed in another room. I wanted to be told not to be foolish, to come to bed, our bed. But she said nothing, absolutely nothing. She took it all for granted ... this was the situation now and no longer could we share a bed. Her silence was deadly confirmation. Or was there a slender possibility (I lay awake in my new bed) that she was simply angry at my moodiness. Now I was really confused. On and on into the night I turned the matter over in my mind. Perhaps she had never even seen Brian. Could the entire matter be of my own imagining? After all, I had had a bad day. But that was absurd, for here was the reality of the situation ... separate beds ... and yet what *should* I have done? What should I have said? I considered every possibility, good lines, cunning silences, terse aphoristic remarks that ripped away at the flimsy veil of appearance. Was she awake now like me, thinking about all this? Or was she fast asleep? How could I find out without appearing to be awake? What would happen if she left me? I was completely at her mercy.

I should bankrupt language if I tried to convey the texture of my existence over the following weeks. It had the arbitrary horror of a nightmare, I seemed a roast on a spit which Helen turned slowly with a free hand. It would be wrong of me to attempt to argue in retrospect that the situation was of my own making; but I do know now that I could have ended my misery sooner. It became established that I slept in the guest room. My pride prevented me from returning to our nuptial bed. I wanted Helen to take the initiative on that. It was she after all who had so much explaining to do. I was adamant on this point, it was my only certainty in a time of bleak confusion. I had to hang on tightly to something … and you see I survived. Helen and I barely talked. We were cold and distant. Each avoided the other's eye. My folly was in thinking that if I remained silent long enough it would somehow break her down and make her want to speak to me, to tell me what she thought was happening to us. And so I roasted. At night I woke from bad dreams shouting and I sulked in the afternoons and tried to think it all out clearly. I had to carry on my business. Often I had to be out of the house, sometimes hundreds of miles away, certain that Brian and Helen were celebrating my absence. Sometimes I phoned home from hotels or airport lounges. No one ever answered, and yet I heard between each throb of the electronic tones Helen in the bedroom gasping with mounting pleasure. I lived in a black valley on the verge of tears. The sight of a small child playing with her dog, the setting sun reflected in a river, a poignant line of advertising copy were enough to dissolve me. When I returned home from business trips, desolate, craving friendship and love, I sensed from the moment I stepped through the door that Brian had been there not long before me. Nothing tangible beyond the *feel* of him in the air, something in the arrangement of the bed, some different smell in the bathroom, the position of the decanter of scotch on its tray. Helen pretended not to see me as I prowled in anguish from room to room, she pretended not to hear my sobs in the bath-room. It might be asked why I did not dismiss my chauffeur. The answer is simple. I feared that if Brian left Helen would follow. I gave my chauffeur no indications of my feelings. I gave him his orders and he drove me, maintaining as he always had his faceless obsequiousness. I observed nothing different in his behaviour, though I did not care to regard him too closely. It is my belief that he never knew that I knew, and this at least gave me the illusion of power over him.

But these are shadowy, peripheral subtleties. Essentially I was a disintegrating man, I was coming apart. I was falling asleep at the telephone. My hair began to loose itself from my scalp. My mouth filled with cankers and my breath had about it the stench of a decaying carcass. I observed my business friends take a step backwards when I spoke. I nurtured a vicious boil in my anus. I was losing. I was beginning to understand the futility of my silent waiting games with Helen. In reality there was no situation between us to play with. All day long she sat in her chair if I was in the house. Sometimes she sat there all night. On many occasions I would have to leave the house early in the morning, leave her sitting in her chair gazing at the figures in the carpet; and when I returned home late at night she would be still there. Heaven knows I wanted to help her. I loved her. But I could do nothing till she helped me. I was locked in the miserable dungeon of my mind and the situation seemed utterly hopeless. Once I was a man hurrying by a shop window and glanc-ing carelessly in, now I was a man with bad breath, boils and cankers. I was coming apart.

In the third week of this nightmare, when there seemed nothing else I could do, I broke the silence. It was all or nothing. Throughout that day I walked in Hyde Park summoning the remaining shreds of my reason, my will power, my suaveness for the confrontation I had decided would take place that evening. I drank a little less than a third of a bottle of scotch, and towards seven o'clock I tiptoed to her bedroom where she had been lying for the past two days. I knocked softly, then, hearing no reply, entered. She lay fully dressed on the bed, arms by her side. She wore a pale cotton smock. Her legs were well apart and her head inclined against a pillow. There was barely a gleam of recognition when I stood before her. My heart was pounding wildly and the stench of my breath filled the room like poisonous smoke. 'Helen,' I said, and had to stop to clear my throat. 'Helen, we can't go on like this. It's time we talked.' And then, without giving her a chance to reply, I told her everything. I told her I knew about her affair. I told her about my boil. I knelt at her bedside. 'Helen,' I cried, 'it's meant so much to both of us. We must fight to save it.' There was silence. My eyes were closed and I thought I saw my own soul recede from me across a vast black void till it was a pinprick of red light. I looked up, I looked into her eyes and saw there quiet, naked contempt. It was all over, and I conceived in that frenzied instant two savage and related desires. To rape and destroy her. With one sudden sweep of my hand I ripped the smock clean off her body. She had nothing on underneath. Before she had time to even draw breath I was on her, I was in her, rammed deep inside while my right hand closed about her tender white throat. With my left I smothered her face with the pillow.

I came as she died. That much I can say with pride. I know her death was a moment of intense pleasure to her. I heard her shouts through the pillow. I will not bore you with rhapsodies on my own pleasure. It was a transfiguration. And now she lay dead in my arms. It was some minutes before I comprehended the enormity of my deed. My dear, sweet, tender Helen lay dead in my arms, dead and pitifully naked. I fainted. I awoke what seemed many hours later, I saw the corpse and before I had time to turn my head I vomited over it. Like a sleepwalker I drifted into the kitchen, I made straight for the Utrillo and tore it to shreds. I dropped the Rodin forgery into the garbage disposal. Now I was running like a naked madman from room to room destroying whatever I could lay my hands on. I stopped only to finish the scotch. Vermeer, Blake, Richard Dadd, Paul Nash, Rothke, I tore, trampled, mangled, kicked, spat and urinated on ... my precious possessions ... oh my precious ... I danced, I sang, I laughed ... I wept long into the night.

In Between the Sheets

That night Stephen Cooke had a wet dream, the first in many years. Afterwards he lay awake on his back, hands behind his head, while its last images receded in the darkness and his cum, strangely located across the small of his back, turned cold. He lay still till the light was blueish-grey, and then he took a bath. He lay there a long time too, staring sleepily at his bright body under water.

That preceding day he had kept an appointment with his wife in a fluorescent café with red formica table tops. It was five o'clock when he arrived and almost dark. As he expected he was there before her. The waitress was an Italian girl, nine or ten years old perhaps, her eyes heavy and dull with adult cares. Laboriously she wrote out the word 'coffee' twice on her notepad, tore the page in half and carefully laid one piece on his table, face downwards. Then she shuffled away to operate the vast and gleaming Gaggia machine. He was the café's only customer.

His wife was observing him from the pavement outside. She disliked cheap cafés and she would make sure he was there before she came in. He noticed her as he turned in his seat to take his coffee from the child. She stood behind the shoulder of his own reflected image, like a ghost, half-hidden in a doorway across the street. No doubt she believed he could not see out of a bright café into the darkness. To reassure her he moved his chair to give her a more complete view of his face. He stirred his coffee and watched the waitress who leaned against the counter in a trance, and who now drew a long silver thread from her nose. The thread snapped and settled on the end of her forefinger, a colourless pearl. She glared at it briefly and spread it across her thighs, so finely it disappeared.

When his wife came in she did not look at him at first. She went straight to the counter and ordered a coffee from the girl and carried it to the table herself.

'I wish,' she hissed as she unwrapped her sugar, 'you wouldn't pick places like this.' He smiled indulgently and downed his coffee in one. She finished hers in careful pouting sips. Then she took a small mirror and some tissues from her bag. She blotted her red lips and swabbed from an incisor a red stain. She crumpled the tissue into her saucer and snapped her bag shut. Stephen watched the tissue absorb the coffee slop and turn grey. He said, 'Have you got another one of those I can have?' She gave him two.

'You're not going to cry are you?' At one such meeting he had cried. He smiled. 'I want to blow my nose.' The Italian girl sat down at a table near theirs and spread out several sheets of paper. She glanced across at them, and then leaned forwards till her nose was inches from the table. She began to fill in columns of numbers. Stephen murmured, 'She's doing the accounts.'

His wife whispered, 'It shouldn't be allowed, a child of that age.' Finding themselves in rare agreement, they looked away from each other's faces.

'How's Miranda?' Stephen said at last.

'She's all right.'

'I'll be over to see her this Sunday.'

'If that's what you want.'

'And the other thing ... ' Stephen kept his eyes on the girl who dangled her legs now and day-dreamed. Or perhaps she was listening.

'Yes?'

'The other thing is that when the holidays start I want Miranda to come and spend a few days with me.'

'She doesn't want to.'

'I'd rather hear that from her.'

'She won't tell you herself. You'll make her feel guilty if you ask her.' He banged the table hard with his open hand.

'Listen!' He almost shouted. The child looked up and Stephen felt her reproach. 'Listen,' he said quietly, 'I'll speak to her on Sunday and judge for myself.'

'She won't come,' said his wife, and snapped shut her bag once more as if their daughter lay curled up inside. They both stood up. The girl stood up too and came over to take Stephen's money, accepting a large tip without recognition. Outside the café Stephen said, 'Sunday then.' But his wife was already walking away and did not hear.

That night he had the wet dream. The dream itself concerned the café, the girl and the coffee machine. It ended in sudden and intense pleasure, but for the moment the details were beyond recall. He got out of the bath hot and dizzy, on the edge, he thought, of an hallucination. Balanced on the side of the bath, he waited for it to wear off, a certain warping of the space between objects. He dressed and went outside, into the small garden of dying trees he shared with other residents in the square. It was seven o'clock. Already Drake, self-appointed custodian of the garden, was down on his knees by one of the benches. Paint-scraper in one hand, a bottle of colourless liquid in the other.

'Pigeon crap,' Drake barked at Stephen. 'Pigeons crap and no one can sit down. No one.' Stephen stood behind the old man, his hands deep in his pockets, and watched him work at the grey and white stains. He felt comforted. Round the edge of the garden ran a narrow path worn to a trough by the daily traffic of dog walkers, writers with blocks and married couples in crisis.

Walking there now Stephen thought, as he often did, of Miranda his daughter. On Sunday she would be fourteen, today he should find her a present. Two months ago she sent him a letter. 'Dear Daddy, are you looking after yourself? Can I have twenty-five pounds please to buy a record-player? With all my love, Miranda.' He replied by return post and regretted it the instant the letter left his hands. 'Dear Miranda, I *am* looking after myself, but not sufficiently to comply with … etc.' In effect it was his wife he had addressed. At the sorting office he spoke to a sympathetic official who led him away by the elbow. You wish to retrieve a letter? This way please. They passed through a glass door and stepped out on to a small balcony. The kindly official indicated with a sweep of his hand the spectacular view, two acres of men, women, machinery and moving conveyor belts. Now where would you like us to start?

Returning to his point of departure for the third time he noticed that Drake was gone. The bench was spotless and smelling of spirit. He sat down. He had sent Miranda thirty pounds, three new ten-pound notes in a registered letter. He regretted that too. The extra five so clearly spelled out his guilt. He spent two days over a letter to her, fumbling, with reference to nothing in particular, maudlin. 'Dear Miranda, I heard some pop music on the radio the other day and I couldn't help wondering at the words which … ' To such a letter he could conceive of no reply. But it came about ten days later. 'Dear Daddy, thanks for the money. I bought a Musivox Junior the same as my friend Charmian. With all my love, Miranda. PS It's got two speakers.'

Back indoors he made coffee, took it into his study and fell into the mild trance which allowed him to work three and a half hours without a break. He reviewed a pamphlet on Victorian attitudes to menstruation, he completed another three pages of a short story he was writing, he wrote a little in his random journal. He typed, 'nocturnal emission like an old man's last gasp' and crossed it out. From a drawer he took a thick ledger and entered in the credit column 'Review ... 1500 words. Short story ... 1020 words. Journal ... 60 words'. Taking a red biro from a box marked 'pens' he ruled off the day, closed the book and returned it to its drawer. He replaced the dust-cover on his typewriter, returned the telephone to its cradle, gathered up the coffee things on to a tray and carried them out, locking the study door behind him, thus terminating the morning's rite, unchanged for twenty-three years.

He moved quickly up Oxford Street gathering presents for his daughter's birthday. He bought a pair of jeans, a pair of coloured canvas running shoes suggestive of the Stars and Stripes. He bought three coloured T-shirts with funny slogans ... It's Raining In My Heart, Still a Virgin, and Ohio State University. He bought a pomander and a game of dice from a woman in the street and a necklace of plastic beads. He bought a book about women heroes, a game with mirrors, a record token for £5, a silk scarf and a glass pony. The silk scarf putting him in mind of underwear, he returned to the shop determined.

The erotic, pastel hush of the lingerie floor aroused in him a sense of taboo, he longed to lie down somewhere. He hesitated at the entrance to the department then turned back. He bought a bottle of cologne on another floor and came home in a mood of gloomy excitement. He arranged his presents on the kitchen table and surveyed them with loathing, their sickly excess and condescension. For several minutes he stood in front of the kitchen table staring at each object in turn, trying to relive the certainty with which he had bought it. The record token he put on one side, the rest he swept into a carrier bag and threw it into the cupboard in the hallway. Then he took off his shoes and socks, lay down on his unmade bed, examined with his finger the colourless stain that had hardened on the sheet, and then slept till it was dark.

Naked from the waist Miranda Cooke lay across her bed, arms spread, face buried deep in the pillow, and the pillow buried deep under her yellow hair. From a chair by the bed a pink transistor radio played methodically through the top twenty. The late afternoon sun shone through closed curtains and cast the room in the cerulean green of a tropical aquarium. Little Charmian sat astride Miranda's buttocks, tiny Charmian, Miranda's friend, plied her finger nails backwards and forwards across Miranda's pale unblemished back.

Charmian too was naked, and time seemed to stand still. Ranged along the mirror of the dressing table, their feet concealed by cosmetic jars and tubes, their hands raised in perpetual surprise, sat the discarded dolls of Miranda's childhood. Chairmian's caresses slowed to nothing, her hands came to rest in the small of her friend's back. She stared at the wall in front of her, swaying abstractedly. Listening.

... They're all locked in the nursery,
They got earphone heads, they got dirty necks,
They're so twentieth century.

'I didn't know *that* was in,' she said. Miranda twisted her head and spoke from under her hair.

'It's come back,' she explained. 'The Rolling Stones used to sing it.'

Don'cha think there's a place for you
In between the sheets?

When it was over Miranda spoke peevishly over the
dj's hysterical routine. 'You've stopped. Why have you
stopped?'

'I've been doing it for ages.'

'You said half an hour for my birthday. You promised.'
Charmian began again. Miranda, sighing as one who
only receives her due, sank her mouth into the pillow.
Outside the room the traffic droned soothingly, the pitch
of an ambulance siren rose and fell, a bird began to sing,
broke off, started again, a bell rang somewhere downstairs
and later a voice called out, over and over again, another
siren passed, this time more distant ... it was all so remote
from the aquatic gloom where time had stopped, where
Charmian gently drew her nails across her friend's back
for her birthday. The voice reached them again. Miranda
stirred and said, 'I think that's my mum calling me. My
dad must've come.'

When he rang the front door bell, this house where he
had lived sixteen years, Stephen assumed his daughter
would answer. She usually did. But it was his wife. She
had the advantage of three concrete steps and she glared
down at him, waiting for him to speak. He had nothing
ready for her.

'Is ... is Miranda there?' he said finally. I'm a little
late,' he added, and taking his chance, advanced up the
steps. At the very last moment she stepped aside and
opened the door wider.

'She's upstairs,' she said tonelessly as Stephen tried to
squeeze by without touching her. 'We'll go in the big
room.' Stephen followed her into the comfortable, un-
changing room, lined from floor to ceiling with books he
had left behind. In one corner, under its canvas cover, was

his grand piano. Stephen ran his hand along its curving edge. Indicating the books he said, 'I must take all these off your hands.'

'In your own good time,' she said as she poured sherry for him. 'There's no hurry.' Stephen sat down at the piano and lifted the cover.

'Do either of you play it now?' She crossed the room with his glass and stood behind him.

'I never have the time. And Miranda isn't interested now.' He spread his hands over a soft, spacious chord, sustained it with the pedal and listened to it die away.

'Still in tune then?'

'Yes.' He played more chords, he began to improvise a melody, almost a melody. He could happily forget what he had come for and be left alone to play for an hour or so, his piano.

'I haven't played for over a year,' he said by way of explanation. His wife was over by the door now about to call out to Miranda, and she had to snatch back her breath to say,

'Really? It sounds fine to me. Miranda,' she called, 'Miranda, Miranda,' rising and falling on three notes, the third note higher than the first, and trailing away inquisitively. Stephen played the three-note tune back, and his wife broke off abruptly. She looked sharply in his direction. 'Very clever.'

'You know you have a musical voice,' said Stephen without irony. She advanced farther into the room.

'Are you still intending to ask Miranda to stay with you?' Stephen closed the piano and resigned himself to hostilities.

'Have you been working on her then?' She folded her arms.

'She won't go with you. Not alone anyway.'

'There isn't room in the flat for you as well.'

'And thank God there isn't.' Stephen stood up and raised his hand like an Indian chief.

'Let's not,' he said. 'Let's not.' She nodded and returned to the door and called out to their daughter in a steady tone, immune to imitation. Then she said quietly, 'I'm talking about Charmian. Miranda's friend.'

'What's she like?'

She hesitated. 'She's upstairs. You'll see her.'

'Ah ... '

They sat in silence. From upstairs Stephen heard giggling, the familiar, distant hiss of the plumbing, a bedroom door opening and closing. From his shelves he picked out a book about dreams and thumbed through. He was aware of his wife leaving the room, but he did not look up. The setting afternoon sun lit the room. 'An emission during a dream indicates the sexual nature of the whole dream, however obscure and unlikely the contents are. Dreams culminating in emission may reveal the object of the dreamer's desire as well as his inner conflicts. An orgasm cannot lie.'

'Hello, Daddy,' said Miranda. 'This is Charmian, my friend.' The light was in his eyes and at first he thought they held hands, like mother and child side by side before him, illuminated from behind by the orange dying sun, waiting to be greeted. Their recent laughter seemed concealed in their silence. Stephen stood up and embraced his daughter. She felt different to the touch, stronger perhaps. She smelt unfamiliar, she had a private life at last, accountable to no one. Her bare arms were very warm.

'Happy birthday,' Stephen said, closing his eyes as he squeezed her and preparing to greet the minute figure at her side. He stepped back smiling and virtually knelt before her on the carpet to shake hands, this doll-like figurine who stood no more than 3 foot 6 at his daughter's side, whose wooden, oversized face smiled steadily back at him.

'I've read one of your books,' was her calm first remark. Stephen sat back in his chair. The two girls still stood before him as though they wished to be described and compared. Miranda's T-shirt did not reach her waist by several inches and her growing breasts lifted the edge of the shirt clear of her belly. Her hand rested on her friend's shoulder protectively.

'Really?' said Stephen after some pause. 'Which one?'

'The one about evolution.'

'Ah ... ' Stephen took from his pocket the envelope containing the record token and gave it to Miranda. 'It's not much,' he said, remembering the bag full of gifts. Miranda retired to a chair to open her envelope. The dwarf however remained standing in front of him, regarding him fixedly. She fingered the hem of her child's dress.

'Miranda told me a lot about you,' she said politely. Miranda looked up and giggled.

'No I didn't,' she protested. Charmian went on.

'She's very proud of you.' Miranda blushed. Stephen wondered at Charmian's age.

'I haven't given her much reason to be,' he found himself saying, and gestured at the room to indicate the nature of his domestic situation. The tiny girl gazed patiently into his eyes and he felt for a moment poised on the edge of total confession. I never satisfied my wife in marriage, you see. Her orgasms terrified me. Miranda had discovered her present. With a little cry she left her chair, cradled his head between her hands and stooping down kissed his ear.

'Thank you,' she murmured hotly and loudly, 'thank you, thank you.' Charmian took a couple of paces nearer till she was almost standing between his open knees. Miranda settled on the arm of his chair. It grew darker.

He felt the warmth of Miranda's body on his neck. She slipped down a little farther and rested her head on his shoulder. Charmian stirred. Miranda said, 'I'm glad you came,' and drew her knees up to make herself smaller. From outside Stephen heard his wife moving from one room to another. He lifted his arm round his daughter's shoulder, careful not to touch her breasts, and hugged her to him.

'Are you coming to stay with me when the holidays begin?'

'Charmian too ... ' She spoke childishly, but her words were delicately pitched between inquiry and stipulation.

'Charmian too,' Stephen agreed. 'If she wants to.' Charmian let her gaze drop and said demurely, 'Thank you.'

During the following week Stephen made preparations. He swept the floor of his only spare room, he cleaned the windows there and hung new curtains. He hired a television. In the mornings he worked with customary numbness and entered his achievements in the ledger book. He brought himself at last to set out what he could remember of his dream. The details seemed to be accumulating satisfactorily. His wife was in the café. It was for her that he was buying coffee. A young girl took a cup and held it to the machine. But now *he* was the machine, now *he* filled the cup. This sequence, laid out neatly, cryptically in his journal, worried him less now. It had, as far as he was concerned, a certain literary potential. It needed fleshing out, and since he could remember no more he would have to invent the rest. He thought of Charmian, of how small she was, and he examined carefully the chairs ranged round the dining-room table. She was small enough for a baby's high chair. In a department store he carefully chose two cushions. The impulse to buy the girls presents he distrusted and resisted. But still he wanted to

do things for them. What could he do? He raked out gobs
of ancient filth from under the kitchen sink, poured dead
flies and spiders from the lamp fixtures, boiled fetid dish-
cloths; he bought a toilet brush and scrubbed the crusty
bowl. Things they would never notice. Had he really
become such an old fool? He spoke to his wife on the
phone.

'You never mentioned Charmian before.'

'No,' she agreed. 'It's a fairly recent thing.'

'Well ... ' he struggled, 'how do you feel about it?'

'It's fine by me,' she said, very relaxed. 'They're good
friends.' She was trying him out, he thought. She hated
him for his fearfulness, his passivity and for all the wasted
hours between the sheets. It took her many years of
marriage to say so. The experimentation in his writing, the
lack of it in his life. She hated him. And now she had a
lover, a vigorous lover. And still he wanted to say, Is it
right, our lovely daughter with a friend who belongs by
rights in a circus or silk-hung brothel serving tea? Our
flaxen-haired, perfectly formed daughter, our tender bud,
is it not perverse?

'Expect them Thursday evening,' said his wife by way
of goodbye.

When Stephen answered the door he saw only Charmian
at first, and then he made out Miranda outside the tight
circle of light from the hall, struggling with both sets of
luggage. Charmian stood with her hands on her hips, her
heavy head tipped slightly to one side. Without greeting
she said, 'We had to take a taxi and he's downstairs
waiting.'

Stephen kissed his daughter, helped her in with the cases
and went downstairs to pay the taxi. When he returned, a
little out of breath from the two flights of stairs, the front
door of his flat was closed. He knocked and had to wait. It

was Charmian who opened the door and stood in his path.

'You can't come in,' she said solemnly. 'You'll have to come back later,' and she made as if to close the door. Laughing in his nasal, unconvincing way, Stephen lunged forwards, caught her under her arms and scooped her into the air. At the same time he stepped into the flat and closed the door behind him with his foot. He meant to lift her high in the air like a child, but she was heavy, heavy like an adult, and her feet trailed a few inches above the ground, it was all he could manage. She thumped his hand with her fists and shouted.

'Put me ... ' Her last word was cut off by the crash of the door. Stephen released her instantly. ' ... down,' she said softly. They stood in the bright hallway, both a little out of breath. For the first time he saw Charmian's face clearly. Her head was bullet shaped and ponderous, her lower lip curled permanently outwards and she had the beginnings of a double chin. Her nose was squat and she had the faint downy greyness of a moustache. Her neck was thick and bullish. Her eyes were large and calm, set far apart, brown like a dog's. She was not ugly, not with these eyes. Miranda was at the far end of the long hall. She wore ready-faded jeans and a yellow shirt. Her hair was in plaits and tied at the end with a scrap of blue denim. She came and stood by her friend's side.

'Charmian doesn't like being lifted about,' she explained. Stephen guided them towards his sitting room.

'I'm sorry,' he said to Charmian and laid his hand on her shoulder for an instant. 'I didn't know that.'

'I was only joking when I came to the door,' she said evenly.

'Yes of course,' Stephen said hurriedly. 'I didn't think anything else.'

During dinner, which Stephen had bought ready-cooked from a local Italian restaurant, the girls talked to

him about their school. He allowed them a little wine and
they giggled a lot and clutched at each other when they
fell about. They prompted each other through a story
about their head master who looked up girls' skirts. He
remembered some anecdotes of his own time at school, or
perhaps they were other people's time, but he told them
well and they laughed delightedly. They became very
excited. They pleaded for more wine. He told them one
glass was enough.

Charmian and Miranda said they wanted to do the
dishes. Stephen sprawled in an armchair with a large
brandy, soothed by the blur of their voices and the homely
clatter of dishes. This was where he lived, this was his
home. Miranda brought him coffee. She sat it down on the
table with the mock deference of a waitress.

'Coffee, sir?' she said. Stephen moved over in his chair
and she sat in close beside him. She moved easily between
woman and child. She drew her legs up like before and
pressed herself against her large shaggy father. She had
unloosened her plaits and her hair spread across Stephen's
chest, golden in the electric light.

'Have you found a boyfriend at school?' he asked.

She shook her head and kept it pressed against his
shoulder.

'Can't find a boyfriend, eh?' Stephen insisted. She sat
up suddenly and lifted her hair clear of her face.

'There are loads of boys,' she said angrily, 'loads of
them, but they're so *stupid*, they're such show-offs.' Never
before had the resemblance between his wife and daughter
seemed so strong. She glared at him. She included him
with the boys at school. 'They're always doing things.'

'What sort of thing?' She shook her head impatiently.

'I don't know ... the way they comb their hair and bend
their knees.'

'Bend their knees?'

'Yes. When they think you're watching them. They stand in front of our window and pretend they're combing their hair when they're just looking in at us, showing off. Like this.' She sprang out of the chair and crouched in the centre of the room in front of an imaginary mirror, bent low like a singer over a microphone, her head tilted grotesquely, combing with long, elaborate strokes; she stepped back, preened and then combed again. It was a furious imitation. Charmian was watching it too. She stood in the doorway with coffee in each hand.

'What about you, Charmian,' Stephen said carelessly, 'do you have a boyfriend?' Charmian set the coffee cups down and said, 'Of course I don't,' and then looked up and smiled at them both with the tolerance of a wise old woman.

Later on he showed them their bedroom.

'There's only one bed,' he told them. 'I thought you wouldn't mind sharing it.' It was an enormous bed, seven foot by seven, one of the few large objects he had brought with him from his marriage. The sheets were deep red and very old, from a time when all sheets were white. He did not care to sleep between them now, they had been a wedding present. Charmian lay across the bed, she hardly took up more room than one of the pillows. Stephen said goodnight. Miranda followed him into the hall, stood on tiptoe to kiss him on the cheek.

'*You're* not a show-off,' she whispered and clung to him. Stephen stood perfectly still. 'I wish you'd come home,' she said. He kissed the top of her head.

'This is home,' he said. 'You've got two homes now.' He broke her hold and led her back to the entrance of the bedroom. He squeezed her hand. 'See you in the morning,' he murmured, left her there and hurried into his study. He sat down, horrified at his erection, elated. Ten minutes passed. He thought he should be sombre, analytical, this was a serious matter. But he wanted to sing, he wanted to play his piano, he wanted to go for a walk. He did none of those things. He sat still, staring ahead, thinking of nothing in particular, and waited for the chill of excitement to leave his belly.

When it did he went to bed. He slept badly. For many hours he was tormented by the thought that he was still awake. He awoke completely from fragmentary, dreams into total darkness. It seemed to him then that for some time he had been hearing a sound. He could not remember what the sound was, only that he had not liked it. It was silent now, the darkness hissed about his ears. He wanted to piss, and for a moment he was afraid to leave his bed. The certainty of his own death came to him now as it occasionally did, as a sick revelation, not the dread of dying, but of dying now, 3.15 am, lying still with the sheet drawn up round his neck and wanting, like all mortal animals, to urinate. He turned the light on and went into the bathroom. His cock was small in his hands, nut brown and wrinkled by the cold, or perhaps the fear. He felt sorry for it. As he pissed his stream split in two. He pulled his foreskin a little and the streams converged. He felt sorry for himself. He stepped back into the hallway, and as he closed the bathroom door behind him and cut off the rumble of the cistern he heard that sound again, the sound he had listened to in his sleep. A sound so forgotten, so utterly familiar that only now as he advanced very cautiously along the hallway did he know it to be the background for all other sounds, the frame of all anxieties. The sound of his wife in, or approaching, orgasm. He stopped several yards short of the girls' bedroom. It was a low moan through the medium of a harsh, barking cough, it rose imperceptibly in pitch through fractions of a tone, then fell away at the end, down but not very far, still higher than the starting-point. He did not dare go nearer the door. He strained to listen. The end came and he heard the bed creak a little, and footsteps across the floor. He saw the door handle turn. Like a dreamer he asked no questions, he forgot his nakedness, he had no expectations.

Miranda screwed up her eyes in the brightness. Her yellow hair was loose. Her white cotton nightdress reached her ankles and its folds concealed the lines of her body. She could be any age. She hugged her arms round her body. Her father stood in front of her, very still, very massive, one foot in front of the other as though frozen mid-step, arms limp by his side, his naked black hairs, his wrinkled, nut-brown naked self. She could be a child or a woman, she could be any age. She took a little step forward.

'Daddy,' she moaned, 'I can't get to sleep.' She took his hand and he led her into the bedroom. Charmian lay curled up on the far side of the bed, her back to them. Was she awake, was she innocent? Stephen held back the bedclothes and Miranda climbed between the sheets. He tucked her in and sat on the edge of the bed. She arranged her hair.

'Sometimes I get frightened when I wake up in the middle of the night,' she told him.

'So do I,' he said and bent over and kissed her lightly on the lips.

'But there's nothing to be frightened of really, is there?'

'No,' he said, 'Nothing.' She settled herself deeper into the deep red sheets and gazed into his face.

'Tell me something though, tell me something to make me go to sleep.' He looked across at Charmian.

'Tomorrow you can look in the cupboard in the hall. There's a whole bag of presents in there.'

'For Charmian too?'

'Yes.' He studied her face by the light from the hall. He was beginning to feel the cold. 'I bought them for your birthday,' he added. But she was asleep and almost smiling, and in the pallor of her upturned throat he thought he saw from one bright morning in his childhood a field of dazzling white snow which he, a small boy of eight, had not dared scar with footprints.

To and Fro

Now Leech pushes his legs out straight till they tremble with the effort, locks his fingers behind his head, cracks them at the joints, chuckles his deliberate, dirty chuckle at what he pretends tó see in the middle distance and bats me gently behind the head with his elbow. Looks like it's over, what would you say?

Is it true? I lie in the dark. It is true, I think the old to and fro rocked her to sleep. The ancient to and fro had no end and the suspension came unnoticed like sleep itself. Rise and fall, rise and fall, rise and fall, between the fall and rise the perilous silent gap, the decision she makes to go on.

The sky a blank yellow-white, the canal odour reduced by distance to the smell of sweet ripe cherries, the melancholy of airliners turning in the stack and here in the office others cut up the day's papers, this is their work. Paste columns to index cards.

If I can lie in the dark I can see in the dark pale skin on the fragile ridge of cheekbone, it carves a dog-leg shape in the dark. The deep-set eyes are open and invisible. Through almost parted lips a point of light glints on saliva and tooth, the thick belt of hair blacker than the surrounding night. Sometimes I look at her and wonder who will die first, who will die first, you or me? The colossal weight of stillness, how many more hours?

Leech. I see Leech in this same corridor in frequent consultation with the Director. I see them, together they pace the long doorless corridor. The Director walks erect, his hands, deep in his pockets, jingle with gewgaws and Leech stoops subordinately, head twisted towards his superior's neck, his hands clasped behind his back, the fingers of one hand rolled around the wrist of the other to check scrupulously his own pulse. I see what the Director sees, our images combine — Leech and this man; twist the bright metal ring and they spring apart, one standing, one sitting, both posing.

Saliva glints on a point of tooth. Listen to her breathing, rhythmic soaring and plunging, deep sleep air, not her now. One animal need tracks another through the night, black-furred sleep smothered pleasure from a low branch, the old tree creaks, gone, memory, listen to her ... house smells sweet. The ancient, soft to and fro rocked her to sleep. Do you remember the small wood, the gnarled and stunted trees, the leafless branches and twigs fused to one canopy, what we found there? What we saw? Ah ... the tiny, patient heroism of being awake, the arctic hole bigger than the surrounding ice widens, too large to assume a shape, inclusive of the optical limits of sight. I lie in the dark and look in, I lie in it and gaze out, and from another room one of her children cries out in her sleep, A bear!

First here comes Leech, no first here am I towards the end on one morning, reclining, sipping, private, and Leech comes by, salutes me, claps me on the back a cordial, vicious blow between the shoulder blades below the neck. He stands at the tea urn, legs apart like a public urinator,

the brown liquid dribbling into his cup and he saying do
I remember (this) or (that) conversation. No, no. He
approaches with his cup. No, no, I tell him, I remember
nothing, I tell him as he settles on the long settee, as close
to me as he can without actually ... becoming me. Ah, the
bitter tang of a stranger's skin wrapped about to conceal
the remoter fecal core. His right leg touches my left.

In the cold hour before dawn her children will climb into
the bed, first one and then the other, sometimes one without the other, they drop between the spicy adult warmth,
attach themselves to her sides like the starfish (remember
the starfish clinging to its rock) and make faint liquid
noises with their tongues. Outside in the street urgent
footsteps approach and recede down the hill. I lie on the
edge of the litter, Robinson Crusoe making his plans for
stockades of finely sharpened stakes, guns that will fire
themselves at the faintest tremor of an alien step, hopes
his goats and dogs will procreate, will not find another
such nest of tolerant creatures. When one of her daughters
comes too early, in the dead of night she wakes and carries
her back, returns and sleeps, her knees drawn up to her
belly. Her house smells sweetly of sleeping children.

In the slow motion of one who feels the need to be
watched, Leech unclips a pen from his breast pocket,
examines it, replaces it, grips my extended arm as I reach
for my book which slid to the floor at the moment of
Leech's blow. A significant space by the door indicates
the Director, the possibility of his arrival.

The colossal weight ... do you remember, sleeper, the
small wood of gnarled stunted trees, the leafless branches
and twigs fused to one canopy, a dark roof leaking light
on to the pungent soil. We tiptoed on the absorbent

vegetable silence, it made us whisper, drew our sibilants through hidden roots beneath our feet, a very old and private wood. Ahead of us brightness, the canopy had collapsed as though a heavy weight once crashed down from the sky. The bright semicircle, the trees' branches and twigs drooping to the ground in a brilliant cascade, and there lodged halfway up the torrent, picked white by the sun and stark against the dull grey wood were bones, white bones of a creature resting there, a flat, socketed skull, a long curving spine diminishing to the delicate point, and at its sides the meticulous heap of other bones, slender with bunch-fisted ends.

Leech's fingers have the tenacity of a chicken's claw. When I prise the fingers loose from my arm they curl back impersonally. Is this a lonely man? To whom, having touched his hand, I feel compelled to speak, as bright-eyed lovers on their backs under a sheet begin a conversation. I hold my own hands in my lap and watch motes fall across a slab of sunlight.

Sometimes I look at her and wonder who will die first ... face to face, wintering in the mess of down and patchwork, she places a hand over each of my ears, takes my head between her palms, regards me with thick, black eyes and pursed smile that does not show her teeth ... then I think, It's me, I shall die first, and you might live forever.

Leech sets down his cup (how brown he has made its rim), settles back, pushes his legs out straight till they tremble from the effort and watches with me motes falling across a slab of sunlight, and beyond that the ice hole, up, out, where I lie beside my sleeping lover, lie staring in, gazing back. I recognise the down and patchwork, the charm of the bed's wrought iron ... Leech sets down his cup, settles back, cracks his finger joints behind his head which he moves to indicate his intention to move, an awareness of the empty space by the door, a wish to be accompanied on the way.

A voice breaks the stillness, a brilliant red flower dropped on the snow, one of her daughters calls out in a dream, A bear! the sound indistinct from its sense. Silence, and then again, A bear, softer this time, with a falling tone of disappointment ... now, a silence dramatic for its absence of the succinct voice ... now imperceptibly ... now, habitual silence, no expectations, the weight of stillness, the luminous after-image of bears in fading orange. I watch them go and lie waiting beside my sleeping friend, turn my head on the pillow and look into her open eyes.

I rise at last and follow Leech across the empty room and along the doorless corridor where I have seen him in frequent consultation, pacing, erect or stooping. The Director and his subordinate, we cannot be told apart from those we fear ... I draw level with Leech and he is feeling the material of his suit, finger and thumb rotate either side of his lapel, the motion slowing to nothing as he considers his words which are, What do you think of it, my suit? accompanied by the faintest smile. We come to a halt in the corridor, face to face, below us our stunted reflections in the polished floor. We see each other's but not our own.

The thick belt of hair is blacker than the surrounding night, and pale skin on the fragile ridge of cheekbone carves a dog-leg shape in the dark ... Was that you? she murmurs, Or the children? Some faint movement where her eyes are say they are closed. The rhythm of her breathing strengthens, it is the impending automation of a sleeping body. It was nothing, it was a dream, a voice in the dark like a red flower on the snow ... she falls backwards, she drifts to the bottom of a deep well and looking up can watch the receding circle of light, of sky broken by the silhouette of my watching head and shoulders far away. She drifts down, her words drift up, passing her on the way and reach me muted by echoes. She calls, Come inside me while I fall asleep, come inside ...

With a similar manoeuvre of finger and thumb I reach out and touch the lapel and then touch my own, the familiar feel of each material, the body warmth they transmit ... the smell of sweet ripe cherries, the melancholy of airliners turning in the stack; this is the work, we cannot be told apart by those we fear. Leech grips my extended arm and shakes it. Open your eyes, open your eyes. You'll see it's not like yours at all. Here the lapels are wider, the jacket has two slits behind at my request and while they are the same shade of blue, mine has little flecks of white and the total effect is lighter. At the sound of footsteps far behind us we continue on our way.

Asleep and so moist? The synaesthesia of the ancient to and fro, the salt water and spice warehouses, a rise beyond which the contours smooth and roll and dip against the skyline like a giant tree hingeing on the sky, a tongue of flesh. I kiss and suck where her daughters sucked. Come away, she said, leave it alone. The white bones of some creature I wanted to approach and touch, the flat-socketed skull, the long curving spine diminishing to the delicate point ... Leave it alone, she said when I put out my arm. No mistaking the terror in those words, she said it was a nightmare and cluched our picnic to her — when we embraced, a bottle rattled against a tin. Holding hands we ran through the wood and out across the slopes, around the knots of gorse, the big valley below us, the good big clouds, the wood a flat scar on the dull green.

Yes, it is the Director's habit to advance several feet into the room and pause to survey the activities of his subordinates. But for a tightening in the air (the very space the air inhabits compresses) nothing changes, everyone looks, no one looks up ... The Director's look is sunk in fat bound by wonderful translucent skin, it has accumulated on the ridge of his cheekbone and now, like a glacier, seeps down into the hollow of his eye. The sunken authoritative eye sweeps the room, desk, faces, the open window, and fixes like a sluggish spinning bottle on me ... Ah Leech, he says.

In her house it smells sweetly of sleeping children, of cats drying in the warmth, of dust warming in the valves of an old radio—is this the news, fewer injured, more dead? How can I be sure the earth is turning towards the morning? In the morning I'll tell her across the empty cups and stains, more memory than dream, I claim waking status in my dreams. Nothing exaggerated but fine points of physical disgust and those exaggerated only appropriately, and all seen through, so I shall claim, a hole so big there was no ice to surround it.

It is tranquil here at the trestle table by the window. This is the work, not happy, not unhappy, sifting through the returned cuttings. This is the work, finding the categories appropriate to the filing system. The sky a blank yellow-white, the canal odour reduced by distance to the smell of sweet ripe cherries, the melancholy of airliners in the stack and elsewhere in the office others cut up the day's papers, paste columns to index cards; pollution/air, pollution/noise, pollution/water, the genteel sound of scissors, the shuffle of glue on pots, a hand pushing open the door. The Director advances several feet into the room and pauses to survey the activity of his subordinates.

I will tell her ... she sighs and stirs, sweeps her unbrushed hair clear of her watery eyes, goes to rise but remains sitting, cups her hands around a jug — a junk shop present to herself. In her eyes the window makes small bright squares, under her eyes cusps of blue twin-moon her white face. She pushes her hair clear, sighs and stirs.

He is walking towards me. Ah Leech, he says as he comes. He calls me Leech. Ah Leech, there's something I want you to do for me. Something I do not hear, mesmerised where I sit by the mouth which forms itself round the syllables. Something I want you to do for me. At the casual, unworried moment he realises his mistake, Leech occurs from behind a bank of cabinets, effusively forgiving. The Director is briskly apologetic. As my colleague will confirm, says Leech, people are always confusing us, and so saying he rests his hand on my shoulder, forgiving me too. A very easy mistake, colleague, to allow yourself to be confused with Leech.

Listen to her breathing, rise and fall, rise and fall, between the rise and fall the perilous gap, the decision she makes to go on ... the weight of hours. I will tell her and avoid confusion. Her eyes will budge from left to right and back, study each of my eyes in turn, compare them for honesty or shift in intent, dip intermittently to my mouth and round and round to make a meaning of a face, and likewise my eyes in hers, round and round our eyes will dance and chase.

I sit wedged between the two standing men and the

Director repeats his instructions, impatiently leaves us, and when he reaches the door turns to look back and smiles indulgently. Yes! I have never seen him smile. I see what he sees—twins as posed for a formal photograph. One stands, his hand settled for ever on the shoulder of the other who sits; possibly a confusion, a trick of the lens, for if we turn this bright metal ring their images coalesce and there is only one. Name of? Hopeful and with good reason ... anxious.

To and fro is my clock, will make the earth turn, the dawn come, bring her daughters to her bed ... to and fro laughs at the stillness, to and fro drops her children between the spicy adult warmth, attaches them to her sides like star-fish, do you remember ... the thrill of seeing what you are not intended to see, the great rock thrust across the wet, striated sand, the water's edge receding against its will to the horizon, and in the rock-thrust the hungry pools sucked and slopped and sucked. A fat black boulder hung across a pool and beneath it there it hung, and stretched its legs and arms, you saw it first, so orange, bright, beautiful, singular, its dripping white dots. It clung to the black rock it commanded, and how the water slapped it against its rock while far away the sea receded. The star-fish did not threaten like the bones for being dead, it threatened for being so awake, like a child's shout in the dead of night.

The body warmth they transmit. Are we the same? Leech, are we? Leech stretches, answers, bats, pushes, pretends, consults, flatters, stoops, checks, poses, approaches, salutes, touches, examines, indicates, grips, murmurs, gazes, trembles, shakes, occurs, smiles, faintly, so very faintly, says, Open your ... the warmth? ... open your eyes, open your eyes.

Is it true? I lie in the dark … it is true, I think it is over. She sleeps, there was no end, the suspension came unnoticed like sleep itself. Yes, the ancient to and fro rocked her to sleep, and in sleep she drew me to her side and placed her leg over mine. The dark grows blue and grey and I feel on my temple, beneath her breast, the ancient tread of her heart to and fro.

Psychopolis

Mary worked in and part-owned a feminist bookstore in Venice. I met her there lunchtime on my second day in Los Angeles. That same evening we were lovers, and not so long after that, friends. The following Friday I chained her by the foot to my bed for the whole weekend. It was, she explained to me, something she 'had to go into to come out of'. I remember her extracting (later, in a crowded bar) my solemn promise that I would not listen if she demanded to be set free. Anxious to please my new friend, I bought a fine chain and diminutive padlock. With brass screws I secured a steel ring to the wooden base of the bed and all was set. Within hours she was insisting on her freedom, and though a little confused I got out of bed, showered, dressed, put on my carpet slippers and brought her a large frying-pan to urinate in. She tried on a firm, sensible voice.

'Unlock this,' she said. 'I've had enough.' I admit she frightened me. I poured myself a drink and hurried out on to the balcony to watch the sun set. I was not at all excited. I thought to myself, If I unlock the chain she will despise me for being weak. If I keep her there she might hate me, but at least I will have kept my promise. The pale orange sun dipped into the haze, and I heard her shout to me through the closed bedroom door. I closed my eyes and concentrated on being blameless.

A friend of mine once had analysis with an elderly man,

a Freudian with a well-established practice in New York. On one occasion my friend spoke at length about his doubts concerning Freud's theories, their lack of scientific credibility, their cultural particularity and so on. When he had done the analyst smiled genially and replied, 'Look around you!' And indicated with his open palm the comfortable study, the rubber plant and the begonia rex, the book-lined walls and finally, with an inward movement of the wrist which both suggested candour and emphasised the lapels of his tasteful suit, said, 'Do you really think I would have got to where I am now if Freud was wrong?'

In the same manner I said to myself as I returned indoors (the sun now set and the bedroom silent), the bare truth of the matter is that I am keeping my promise.

All the same, I felt bored. I wandered from room to room turning on the lights, leaning in doorways and staring in at objects that already were familiar. I set up the music stand and took out my flute. I taught myself to play years ago and there are many errors, strengthened by habit, which I no longer have the will to correct. I do not press the keys as I should with the very tips of my fingers, and my fingers fly too high off the keys and so make it impossible to play fast passages with any facility. Furthermore my right wrist is not relaxed, and does not fall, as it should, at an easy right angle to the instrument. I do not hold my back straight when I play, instead I slouch over the music. My breathing is not controlled by the muscles of my stomach, I blow carelessly from the top of my throat. My embouchure is ill-formed and I rely too often on a syrupy vibrato. I lack the control to play any dynamics other than soft or loud. I have never bothered to teach myself the notes above top G. My musicianship is poor, and slightly unusual rhythms perplex me. Above all I have no ambition to play any other than the same half-dozen pieces and I make the same mistakes each time.

Several minutes into my first piece I thought of her listening from the bedroom and the phrase 'captive audience' came into my mind. While I played I devised ways in which these words could be inserted casually into a sentence to make a weak, light-hearted pun, the humour of which would somehow cause the situation to be elucidated. I put the flute down and walked towards the bedroom door. But before I had my sentence arranged, my hand, with a kind of insensible automation, had pushed the door open and I was standing in front of Mary. She sat on the edge of the bed brushing her hair, the chain decently obscured by blankets. In England a woman as articulate as Mary might have been regarded as an aggressor, but her manner was gentle. She was short and quite heavily built. Her face gave an impression of reds and blacks, deep red lips, black, black eyes, dusky apple-red cheeks and hair black and sleek like tar. Her grandmother was Indian.

'What do you want?' she said sharply and without interrupting the motion of her hand.

'Ah,' I said. 'Captive audience!'

'What?' When I did not repeat myself she told me that she wished to be left alone. I sat down on the bed and thought, If she asks me to set her free I'll do it instantly. But she said nothing. When she had finished with her hair she lay down with her hands clasped behind her head. I sat watching her, waiting. The idea of asking her if she wished to be set free seemed ludicrous, and simply setting her free without her permission was terrifying. I did not even know whether this was an ideological or psycho-sexual matter. I returned to my flute, this time carrying the music stand to the far end of the apartment and closing the intervening doors. I hoped she couldn't hear me.

On Sunday night, after more than twenty-four hours of unbroken silence between us, I set Mary free. As the lock sprang open I said, 'I've been in Los Angeles less than a week and already I feel a completely different person.'

Though partially true, the remark was designed to give pleasure. One hand resting on my shoulder, the other massaging her foot Mary said, 'It'll do that. It's a city at the end of cities.'

'It's sixty miles across!' I agreed.

'It's a thousand miles deep!' cried Mary wildly and threw her brown arms about my neck. She seemed to have found what she had hoped for.

But she was not inclined to explanations. Later on we ate out in a Mexican restaurant and I waited for her to mention her weekend in chains and when, finally, I began to ask her she interrupted with a question. 'Is it really true that England is in a state of total collapse?'

I said yes and spoke at length without believing what I was saying. The only experience I had of total collapse was a friend who killed himself. At first he only wanted to punish himself. He ate a little ground glass washed down with grapefruit juice. Then when the pains began he ran to the tube station, bought the cheapest ticket and threw himself under a train. The brand new Victoria line. What would that be like on a national scale? We walked back from the restaurant arm in arm without speaking. The air hot and damp around us, we kissed and clung to each other on the pavement beside her car.

'Same again next Friday?' I said wryly as she climbed in, but the words were cut by the slam of her door. Through the window she waved at me with her fingers and smiled. I didn't see her for quite a while.

I was staying in Santa Monica in a large, borrowed apartment over a hire shop which specialised in renting out items for party givers and, strangely, equipment for 'sickrooms'. One side of the shop was given over to wine-

glasses, cocktail shakers, spare easy chairs, a banqueting
table and a portable discotheque, the other to wheel-
chairs, tilting beds, tweezers and bedpans, bright tubular
steel and coloured rubber hoses. During my stay I noticed
a number of these stores throughout the city. The manager
was immaculately dressed and initially intimidating in his
friendliness. On our first meeting he told me he was 'only
twenty-nine'. He was heavily built and wore one of those
thick drooping moustaches grown throughout America
and England by the ambitious young. On my first day he
came up the stairs and introduced himself as George
Malone and paid me a pleasant compliment. 'The
British,' he said, 'make damn good invalid chairs. The
very best.'

'That must be Rolls-Royce,' I said. Malone gripped my
arm.

'Are you shitting me? Rolls-Royce make ... '

'No, no,' I said nervously. 'A ... a joke.' For a moment
his face was immobilised, the mouth open and black, and
I thought, He's going to hit me. But he laughed.

'Rolls-Royce! That's neat!' And the next time I saw
him he indicated the sickroom side of his shop and called
out after me, 'Wanna buy a Rolls?' Occasionally we
drank together at lunchtime in a red-lit bar off Colorado
Avenue where George had introduced me to the barman
as 'a specialist in bizarre remarks'.

'What'll it be?' said the barman to me.

'Pig oil with a cherry,' I said, cordially hoping to live up
to my reputation. But the barman scowled and turning to
George spoke through a sigh.

'What'll it be?'

It was exhilarating, at least at first, to live in a city of
narcissists. On my second or third day I followed George's
directions and walked to the beach. It was noon. A
million stark, primitive figurines lay scattered on the fine,

pale, yellow sand till they were swallowed up, north and south, in a haze of heat and pollution. Nothing moved but the sluggish giant waves in the distance, and the silence was awesome. Near where I stood on the very edge of the beach were different kinds of parallel bars, empty and stark, their crude geometry marked by silence. Not even the sound of the waves reached me, no voices, the whole city lay dreaming. As I began walking towards the ocean there were soft murmurs nearby, and it was as if I overheard a sleep-talker. I saw a man move his hand, spreading his fingers more firmly against the sand to catch the sun. An icebox without its lid stood like a gravestone at the head of a prostrate woman. I peeped inside as I passed and saw empty beercans and a packet of orange cheese floating in water. Now that I was moving among them I noticed how far apart each solitary sunbather was. It seemed to take minutes to walk from one to another. A trick of perspective had made me think they were jammed together. I noticed too how beautiful the women were, their brown limbs spread like starfish; and how many healthy old men there were with gnarled muscular bodies. The spectacle of this common intent exhilarated me and for the first time in my life I too urgently wished to be brown-skinned, brown-faced, so that when I smiled my teeth would flash white. I took off my trousers and shirt, spread my towel and lay down on my back thinking, I shall be free, I shall change beyond all recognition. But within minutes I was hot and restless, I longed to open my eyes. I ran into the ocean and swam out to where a few people were treading water and waiting for an especially huge wave to dash them to the shore.

Returning from the beach one day I found pinned to my door a note from my friend Terence Latterly. 'Waiting for you,' it said, 'in the Doggie Diner across the street.' I had met Latterly years ago in England when he was researching a still uncompleted thesis on George Orwell, and it was not till I came to America that I realised how rare an American he was. Slender, extraordinarily pallid, fine black hair that curled, doe eyes like a Renaissance princess, long straight nose with narrow black slits for nostrils, Terence was unwholesomely beautiful. He was frequently approached by gays, and once, in Polk Street San Francisco, literally mobbed. He had a stammer, slight enough to be endearing to those endeared by such things, and he was intense in his friendships to the point of occasionally lapsing into impenetrable sulks about them. It took me some time to admit to myself I actually disliked Terence and by that time he was in my life and I accepted the fact. Like all compulsive monologuists he lacked curiosity about other people's minds, but his stories were good and he never told the same one twice. He regularly became infatuated with women whom he drove away with his labyrinthine awkwardness and consumptive zeal, and who provided fresh material for his monologues. Two or three times now quiet, lonely, protective girls had fallen hopelessly for Terence and his ways, but, tellingly, he was not interested. Terence cared for long-legged, tough-minded, independent women who were rapidly bored by Terence. He once told me he masturbated every day.

He was the Doggie Diner's only customer, bent morosely over an empty coffee cup, his chin propped in his palms.

'In England,' I told him, 'a dog's dinner means some kind of unpalatable mess.'

'Sit down then,' said Terence. 'We're in the right place. I've been so humiliated.'

'Sylvie?' I asked obligingly.

'Yes yes. Grotesquely humiliated.' This was nothing new. Terence dined out frequently on morbid accounts of blows dealt him by indifferent women. He had been in love with Sylvie for months now and had followed her here from San Francisco, which was where he first told me about her. She made a living setting up health food restaurants and then selling them, and as far as I knew, she was hardly aware of the existence of Terence.

'I should never've come to Los Angeles,' Terence was saying as the Doggie Diner waitress refilled his cup. 'It's OK for the British. You see everything here as a bizarre comedy of extremes, but that's because you're out of it. The truth is it's psychotic, totally psychotic.' Terence ran his fingers through his hair which looked lacquered and stiff, and stared out into the street. Wrapped in a constant, faint blue cloud, cars drifted by at twenty miles an hour, their drivers propped their tanned forearms on the window ledges, their car radios and stereos were on, they were all going home or to bars for happy hour.

After a suitable silence I said, 'Well ... ?'

From the day he arrives in Los Angeles Terence pleads with Sylvie over the phone to have a meal with him in a restaurant, and finally, wearily, she consents. Terence buys a new shirt, visits a hairdresser and spends an hour in the late afternoon in front of the mirror, staring at his face. He meets Sylvie in a bar, they drink bourbon. She is relaxed and friendly, and they talk easily of Californian politics, of which Terence knows next to nothing. Since Sylvie knows Los Angeles she chooses the restaurant. As they are leaving the bar she says, 'Shall we go in your car or mine?'

Terence, who has no car and cannot drive, says, 'Why not yours?'

By the end of the *hors d'oeuvres* they are starting in on their second bottle of wine and talking of books, and then of money, and then of books again. Lovely Sylvie leads Terence by the hand through half a dozen topics; she

smiles and Terence flushes with love and love's wildest
ambitions. He loves so hard he knows he will not be able
to resist declaring himself. He can feel it coming on, a mad
confession. The words tumble out, a declaration of love
worthy of the pages of Walter Scott, its main burden being
that there is nothing, absolutely nothing, in the world
Terence would not do for Sylvie. In fact, drunk, he
challenges her now to test his devotion. Touched by the
bourbon and wine, intrigued by this wan, *fin de siècle*
lunatic, Sylvie gazes warmly across the table and returns
his little squeeze to the hand. In the rarefied air between
them runs a charge of goodwill and daredevilry. Pro-
pelled by mere silence Terence repeats himself. There is
nothing, absolutely nothing, in the etc. Sylvie's gaze shifts
momentarily from Terence's face to the door of the
restaurant through which a well-to-do middle-aged
couple are now entering. She frowns, then smiles.

'Anything?' she says.

'Yes yes, anything.' Terence is solemn now, sensing the
real challenge in her question. Sylvie leans forward and
grips his forearm.

'You won't back out?'

'No, if it's humanly possible I'll do it.' Again Sylvie is
looking over at the couple who wait by the door to be
seated by the hostess, an energetic lady in a red soldier-
like uniform. Terence watches too. Sylvie tightens her
grip on his arm.

'I want you to urinate in your pants, now. Go on now!
Quick! Do it now before you have time to think about it.'

Terence is about to protest, but his own promises still
hang in the air, an accusing cloud. With drunken sway,
and with the sound of an electric bell ringing in his ears,
he urinates copiously, soaking his thighs, legs and backside
and sending a small, steady trickle to the floor.

'Have you done it?' says Sylvie.

'Yes,' says Terence, 'But why ... ?' Sylvie half-rises from her seat and waves prettily across the restaurant at the couple standing by the door.

'I want you to meet my parents,' she says. 'I've just seen them come in.' Terence remains seated for the introductions. He wonders if he can be smelled. There is nothing he will not say to dissuade this affable, greying couple from sitting down at their daughter's table. He talks desperately and without a break ('as if I was some kinda bore'), referring to Los Angeles as a 'shithole' and its inhabitants as 'greedy devourers of each other's privacy'. Terence hints at a recent prolonged mental illness from which he has hardly recovered, and he tells Sylvie's mother that all doctors, especially women doctors, are 'assholes' (arseholes). Sylvie says nothing. The father cocks an eyebrow at his wife and the couple wander off without farewell to their table on the far side of the room.

Terence appeared to have forgotten he was telling his story. He was cleaning his nails with the tooth of a comb. I said, 'Well, you can't stop there. *What happened?* What's the explanation for all this?' Around us the diner was filling up, but no one else was talking.

Terence said, 'I sat on a newspaper to keep her car seat from getting wet. We didn't speak much and she wouldn't come in when we got to my place. She told me earlier she didn't like her parents much. I guess she was just fooling around.' I wondered if Terence's story was invented or dreamed for it was the paradigm of all his rejections, the perfect formulation of his fears or, perhaps, of his profoundest desires.

'People here,' Terence said as we left the Doggie Diner, 'live so far from each other. Your neighbour is someone forty minutes' car ride away, and when you finally get together you're out to wreck each other with the frenzy of having been alone.'

Something about that remark appealed to me and I invited Terence up to my place to smoke a joint with me. We stood about on the pavement a few minutes while he tried to decide whether he wanted to or not. We looked across the street through the passing traffic and into the store where George was demonstrating the disco equipment to a black woman. Finally Terence shook his head and said that while he was in this part of town he would go and visit a girl he knew in Venice.

'Take some spare underwear,' I suggested.

'Yeah,' he called over his shoulder as he walked away. 'See you!'

There were long pointless days when I thought, Everywhere on earth is the same. Los Angeles, California, the whole of the United States seemed to me then a very fine and frail crust on the limitless, subterranean world of my own boredom. I could be anywhere, I could have saved myself the effort and the fare. I wished in fact I was nowhere, beyond the responsibility of place. I woke in the morning stultified by oversleep. Although I was neither hungry nor thirsty, I ate breakfast because I dared not be without the activity. I spent ten minutes cleaning my teeth knowing that when I finished I would have to choose to do something else. I returned to the kitchen, made more coffee and very carefully washed the dishes. Caffeine aided my growing panic. There were books in the living room that needed to be studied, there was writing that needed completion but the thought of it all made me flush hot with weariness and disgust. For that reason I tried not to think about it, I did not tempt myself. It hardly occurred to me to set foot inside the living room.

Instead I went to the bedroom and made the bed and took great care over the 'hospital corners'. Was I sick? I lay down on the bed and stared at the ceiling without a thought in my head. Then I stood up and with my hands in my pockets stared at the wall. Perhaps I should paint it another colour, but of course I was only a temporary resident. I remembered I was in a foreign city and hurried to the balcony. Dull, white, box-shaped shops and houses, parked cars, two lawn sprinklers, festoons of telephone cable everywhere, one palm tree teetering against the sky, the whole lit by a cruel white glow of a sun blotted out by high cloud and pollution. It was as obvious and self-explanatory to me as a row of suburban English bungalows. What could I do about it? Go somewhere else? I almost laughed out loud at the thought.

More to confirm my state of mind than change it, I returned to the bedroom and grimly picked up my flute. The piece I intended to play, dog-eared and stained, was already on the music stand, Bach's Sonata No. 1 in A minor. The lovely opening Andante, a series of lilting arpeggios, requires a flawless breathing technique to make sense of the phrasing, yet from the beginning I am snatching furtively at breaths like a supermarket shoplifter, and the coherence of the piece becomes purely imaginary, remembered from gramophone recordings and superimposed over the present. At bar fifteen, four and a half bars into the Presto, I fumble over the octave leaps but I press on, a dogged, failing athlete, to finish the first movement short of breath and unable to hold the last note its full length. Because I catch most of the right notes in the right order, I regard the Allegro as my showpiece. I play it with expressionless aggression. The Adagio, a sweet thoughtful melody, illustrates to me every time I play it how out of tune my notes are, some sharp, some flat, none sweet, and the semi-demi quavers are always mis-timed. And so to the two Minuets at the end which I play with dry, rigid persistence, like a mechanical organ turned by a monkey. This was my performance of Bach's Sonata, unaltered now in its details for as long as I could remember.

I sat down on the edge of the bed and almost immediately stood up again. I went to the balcony to look once more at the foreign city. Out on one of the lawns a small girl picked up a smaller girl and staggered a few steps with her. More futility. I went inside and looked at the alarm clock in the bedroom. Eleven forty. Do something, quick! I stood by the clock listening to its tick. I went from room to room without really intending to, sometimes surprised to find that I was back in the kitchen again fiddling with the cracked plastic handle of the wall can-opener. I went into the living room and spent twenty minutes drumming with my fingers on the back of a book. Towards the middle of the afternoon I dialled the time and set the clock exactly. I sat on the lavatory a long time and decided then not to move till I had planned what to do next. I remained there over two hours, staring at my knees till they lost their meaning as limbs. I thought of cutting my fingernails, that would be a start. But I had no scissors! I commenced to prowl from room to room once more, and then, towards the middle of the evening, I fell asleep in an armchair, exhausted with myself.

George at least appeared to appreciate my playing. He came upstairs once, having heard me from the shop, and wanted to see my flute. He told me he had never actually held one in his hands before. He marvelled at the intricacy and precision of its levers and pads. He asked me to play a few notes so he could see how it was held, and then he wanted me to show him how he could make a note for himself. He peered at the music on the stand and said he thought it was 'brilliant' the way musicians could turn such a mess of lines and dots into sounds. The way composers could think up whole symphonies with dozens of different instruments going at once was totally beyond him. I said it was beyond me too.

'Music,' George said with a large gesture of his arm, 'is a sacred art.' Usually when I wasn't playing my flute I left it lying about collecting dust, assembled and ready to play. Now I found myself pulling it into its three sections and drying them carefully and laying each section down like a favourite doll, in the felt-lined case.

George lived out in Simi Valley on a recently reclaimed stretch of desert. He described his house as 'empty and smelling of fresh paint still'. He was separated from his wife and two weekends a month had his children over to stay, two boys aged seven and eight. Imperceptibly George became my host in Los Angeles. He had arrived here penniless from New York city when he was twenty-two. Now he made almost forty thousand dollars a year and felt responsible for the city and my experience in it. Sometimes after work George drove me for miles along the freeway in his new Volvo.

'I want you to get the feel of it, the insanity of its size.'

'What's that building?' I would say to him as we sped past an illuminated Third Reichian colossus mounted on a manicured green hill. George would glance out of his window.

'I dunno, a bank or temple or something.' We went to bars, bars for starlets, bars for 'intellectuals' where screen-writers drank, lesbian bars and a bar where the waiters, lithe, smooth-faced young men, dressed as Victorian serving-maids. We ate in a diner founded in 1947 which served only hamburgers and apple pie, a renowned and fashionable place where waiting customers stood like hungry ghosts at the backs of those seated.

We went to a club where singers and stand-up comedians performed in the hope of being discovered. A thin girl with bright red hair and sequined T-shirt reached the end of her passionately murmured song on a sudden shrill, impossible top note. All conversation ceased. Someone, perhaps maliciously, dropped a glass. Halfway through, the note became a warbling vibrato and the singer collapsed on the stage in an abject curtsy, arms held stiffly in front of her, fists clenched. Then she sprang to her tiptoes and held her arms high above her head with the palms flat as if to forestall the sporadic and indifferent applause.

'They all want to be Barbara Streisand or Liza Minnelli,' George explained as he sucked a giant cocktail through a pink plastic straw. 'But no one's looking for that kind of stuff anymore.'

A man with stooped shoulders and wild curly hair shuffled on to the stage. He took the microphone out of its rest, held it close to his lips and said nothing. He seemed to be stuck for words. He wore a torn, muddied denim jacket over bare skin, his eyes were swollen almost to the point of closing and under the right there ran a long scratch which ended at the corner of his mouth and gave him the look of a partly made-up clown. His lower lip trembled and I thought he was going to weep. The hand that was not holding the microphone worried a coin and looking at that I noticed the stains down his jeans, yes, fresh wet vomit clung there. His lips parted but no sounds came out. The audience waited patiently. Somewhere at the back of the room a wine bottle was opened. When he spoke finally it was to his fingernails, a low, cracked murmur.

'I'm such a goddamn mess!'

The audience broke into fallabout laughter and cheering, which after a minute gave way to footstamping and rhythmic clapping. George and I, perhaps constrained by each other's company, smiled. The man reappeared by the microphone the moment the last clapping died away.

Now he spoke rapidly, his eyes still fixed on his fingers. Sometimes he glanced worriedly to the back of the room and we caught the flash of the whites of his eyes. He told us he had just broken up with his girl-friend, and how, as he was driving away from her house, he had started to weep, so much so that he could not see to drive and had to stop his car. He thought he might kill himself but first he wanted to say goodbye to *her*. He drove to a call box but it was out of order and this made him cry again. Here the audience, silent till now, laughed a little. He reached his girl-friend from a drug store. As soon as she picked up the phone and heard his voice she began to cry too. But she didn't want to see him. She told him, 'It's useless, there's nothing we can do.' He put the phone down and howled with grief. An assistant in the drug store told him to leave because he was upsetting the other customers. He walked along the street thinking about life and death, it started to rain, he popped some amyl nitrate, he tried to sell his watch. The audience was growing restless, a lot of people had stopped listening. He bummed fifty cents off a bum. Through his tears he thought he saw a woman aborting a foetus in the gutter and when he got closer he saw it was cardboard boxes and a lot of old rags. By now the man was talking over a steady drone of conversation. Waitresses with silver trays circulated the tables. Suddenly the speaker raised his hand and said, 'Well, see you,' and he was gone. A few people clapped but most did not notice him leave.

Not long before I was due to leave Los Angeles George invited me to spend Saturday evening at his house. I would be flying to New York late the following day. He wanted me to bring along a couple of friends to make a small farewell party, and he wanted me to bring along my flute.

'I really want to sit,' said George, 'in my own home with a glass of wine in my hand and hear you play that thing.' I phoned Mary first. We had been meeting intermittently since our weekend. Occasionally she had come and spent the afternoon at my apartment. She had another lover she more or less lived with, but she hardly mentioned him and it was never an issue between us. After agreeing to come, Mary wanted to know if Terence was going to be there. I had recounted to her Terence's adventure with Sylvie, and described my own ambivalent feelings about him. Terence had not returned to San Francisco as he had intended. He had met someone who had a friend 'in screen writing' and now he was waiting for an introduction. When I phoned him he responded with an unconvincing parody of Semitic peevishness. 'Five weeks in this town and I'm invited out already?' I decided to take seriously George's wish to hear me play the flute. I practised my scales and arpeggios, I worked hard at those places in the Sonata No. 1 where I always faltered and as I played I fantasised about Mary, George and Terence listening spellbound and a little drunk, and my heart raced.

Mary arrived in the early evening and before driving to pick up Terence we sat around on my balcony watching the sun and smoked a small joint. It had been on my mind before she came that we might be going to bed for one last time. But now that she was here and we were dressed for an evening elsewhere, it seemed more appropriate to talk. Mary asked me what I had been doing and I told her about the night club act. I was not sure whether to present the man as a performer with an act so clever it was not funny, or as someone who had come in off the street and taken over the stage.

'I've seen acts like that here,' said Mary. 'The idea, when it works, is to make your laughter stick in your throat. What was funny suddenly gets nasty.' I asked

Mary if she thought there was any truth in my man's story. She shook her head.

'Everyone here,' she said, gesturing towards the setting sun, 'has got some kind of act going like that.'

'You seem to say that with some pride,' I said as we stood up. She smiled and we held hands for an empty moment in which there came to me from nowhere a vivid image of the parallel bars on the beach; then we turned and went inside.

Terence was waiting for us on the pavement outside the house where he was staying. He wore a white suit and as we pulled up he was fixing a pink carnation into his lapel. Mary's car had only two doors. I had to get out to let Terence in, but through a combination of sly manoeuvring on his part and obtuse politeness on my own, I found myself introducing my two friends from the back seat. As we turned on to the freeway Terence began to ask Mary a series of polite, insistent questions and it was clear from where I sat, directly behind Mary, that as she was answering one question he was formulating the next, or falling over himself to agree with everything she said.

'Yes, yes,' he was saying, leaning forwards eagerly, clasping together his long, pale fingers, 'That's a really good way of putting it.' Such condescension, I thought, such ingratiation. Why does Mary put up with it? Mary said that she thought Los Angeles was the most exciting city in the USA. Before she had even finished Terence was outdoing her with extravagant praise.

'I thought you hated it,' I interjected sourly. But Terence was adjusting his seat belt and asking Mary another question. I sat back and stared out the window, attempting to control my irritation. A little later Mary was craning her neck trying to find me in her mirror.

'You're very quiet back there,' she said gaily. I fell into sudden, furious mimicry.

'That's a really good way of putting it, yes, yes.' Neither
Terence nor Mary made any reply. My words hung over
us as though they were being uttered over and over again.
I opened my window. We arrived at George's house with
twenty-five minutes of unbroken silence behind us.

The introductions over, the three of us held the centre
of George's huge living room while he fixed our drinks at
the bar. I held my flute case and music stand under my
arm like weapons. Apart from the bar the only other
furniture was two yellow, plastic sag chairs, very bright
against the desert expanse of brown carpet. Sliding doors
took up the length of one wall and gave on to a small back
yard of sand and stones in the centre of which, set in
concrete, stood one of those tree-like contraptions for
drying clothes on. In the corner of the yard was a scrappy
sagebrush plant, survivor of the real desert that was here a
year ago. Terence, Mary and I addressed remarks to
George and said nothing to each other.

'Well,' said George when the four of us stood looking at
each other with drinks in our hands, 'Follow me and I'll
show you the kids.' Obediently we padded behind George
in single file along a narrow, thickly carpeted corridor. We
peered through a bedroom doorway at two small boys in a
bunk bed reading comics. They glanced at us without
interest and went on reading.

Back in the living room I said, 'They're very subdued,
George. What do you do, beat them up?' George took my
question seriously and there followed a conversation about
corporal punishment. George said he occasionally gave
the boys a slap on the back of the legs if things got really
out of hand. But it was not to hurt them, he said, so much
as to show them he meant business. Mary said she was
dead against striking children at all, and Terence, largely
to cut a figure I thought, or perhaps to demonstrate to me
that he could disagree with Mary, said that he thought a

sound thrashing never did anyone any harm. Mary laughed, but George, who obviously was not taking to this faintly foppish, languid guest sprawled across his carpet, seemed ready to move into the attack. George worked hard. He kept his back straight even when he sat in the sag chair.

'You were thrashed when you were a kid?' he asked as he handed round the scotch.

Terence hesitated and said, 'Yes.' This surprised me. Terence's father died before he was born and he had grown up with his mother in Vermont.

'Your mother beat you?' I said before he had time to invent a swaggering bully of a father.

'Yes.'

'And you don't think it did you any harm?' said George. 'I don't believe it.'

Terence stretched his legs. 'No harm done at all.' He spoke through a yawn that might have been a fake. He gestured towards his pink carnation. 'After all, here I am.'

There was a moment's pause then George said, 'For example, you never had any problem making out with women?' I could not help smiling.

Terence sat up. 'Oh yes,' he said. 'Our English friend here will verify that.' By this Terence referred to my out-burst in the car. But I said to George, 'Terence likes to tell funny stories about his own sexual failures.'

George leaned forwards to catch Terence's full attention. 'How can you be sure they're not caused by being thrashed by your mother?'

Terence spoke very quickly. I was not sure whether he was very excited or very angry. 'There will always be problems between men and women and everyone suffers in some way. I conceal less about myself than other people do. I guess you never had your backside tanned by your mother when you were a kid, but does that mean you never have any hang-ups with women? I mean, where's your wife … ?'

Mary's interruption had the precision of a surgeon's knife.

'I was only ever hit once as a kid, by my father, and do you know why that was? I was twelve. We were all sitting round the table at suppertime, all the family, and I told everyone I was bleeding from between my legs. I put some blood on the end of my finger and held it up for them all to see. My father leaned across the table and slapped my face. He told me not to be dirty and sent me up to my room.'

George got up to fetch more ice for our glasses and muttered 'Simply grotesque' as he went. Terence stretched out on the floor, his eyes fixed on the ceiling like a dead man's. From the bedroom came the sound of the boys singing, or rather chanting, for the song was all on one note. I said to Mary something to the effect that between people who had just met, such a conversation could not have taken place in England.

'Is that a good thing do you think?' Mary asked.

Terence said, 'The English tell each other nothing.'

I said, 'Between telling nothing and telling everything there is very little to choose.'

'Did you hear the boys?' George said as he came back.

'We heard some kind of singing,' Mary told him. George was pouring more scotch and spooning ice into the glasses.

'That wasn't singing. That was praying. I've been teaching them the Lord's Prayer.' On the floor Terence groaned and George looked round sharply.

'I didn't know you were a Christian, George,' I said.

'Oh, well, you know … ' George sank into his chair. There was a pause, as if all four of us were gathering our strength for another round of fragmentary dissent.

although I was not sure who he was talking to. Terence was pressing on loudly with his own speech. I heard him mention the Crusades and the Inquisition.

'This has nothing to do with Christianity.' George was almost shouting. His face was flushed.

'More evil perpetrated in the name of Christ than ... this has nothing to do with ... to the persecution of women herbalists as witches ... Bullshit. It's irrelevant ... corruption, graft, propping up tyrants, accumulating wealth at the altars ... fertility goddess ... bullshit ... phallic worship ... look at Galileo ... this has nothing to ... ' I heard little else because now I was shouting my own piece about Christianity. It was impossible to stay quiet. George was jabbing his finger furiously in Terence's direction. Mary was leaning forwards trying to catch George by the sleeve and tell him something. The whisky bottle lay on its side empty, someone had upset the ice. For the first time in my life I found myself with urgent views on Christianity, on violence, on America, on everything, and I demanded priority before my thoughts slipped away.

' ... and starting to think objectively about this ... their pulpits to put down the workers and their strikes so ... objective? You mean male. All reality now is male rea ... always a violent God ... the great capitalist in the sky ... protective ideology of the dominant class denies the conflict between men and women ... bullshit, total bullshit ... '

Suddenly I heard another voice ringing in my ears. It was my own. I was talking into a brief, exhausted silence.

' ... driving across the States I saw this sign in Illinois along Interstate 70 which said, "God, Guts, Guns made America great. Let's keep all three." '

'Hah!' Mary and Terence exclaimed in triumph. George was on his feet, empty glass in hand.

'That's right,' he cried. 'That's right. You can put it

down but it's right. This country has a violent past, a lot
of brave men died making ... '

'Men!' echoed Mary.

'All right, and a lot of brave women too. America was
made with the gun. You can't get away from that.'
George strode across the room to the bar in the corner and
drew out something black from behind the bottles. 'I keep
a gun here,' he said, holding the thing up for us to see.

'What for?' Mary asked.

'When you have kids you begin to have a very different
attitude towards life and death. I never kept a gun before
the kids were around. Now I think I'd shoot at anyone who
threatened their existence.'

'Is it a real gun?' I said. George came back towards us
with the gun in one hand and a fresh bottle of scotch in the
other. 'Dead right it's a real gun!' It was very small and
did not extend beyond George's open palm.

'Let me see that,' said Terence.

'It's loaded,' George warned as he handed it across. The
gun appeared to have a soothing effect on us all. We no
longer shouted, we spoke quietly in its presence. While
Terence examined the gun George filled our glasses. As he
sat down he reminded me of my promise to play the flute.
There followed a bleary silence of a minute or two, broken
only by George to tell us that after this drink we should eat
dinner. Mary was far away in thought. She rotated her
glass slowly between her finger and thumb. I lay back on
my elbows and began to piece together the conversation
we had just had. I was trying to remember how we
arrived at this sudden silence.

Then Terence snapped the safety catch and levelled the
gun at George's head.

'Raise your hands, Christian,' he said dully.

George did not move. He said, 'You oughtn't to fool
around with a gun.' Terence tightened his grip. Of course

he was fooling around, and yet I could see from where I was that his finger was curled about the trigger, and he was beginning to pull on it.

'Terence!' Mary whispered, and touched his back gently with her foot. Keeping his eyes on Terence, George sipped at his drink. Terence brought his other hand up to steady the gun which was aimed at the centre of George's face.

'Death to the gun owners.' Terence spoke without a trace of humour. I tried to say his name too, but hardly a sound left my throat. When I tried again I said something in my accelerating panic that was quite irrelevant.

'Who is it?' Terence pulled the trigger.

From that point on the evening collapsed into conventional, labyrinthine politenesses at which Americans, when they wish, quite outstrip the English. George was the only one to have seen Terence remove the bullets from the gun, and this united Mary and me in a state of mild but prolonged shock. We ate salad and cold cuts from plates balanced on our knees. George asked Terence about his Orwell thesis and the prospects of teaching jobs. Terence asked George about his business, fun party hire and sickroom requisites. Mary was questioned about her job in the feminist bookshop and she answered blandly, carefully avoiding any statement that might provoke discussion. Finally I was called on to elaborate on my travel plans, which I did in great and dull detail. I explained how I would be spending a week in Amsterdam before returning to London. This caused Terence and George to spend several minutes in praise of Amsterdam, although it was quite clear they had seen very different cities.

Then while the others drank coffee and yawned, I played my flute. I played my Bach sonata no worse than usual, perhaps a little more confidently for being drunk, but my mind ran on against the music. For I was weary of this music and of myself for playing it. As the notes transferred themselves from the page to the end of my fingers I thought, Am I still playing *this*? I still heard the echo of our raised voices, I saw the black gun in George's open palm, the comedian reappear from the darkness to take the microphone again, I saw myself many months ago setting out for San Francisco from Buffalo in a drive-away car, shouting out for joy over the roar of the wind through the open windows, It's me, I'm here, I'm coming ... where was the music for all this? Why wasn't I even looking for it? Why did I go on doing what I couldn't do, music from another time and civilisation, its certainty and perfection to me a pretence and a lie, as much as they had once been, or might still be, a truth to others. What should I look for? (I tooled through the second movement like a piano roll.) Something difficult and free. I thought of Terence's stories about himself, his game with the gun, Mary's experiment with herself, of myself in an empty moment drumming my fingers on the back of a book, the vast, fragmented city without a centre, without citizens, a city that existed only in the mind, a nexus of change or stagnation in individual lives. Picture and idea crashed drunkenly one after the other, discord battened to bar after bar of implied harmony and inexorable logic. For the pulse of one beat I glanced past the music at my friends where they sprawled on the floor. Then their after-image glowed briefly at me from the page of music. Possible, even likely, that the four of us would never see each other again, and against such commonplace tran-sience my music was inane in its rationality, paltry in its over-determination. Leave it to others, to professionals who could evoke the old days of its truth. To me it was nothing, now that I knew what I wanted. This genteel escapism ... crossword with its answers written in, I could play no more of it.

I broke off in the slow movement and looked up. I was about to say, 'I can't go on any more', but the three of them were on their feet clapping and smiling broadly at me. In parody of concert-goers George and Terence cupped their hands round their mouths and called out 'Bravo! Bravissimo!' Mary came forward, kissed me on the cheek and presented me with an imaginary bouquet. Overwhelmed by nostalgia for a country I had not yet left, I could do no more than put my feet together and make a bow, clasping the flowers to my chest.

Then Mary said, 'Let's go. I'm tired.'